SKIRT 3

THE RISE OF LIL' C

MIKAL MALONE

CARTEL PUBLICATIONS
PRESENTS

PUBLISHER'S NOTE:
This book is a work of fiction. Names, characters, businesses, Organizations, places, events and incidents are the product of the Author's imagination or are used fictionally. Any resemblance of Actual persons, living or dead, events, or locales are entirely coincidental.

Library of Congress Control Number: 2007940747
ISBN 10: 0984303006
ISBN 13: 978-0984303007
Cover Design: Davida Baldwin www.oddballdsgn.com
Editor: Advanced Editorial Services
Graphics: Davida Baldwin
www.thecartelpublications.com
First Edition

Printed in the United States of America

CHECK OUT OTHER TITLES BY THE CARTEL PUBLICATIONS

SHYT LIST 1
SHYT LIST 2
SHYT LIST 3
PITBULLS IN A SKIRT 1
PITBULLS IN A SKIRT 2
PITBULLS IN A SKIRT 3
POISON 1
POISON 2
VICTORIA'S SECRET
HELL RAZOR HONEYS 1
HELL RAZOR HONEYS 2
BLACK AND UGLY AS EVER
A HUSTLER'S SON 2
THE FACE THAT LAUNCHED A THOUSAND BULLETS
YEAR OF THE CRACKMOM
THE UNUSUAL SUSPECTS
MISS WAYNE AND THE QUEENS OF DC
LA FAMILIA DIVIDED
RAUNCHY

What Up Superstars!

Well, Pitbulls In A Skirt 3 is finally here! And to think, Pitbulls In A Skirt 1 is soon to be a movie. We not playing in 2011, babies! We're on fire and working overtime to deliver the stories you love both visually and mentally.

Now, Pitbulls in A Skirt 3 is sure to be a favorite with Pitbulls fans everywhere. This book is full of drama, nastiness, anger, deceit and love. And although a lot of fans are sure to be devastated upon reading this book, we feel we are keeping it real with the storyline. Things change. Life changes and so it was important that we depict real life in Pitbulls 3.

So in regular Cartel Fan fashion, grab a seat, grab a drink and turn your phone off and let us take you on a Cartel ride!

Lastly, and as always, we want to pay respect to an author we love and appreciate for his/her literary journey or pen game. So it is with great pleasure that we pay homage to:

"James Henderson"

I stumbled on Mr. James Henderson's novel *'Baby Huey: A Cautionary Tale of Addiction'* by mistake. Browsing around for Kindle books, I figured I'd download it to see what was what. I couldn't believe my eyes as I laughed at every other sentence. And if laughter wasn't enough, he kept me in suspense wondering how his main character would get out of the mess he stayed in. It's just a great book and I really hope it reaches lovers of urban fiction. Please cop this book! It's a sleeper!

Well, until I hug you later,

T. Styles
President & CEO, The Cartel Publications
www.thecartelpublications.com
www.facebook.com/authortstyles
http://www.ustream.tv/channel/tstyles/v3
http://www.youtube.com/user/tstyles74

PROLOGUE

BEWARE OF THE BLACK WATER KLAN

Tamir, one of Black Water's oldest sons was on top of his newest girlfriend, Gia. They had just finishing having sex and he was ready for another round as Trey Songz', "Wonder Woman", played loudly on the radio to conceal their lustful noises from the girl's mother. And even though he was on his fifth stroke, his mind was filled with thoughts of Lil C. He hated how he and his family were responsible for his father's murder and vowed before he died to get them back.

Tiring of her pussy, he took his dick out and entered her ass.

"Ouch!"

"What's wrong? You know how I like it." He said, as he pushed his manhood deeper into her ass from the front, without mercy.

"I know and I want to please you."

"I can't tell. You seem like you got something on your mind."

It was hard for her to look at Tamir directly in the eyes because his handsome features made her weak. He was tall and attractive and his skin was as smooth and silky as melted chocolate. He kept his hair in a long silky ponytail if it wasn't braided like it was now.

"Tamir, I wanna know if you like me." She said trying to breathe regularly, as the weight of his warm body pressed against hers.

"If I like you?" He laughed and pulled out of her. "Why you asking me that shit right now?"

"I knew I was gonna sound stupid." She said turning away.

"You know I like you."

"Then...then...why don't you come around as much?" She said looking into his eyes. "You sending me mix messages, Tamir."

"I don't come around a lot because you not willing to be the wifey I need you to be. You force me to hang out more with my other girls. I mean, I wanna be here but you gotta step up and you gotta do it quick. The world and everything around us is getting ready for war and I need people in my life who understand that."

"Why you always talking about war?"

"Why not?"

She swallowed hard and tried to adjust her breathing to be comfortable. But for some reason, it seemed as if Tamir was pushing all of his weight on top of her on purpose.

"Tamir, can I ask you one more question?"

"Yeah, but make this the last one, I'm trying to fuck."

"Okay...um...why do you have to have other girls? How come I'm not good enough for you, by myself?"

"'Cause I'm a man who has needs to be fulfilled. Most niggas would just cheat and not tell you the truth but that ain't my style." He kissed her neck and then sucked her lips passionately. "Now, if you can't deal with what I need," he said as he opened her legs wider and pushed his dick back into her pussy. "Then that'll be your choice. I'll just have to let you go."

"I...don't want you to do that. I...I just never heard of someone having more than one girlfriend and it be okay."

"Now you have. My father had 10 wives before he died."

"Ten wives? I thought you couldn't have but just one."

"You can have whatever you want in life." He paused. "Now stop fucking up my flow."

"I'll...I'll do anything for you."

"Anything?"

"Yes." She moaned.

"Good...now tell me you'll have my baby."

He'd asked her before but in the past she said no fearing what her mother would do once she found out. But he'd long since snatched her from her mother's authority and now she was wrapped up like a gift and he knew it.

"I'm scared," she cried. "I...I don't know if I can do that. I don't know if I can have a baby right now. What about school and stuff?"

He stopped moving and looked at her as if she'd just disrespected his mother. Already she felt incomplete, like someone had taken a limb from her.

"You know what," he said pulling his dick out of her pussy. "I'm not fucking with you no more. When you know what you want, and you ready to do what I ask, you come see me then."

Gia's mind quickly went through what life would be like without Tamir. How bored she'd be with her friends and how broke she'd be without him. Her mother didn't allow boys in the house, but he was the only boy who could come over anytime he wanted because Tamir paid her mother off handsomely to allow him to sleep with her child in her home. So if Tamir left, all that would end and she'd be shit out of luck.

"Please...don't leave," she stopped him pulling him back into her. "I wanna have your baby. I wanna do whatever I gotta do to keep you."

As she said that, he reentered her body quickly releasing his poisonous semen into her bloodstream. Nineteen-year-old Tamir was just like his father in all senses. Although Black Water was murdered, he still had dreams of growing the Black Water Klan just like his father had. To date he'd fathered six children, but he'd need to father at least fifty more to be as deep as he wanted. With his father's children, wives, and grandchildren, the Black Water Klan was already over very deep and growing.

But Tamir was unlike his father in one way. The semen he used to breed his direct bloodline was infected with HIV. And when he was diagnosed a year earlier, he chose to ignore the doctor's orders to inform his sexual partners.

He was all about the Klan and doing what was necessary to grow the family in order to get them out of Virginia, where they retreated after Black Water was murdered and Dreyfus cut them off. His family had to murder, rob and steal to help out, too.

When his phone rang next to his bed he picked it up and handed it to Gia. "Hold it to my ear."

She did and he fucked her while on the call. Although he had already busted his nut, he was hard and still deep inside Gia. "Who's this?" He said not missing a stroke.

"It's me, Energy. Are you coming home tonight?"

"Fuck is you asking me something like that for?" he said, fucking Gia harder. "I get in there when I come in there."

"I'm only asking because everything is in place for our buildings, baby. We just have to sign the deeds. And I wanted to celebrate that's all."

Tamir smiled thinking of what he had achieved, being able to put his entire family up in places of their own.

"Cool, I'ma see you later. I'm busy right now though." He looked at Gia and said, "Hang up."

But instead of hanging up Gia left the phone on. She wanted whoever was on the other end, to hear the passion in Tamir's voice.

"Tell me how good my pussy is." Gia demanded.

"Oh you talking nasty now?"

"Yeah, baby. Tell me how much you like it."

"I like it a lot." He said before gripping her throat so hard he almost crushed her windpipe. "But if you ever try to do some sneaky shit behind my back again, I won't hesitate to kill you." He released her throat and said, "Now hang up the phone. This time let me see you do it."

As she ended the call cutting off Energy's connection, Tamir's mind raced. After hearing the news about the buildings, everything was coming together. He was finally going back to DC to seek revenge for his father's murder. He'd start by breaking down Lil C's friends and family and when the time was right, he'd personally kill him.

"I'm coming for you, nigga." He said, out loud causing Gia to wonder what he was talking about. "Get ready for us."

THE PRESENT

"WHY YOU MAKE ME DO THIS? I LOVED YOU."

- LIL C

Lil C sat quietly in the back seat of his silver Maybach, the hum of the engine was almost non-existent and was perfect for what he was doing, scoping out the scene. The migraines he'd been plagued with since his father died consumed him and the anger he felt inside because of her betrayal made matters worse. The lies came one after another, until eventually they spelled truth, and her cover was blown.

But he was different now in so many ways he wasn't the boy he used to be, the one who longed for the direction of his father or the love of his mother. He was a man and a drug lord with very tough decisions to make, and he was ready to make them all.

"Sir, where would you like me to take you now?"

Lil C looked up at his chauffeur and said, "When I tell you I'm ready, you'll know. Until then don't open your fucking mouth, 'till I address you."

Wallace, who was ten years his senior, turned around without another word. Besides, he knew what could happen if he spoke back to his 'young king', a moniker Lil C demanded everyone who reported to him call him. He was in charge. He was the boss. And he ruled all, and because of it, he had a decision to make.

Lil C rolled the window down and the cold air rushed inside and teased his chocolate colored fur. The glow from the streetlight brightened his platinum chain with the word 'Camelot' dressed in diamonds. He'd changed the name of Tyland Towers to Camelot, in his deceased father's honor. And he felt if Cameron were alive today, he'd surely be proud.

As far as he was concerned their bond was too brief, there were still so many things he wanted to ask his father, there were still so many things he needed to know in order to be a man. He didn't tell anybody about the nights he woke up to a damp pillow due to grieving over his father in his sleep. Just like his father, his cockiness wouldn't dare let him grieve when he was awake, unless he was crashing at walls with his bare fists, later lying about the reason for his outburst. He missed his father, and he missed him dearly.

With his window down, he could see his mother and her friend standing outside of a house, in an upscale neighborhood.

"What do you want me to do? First you tell me to end their relationship and I did it! And then I learn you betray me by telling her something you never should have!" Mercedes screamed.

"This isn't about us! And just so you know, I didn't think she would tell him. I was drunk when I told her, and she must've remembered."

"It doesn't matter. He hates me now and I think it's best for them to stay apart."

"Well, I can't stand by anymore and watch her cry. She's fucking pregnant, Mercedes!" Carissa added.

"She's what?"

"You heard me."

Mercedes and Carissa were so involved in a heated argument that they could not see him hidden within the night.

"Why you make me do this? I loved you." He said to himself as he watched his mother.

He looked at the platinum .45-handgun in his lap and examined its features. It represented revenge, death and new beginnings and there was no doubt in his heart he'd have to use it, the only question was when. He never thought it would come to this, yet he understood how it all began. It started with vicious lies and ended with a bloody murder.

Seeing her face, a face he'd known all of his life, he decided it was time. It was now or never. And his decision to pull the trigger would change the course of everything in his life, forever.

SOME MONTHS EARLIER

"HE SMUTTIN' HER OUT AND THIS SHIT IS TEARING ME UP!"

-MERCEDES

"Mam…mam." My driver said. "Did you want me to pull off?"

"Huh?"

"Is everything okay?" He asked me with concern in his voice.

"Oh…yes. Let's hit the road."

I had so much on my mind I was missing the world around me. If I wasn't thinking of what I had done to my son, by murdering his father who he loved dearly, I was thinking of a husband who didn't want me anymore. To make matters worse, it was that time of the month again...the time when we discussed Emerald City business and any issues at hand. Only this time the meeting wasn't about Emerald as much as it was about my girls. And even though I knew my mind should be here, other thoughts consumed me. Like the fact that I texted my husband five times and he still hadn't responded.

Irritated and wondering about our future, I threw my iPhone in my lap and looked out of the window of my silver Mercedes Limousine. My white fur coat is still on, because I had just stepped inside from the cold. I knew before the meeting started that this night wasn't going to end well and I tried to calm down to deal with the matter in the best way possible.

"Mrs. Ganger, would you like me to pick up Ms. Tailor or Ms. Shawnville and Ms. Packer first?

Since most of our conversation was about Carissa and Kenyetta was with her, I decided that it was best to scoop Yvette first. She needed a heads up about the information that was plaguing me.

This drug lifestyle is getting on my fucking nerves. I was finally realizing that I was meant to be a hustler's wife and not a hustler. Don't get me wrong, I loved the money and because of it, I would never be able to step into another lifestyle that couldn't afford me the same privileges, still, I'd be lying if I'd say I wasn't sick of it all.

Why did life have to change so much? It's funny, you think having money would get rid of your problems but once you have all the money you desire, you discover it ain't true. In the end all you want is love and safety for yourself and family. And lately with me and my husband Derrick fighting all the time, and Lil C fucking with me about being a part of the Emerald City drug organization like his father, happiness was the last thing going on in my home.

I decided to text Derrick again in the hopes he'd answer, but was sure they'd all end up in the 'Pressed Wife Graveyard' with the rest of my texts.

'Derrick, where are you? Please respond back. I miss you and was going to come home early if you were there. Please text me back, I love you.'

When we slid in front of Yvette and Chris's townhome in Georgetown, the way Yvette walked out, I could tell something was wrong. She pulled up the collar of her black fur coat, buried her head deeper into it and the sound of her Dior heels clicked quickly to my limo. But before she reached the gate that enclosed her small yard, she suddenly fell.

I quickly got out of the car to help her up. And when I did, my Jimmy Choo heel landed in the middle of a pile of dog shit.

"Yvette, you gotta get rid of them dogs!" I yelled wiping the heel of my shoe on the curb scraping them a little. "Or clean up behind them at least."

"Fuck that shit! Them dogs are my kids I ain't never getting rid of them."

We finally made it to the car and I could tell she was both angry and eager to get out of the cold. It was 30 degrees outside and the wind was brisk. My driver parked and opened the door for us and the moment she got inside she said, "No I don't want to talk about it so don't ask me!"

"*Okay*," I said looking the other way. "But you could say thank you for helping your ass up."

"Thank you." She said dryly. "But wait, what's wrong with you?" She said in a concerned voice. I didn't answer. "Bitch, you heard me talking to you! What's up?"

"Nothing. Just drop it."

"Mercedes, let's not play this game tonight. You know you gonna tell me so you might as well do it now."

"Am I ugly?"

"What?"

"You heard me." I paused. "I want to know if you think I'm attractive."

"Why you asking me, because I fuck another woman or something?"

"Yvette! I'm serious."

"Mercedes, please! You can't be serious. I mean look at you." She said gripping a few strands of my hair. "You in your thirties and you look like you about twenty something. You got the yellow skin men love and your natural black hair hangs down your back. Let's not even talk about your body. That shit is on point!"

"Ughhhh…dike! Why you looking at me like that?"

"Bitch, please!" Yvette laughed hitting me. "You wish I looked at you like that. I don't even want the bitch I got at home, I damn sure ain't recruiting no more split tails."

"All jokes aside, thank you," I said touching her hand. "I needed to hear that."

"Don't thank me. I ain't telling you nothing that ain't true." I faced my window again and wondered where Derrick was. "Now what's wrong?"

"Everything." I said.

Yvette rolled her eyes and said, "Well when you get ready to tell me, know that I'm here," she said turning one of the heat vents in her direction." "Girl, it's cold as shit out there! Fuck!" She flung her Louis Vuitton bag on the floor next to my Gucci and shivered in her seat.

"You telling me! I had to buy me another fur coat because the other one wasn't warm enough."

"Bitch, you stay buying shit. I peeped the new diamond rings, too." She said smoothing on some Chapstick. "I don't see how you do it! I hate fucking shopping."

"Girl, I ain't tripping off this dope money…might as well spend it because I damn sure can't take it with me."

We laughed.

"So what's up? Who did what this time? 'Cause if you picked me up before Carissa and Kenyetta who are closer, you must want to rap about something. What is it, Mercedes? Stop fucking around because something is up with you."

"You are too much."

"I'm serious! You brought the big boy out today and whenever you pick us up in your Mercedes stretch, it means somebody is fucking up. So which of us bitches got you wrong?"

Damn, she was on to me. I looked away and said, "I wish ya'll didn't know me so well."

"We're sisters, I know everything about you. Now what's up, bitch, you scaring me?"

I picked up the iPhone in my lap, selected the Email app, opened the message from Toi who found the video and pressed play. She took it out of my hands with her manicured Minx nails. It didn't take long for her normal expression on her face to change fifteen seconds into the video.

Her eyes rose up from the video and her jaw dropped. "No...that can't be. Please stop playing. Is it...really?"

"Yes." I said sadly. "It's her."

"But, why would she allow him to do this to her? She a boss, Mercedes! Does she have any idea how bad this looks for us? How bad this looks for her daughters?" I took the phone from her hand when I heard it ding with a text message. "Derrick just texted you."

"Thanks."

"And who is the nigga who taped that bullshit anyway?"

I ignored her momentarily to focus on the text I received. My heart raced before I even knew what he said. When I finally opened his text the message read, *'Take your time coming home. I'm gonna be late.'*

What was going on with him? Why was he doing this to our family?

"Mercedes! Are you listening to me?!"

"Huh?" I said snapping out of my gaze.

"Bitch, snap out of it!" She yelled, snapping her fingers. "Who is that in the video?"

"I don't know. You see he's hiding his face." I said wondering who had Derrick's attention. I threw my iphone in my lap frustrated with everything. "But whoever he is, he posted this shit to the web, Yvette. He smuttin' her out and this shit is tearing me up."

The video was raunchy and it was co-starring one of the pitbulls. Carissa was being fucked from behind by some dude with a tattoo of the letters NC on his back. Then it went to her giving him head and that's when it got too hard to watch. Several times she gagged and threw up on his dick and each time he'd slap her in the face demanding that she'd open her mouth wider. She'd do as she was told until finally he busted his nut all over her face. It was vicious, disgusting and smutty.

"Maybe it's not her, Mercedes. You know how niggas are, anybody could've edited that shit."

"It was her, Yvette. Stop making excuses."

She smoothed the back of her cute spiky haircut with her hands and stared out in front of her. Overtime, Yvette was starting to look prettier because of all of the time she'd spent in the gym.

"But how do we know? You know they still mad because our operation is tighter than ever, even with the niggas dead and gone."

"Our operation tighter than ever? Really?" I said in a condescending tone.

"What you mean?"

"Yvette, we don't pick up the money on time the way we use to, we barely meet Dreyfus for the package, it's like we don't care anymore."

"Speak for yourself."

"Maybe I am."

Yvette turned to me and said, "We got this. Ya'll just got too much shit going on that you're not willing to put on the back burner no more. I put my relationship and everything on the line for the love of EC. I just wished ya'll met me half way."

"I don't know about all of that anymore." I said not wanting to tell her how I really didn't want to focus on anything but my family right now. “And as far as Carissa, I’m fucked up that she would get caught out here like this.”

“Maybe it’s the Black Water Klan.” Yvette said.

“Bitch, that’s an urban legend! Ain’t no fucking Black Water Klan out there.”

“Oh yeah? Because Kenyetta said they were deep, and even tried to bring her into their fold when she use to fuck with him.”

“Well I don’t believe it.”

“Shit I do,” Yvette said. “And folks are saying they not in Virginia no more. Maybe they trying to make us look bad in front of Dreyfus by getting a girl who looks like Carissa to play her."

“And the purpose?”

“If we are reckless, why would he want us connected to him? If you get caught on tape fucking, you could get caught on tape smuggling drugs which leads directly back to him.”

"Look at the video again at the minute and a half mark. The tattoo of Lavelle's name is on her leg. It’s her."

I handed her the phone but she didn’t accept it saying, "I can't watch that shit again, ‘Cedes. I believe you."

Yvette looked as hurt as I did when Toi first sent me the video. Ever since Toi helped me kill Cameron, we'd been cool and I liked her even though I figured her for a square. It didn’t take me long to see that she was feisty and could be loyal to me even though we’d fucked the same nigga. I guess Cameron fucked up when he picked two bitches who would turn on him in a heartbeat if done wrong. May he rest in peace.

"How you get that shit, anyway? Let’s talk about that…what were you on some type of porn site or something?"

"Fuck no! Toi sent that shit to me."

"Where she find it at?" Yvette asked with raised eyebrows.

"She fucks with some nigga who likes porn. I think he spotted Lavelle's name on her tattoo and they sent it to me."

When we pulled up in southwest, at the waterfront, the place where Carissa kept her Yacht, I saw five dudes who judging by the parked cars, looked like they had cash. Three I recognized from Emerald City and the other two I had only seen once.

When the girls saw us, Carissa gave them all hugs and Kenyetta tongued the dude, I knew as Cheese, down. Carissa slobbered down the other dude I knew as Slack. To make matters worse, our three workers who should have been in EC threw up deuces our way, I guess saying hello.

The deuces pissed Yvette off and she clutched her gun and said, "Did this nigga just throw up deuces at us? I will shoot them two fucking fingers off his hand! I'm 'bout to go on these mothafuckas…"

"Stop, Yvette!" I said grabbing her before she got out. "We got other shit to worry about and now is not the time."

"But they fucking hanging out with our employees. Block niggas at that. Foot soldiers! What kind of shit is that, 'Cedes?"

"Just let it play out, damn! You always wanna push the red button. Relax."

She fell back into the seat and said, "I wonder if it's one of them niggas." Then she looked at me and said, "Do Slack got a tattoo of the letters NC on his back?"

"How the fuck should I know?"

"Fuck!" Yvette said with hate in her voice. "If I find out he do, I'ma murder this nigga, 'Cedes. I'm all the way serious about that right there and it ain't gonna be nothing ya'll can do to stop me."

"Hold fast, 'Vette. You already to get into some gangsta shit when you don't even know what's going on yet. Let's get to the bottom of things first."

Yvette gave me the look, and I knew what that meant. She didn't care if Carissa would hate her for the rest of her life, she'd kill any nigga who disrespected any of us before she gave two fucks about the consequences of our friendship. She was confrontational and when it came to Emerald City, or us, she could fly off the handle. I often wondered how she and her girlfriend Chris stayed together so long since she always chose us.

"Let's just wait and see first," I told her even though I didn't know what difference it would make later.

Carissa and Kenyetta slid inside of the car with bottles of liquor in their hands. Carissa had a bottle of Coconut Ciroc and Kenyetta carried Hennessy Black. They were already tipsy and I knew I was about to be blown for the rest of the night.

"Really?" I said looking at them. "You're drunk? Really?"

They knew tonight was the first night back to Emerald to discuss business yet they show up like this?

"Relax." Kenyetta laughed. "Besides…Lil C or the girls ain't in this car so you ain't gotta play mama tonight. I'm a grown ass woman, dawg."

Carissa and Kenyetta were virtually twins the way they hung up under each other's asses. If they weren't on the Yacht riding around the city together, they were hosting parties, which catered to big time drug dealers. All the major rap artist frequented their parties, too, from Jay Z to Rick Ross. When they were in DC, they knew who to call, but sometimes I think they were bad representations of what the Nation's Capital was really about. And then it dawned on me, maybe NC stood for Nation's Capital.

"Relax?" Yvette said. "Bitch, ya'll are out there fucking with our workers. Workers who as far as I'm concerned don't deserve to be off post let alone hanging with two bosses."

"Girlllllll, please!" Kenyetta screamed. "Niggas who run drug operations fuck with who they want all the time and don't nobody say nothing."

"What?" I asked confused.

"They just friends! Is that a problem?" She paused. "Miss me with that shit."

"Whatever. You can do whatever you fucking want to do."

"Exactly, now what did we do to warrant all this?!!!" Carissa said looking around the limo.

"What are you talking about, Carissa?" Yvette asked.

Carissa had a drunk smile on her face and she was loud and belligerent. "You pulled the limo out on our ass tonight so I know something's up!"

Yvette and I looked at each other in disgust. This bitch was doing the most and she didn't even know it. She was playing herself so badly that I didn't even notice her anymore. Don't get me wrong, there are seven people I would put my life on the line for, but when you wrong you wrong and I wouldn't be me if I didn't call her out about it. The way Carissa pushed the issue made me think she knew the meeting was about her all along.

"We had to meet up regardless this week. You know that." I said.

"Awww, this about business for real?" Kenyetta whined.

"What you think?" Yvette said.

"Man, I was hoping we'd have a good time tonight," She continued. "I ain't seen ya'll in two weeks and figured we could celebrate." She said grabbing a glass and pouring a drink.

"Celebrate what? It's not one of our birthdays."

"I figured we'd celebrate life and the fact that we still living and our niggas ain't." Her words were all over the place. "That we still running shit after all these years with no indictments, with no problems and no bullshit."

There was silence. Indictments were something we hated even thinking about, feeling we might will that shit into our existence.

"This is a business night, and ya'll know that." Yvette said. "So I'm not understanding why ya'll would even step in here like that."

Carissa sighed and rolled her eyes and I knew if the driver wasn't floating on the way to Emerald City she would have asked to get out.

"What is the problem?" Carissa said. "All we trying to do is have fun. We may be business partners, but we still friends, too right?"

"Don't ask dumb questions." I said.

Carissa rolled her eyes and said, "Then let's get on with the meeting. Why wait 'til we get back to EC?"

"Well let's do it then." I said. "First we have to talk about Tyland Towers. It's more difficult to run than we thought, so we gonna have Dreyfus pull us off the project. We got our hands full enough as is and I don't like the people who work for us there. They don't respect us and are more problem than they're worth. And since we aren't buying the package for Tyland…just taking points per our arrangements with Dreyfus, it ain't worth it."

Carissa and Kenyetta looked at each other and Kenyetta said, "But we'll lose about two hundred thousand dollars a month if we do that shit. That don't sound like a smart move to me."

"We'll lose more than that if we try to run it with their lieutenants." Yvette said leaning in closer to her. "I don't trust nobody over there." Yvette continued taking the Ciroc from Carissa's hand to pour her a glass. Carissa looked like she was stealing out of her purse so Yvette said, "What...I can't have none? Just a minute ago you were all like we trying to have fun."

"Oh girl, I'm not tripping off that. Go 'head." Carissa and this drunk shit was making me want to punch her in the face.

"I'm not feeling letting go." Carissa said, interrupting my stare. "We haven't even tried hard enough yet. I mean…maybe we can put more of our men in Tyland from Emerald. I've been watching a few niggas, especially Kirk and his soldiers. They would be perfect."

I sat up straight and leaned toward them. "*WE* have tried everything." I said pointing at Yvette and then me. "And Kirk is too valuable to lose to Tyland. But if *WE* had more help as it pertains to management, before shit got too hard to handle, maybe we wouldn't have to do this." I sat back into my seat. "We pulling out of Tyland and we pulling out now."

Silence.

"So what you trying to say, me and Carissa haven't been helping, too?" Kenyetta said with an attitude.

"Naw, ya'll been too busy throwing parties and shit. And that's cool if that's ya'll thing, but it ain't helping us none." Yvette said. "So we have to look out for ourselves and let Tyland go. And there ain't no need in complaining about it because the decision has been made."

"Dreyfus know yet?" Carissa said, eyes rolling up in her head. She was starting to look real bad. "'Cause I know he gonna flip when he find out if he don't know already."

"Yeah…well…we don't work for Dreyfus now do we? He supplies us for Tyland and that's about it. We purchase outright our package for Emerald." I said. "But we are our own persons and he knows that."

"Come on, girl. You and I both know that Dreyfus has always been the silent partner in both the Emerald and Tyland Tower operations. And if you think I'm lying, tell me his reaction once you let him know." Carissa added.

"We don't give a fuck about none of that." Yvette said. "This is about what we can handle and what we wanna handle. And we smart enough to walk away."

Silence.

"Well, whatever. We making enough money anyway throwing the parties, Kenyetta. So let's not even trip."

Me and Yvette looked at each other and Yvette whispered, "Do you see this shit?"

"Yeah," I whispered back.

I hated how she was acting because the drunk Carissa wasn't the same. She was young and dumb and not smart enough to run an operation or anything else for that matter. And at the rate she was going, she wasn't even smart enough to run her mouth. To think, this bitch has two kids, Persia and Treasure who were just as grown as her. What kind of mother is she anyway?

"Is there something else? 'Cause ya'll blowing me." Carissa said.

"Yeah, we have to show you something," I said handing her my iPhone, which was already cued up and ready to go.

"What's this?"

"Just hit play."

She hit play and her and Kenyetta looked at it first as if they didn't know who it was and when Carissa noticed herself she leaned to the side so Kenyetta couldn't see anymore. I was surprised when Carissa let the whole video play out.

"So what's this supposed to mean?" Carissa asked a little embarrassed, handing me back my phone.

"It means whoever you fucking taped you, and that you need to slow your roll." I said.

"Slow my roll?" She frowned.

"Yes, bitch, slow your mothafucking roll!" I said leaning into her. "You were caught on tape letting a nigga gag you with his dick and you alright with that?"

"Are we getting in each other business now?" She paused. "Because we all know Derrick is fucking Bucky again and he not even tripping off you no more."

Silence.

"Why would you say some shit like that?!" Yvette yelled.

"She know I'm telling the truth. Bucky got the whole Emerald City screaming about how she took your man." Then she laughed. "I can't believe Derrick choosing Bucky, a bitch who banks at the liquor store over you…but I guess you're lacking in the bedroom department or something."

"Carissa, don't go too far," Kenyetta said finally realizing how bad her right hand had gotten. "We still family.

I hadn't known he was fucking Bucky but I did know he was cheating. Bucky been wanting his ass since the day she met him, and I should've murdered her when I had the chance. But all the deaths I've caused were starting to weigh on my conscious and I didn't…at least I wasn't trying to bust my gun again unless I had a real good reason.

"So what's this, Carissa? You go on a friend who looking out for you?" I asked. "I mean if you still mad that you gave the word to have Lavelle killed then let's talk about it. But please don't talk about my husband when you know how I feel about that kind of shit."

"I gave the word to have Lavelle killed because I don't give a fuck about him anymore. He tried to do me wrong and I got back at him and if you think I'm still tripping off of that, you got me fucked up."

"Stop lying to yourself, Carissa!" I said. "You loved that nigga just like we loved our men. If anything we all lost when we caused their murders. I mean think about it, Yvette took care of Thick, Dyson was murdered on the streets and even I had to off Cam. The difference is we ain't getting busted and running around town making fools of ourselves."

"Yeah, you wilding out now." Yvette added. "Big time."

"Don't try to skip the subject," Carissa said slyly. "Is Derrick stepping out on you or what?"

Silence.

"Okay…okay…if you must know, yes, my marriage is in trouble." I said in a low voice.

"I'm sorry, Mercedes. I didn't know." Yvette lied.

I know they knew, it was news around town. I just didn't expect it to be used as a slight against me simply because I cared enough to show my friend a slut video co-starring her mouth and ass.

"It's okay, Yvette." I paused. "But at least he's not gagging me with his dick on camera either. He has enough respect for me not to do that at least. But what about you, Carissa? You acting like you're a teenager and your daughter Persia is taking notice." I saw I struck a nerve when her facial expression went from conniving to shock. "Oh yes, them same parties you be throwing, Persia be at each and every one of them and she be fucking all them drug dealers under her mother's watch, too. Including freaky ass Zulo. And you know why, because you're too drunk and busted to give a fuck!"

Now she looked mad and Yvette said, "Now you deserved that shit."

Hearing Yvette's voice Carissa turned her head in her direction and said, "Oh do I?"

"Yes. You came in here with some off the wall bullshit and deserved to get called out about it. So I don't even know why you looking all dumb."

"Okay, you may be right and I'ma eat that. But what about you?"

"What about me?"

"After all this time you still fucking a woman." Then she laughed slyly. "I gotta tell you though, we took a bet and none of us in this limo thought that bullshit would last *this* long. I guess I gotta pay up though because Kenyetta thought differently."

Yvette looked at me and then Kenyetta.

"I didn't think you would stay with her, Yvette. But now I realize you really care about her and as long as you're happy, I'm good." I said trying to clean up my part of the personal conversations we had behind her back.

"Yeah, we were worried at first because we know you ain't got no kids. I mean, I know you don't want none now but what if you do?" Kenyetta said. "We just wanted to be sure you knew what you were really getting in to. But we weren't talking about you like you were a dog or nothing."

"Don't try to clean it up, Kenyetta. Let's give her a round of applause," Carissa said clapping her hands. "Congratulations, Yvette, you are officially a bull dagger."

I didn't even see it happen at first. All I saw was a black blur move so fast that I had to look again to see what happened. Yvette had jumped up and smacked her so hard in the face it left an imprint. The next thing I know a rumble ensued and Kenyetta was pulling Carissa and I was doing my best to hold Yvette who already busted her five times in the face to Carissa's none.

My driver pulled over on the side of a busy highway and everyone jumped out. Cars zipped by as we yelled and screamed at the top of our lungs.

"You wrong as shit for putting your hands on me!" Carissa cried wiping tears from her face, her makeup streaking. Kenyetta held onto her as if she was a wild dog about to attack. "If you can lick a pussy you can take a joke!"

"Fuck you, bitch! I wouldn't give a fuck if both of you bitches keeled over! I'm sick of both of ya'll shit!"

Yvette went too far but that's how she was when she got real mad. Just like she cut her face when Thick tested her loyalty, she believed in going to the extreme to prove her point. And there was no need in me telling her otherwise either because if I did, she would have three people instead of two to apologize to in the morning. Although this fight was official, I knew we could get past it, at least I hoped.

"You being so extra! Get back in the fucking car!" I said.

"I'm not getting back in that car with that bitch!" Carissa said. "Kenyetta, call Slack and Cheese to come scoop us!"

"We can take ya'll home." I said tiring of all this shit. It was entirely too cold to be standing outside. "This is not Broadway, Carissa. You can cut your fucking performance."

"Fuck you and fuck you!" Carissa said to me and Yvette.

I threw my hands up in the air because I was done with her shit for tonight. I was just happy she had someone to call to pick her up and wanted my offer to take her home on record in case she tried to call me on it in the morning.

Yvette got back in the car and I saw her mouth, 'I'm sorry', to Kenyetta.

Kenyetta mouthed, 'I'm sorry, too.'

Yvette and I sat in the car while Kenyetta and Carissa stayed outside. I shook my head and said, "She family, Yvette, no matter what she says or does. Don't forget that."

Cars whizzed by moving the fur on their coats and their hair. We didn't pull off until a black BMW pulled up and took them both away. It was our biggest fight yet, and one I hoped to forget.

"BUT AIN'T I WORTH IT? NOW YOU GET TO LOOK AT A PRETTY ASS NIGGA FOR THE NEXT COUPLE OF HOURS."

- Lil C

Lil C tugged at his black Gucci knit cap as he sat in the backseat of his Benz talking on the phone. His mother had Wallace drive him wherever he wanted to go in the DMV (D.C, Maryland Virginia). Wallace took a bullet for the city when Black Water's son Nathan shot him in the arm and Mercedes felt indebted to him so she trusted him with C's life. Kit saved Mercedes by feeding her when niggas gang raped her, an event even now she hadn't fully shared with her son, so she also blessed him with gainful employment. Little did C know that one incident had a lot to do with why she chose to take Cameron's life. Kit, who was in the passenger seat of the Benz, was C's bodyguard while Wallace was his driver. She didn't want C being by himself and wanted him protected at all times, even when he didn't want to be.

"I told you I'm 'bout to scoop Monie. Why you keep asking, nigga?" C checked the pockets of his leather coat looking for his Twix candy bar. It wasn't there.

"You act like it's top secret or something."

C laughed and said, "Me and Monie gonna grab something to eat and then I'ma go bang Cute Nikki's back out after I leave the gym."

"I still can't believe you bagged that bitch! How the fuck you do that?" Ryan said.

"Nigga, I'm C, of Emerald City. Ain't no nigga around here richer or better looking than me. You know this."

"Yeah, whatever." Ryan responded knowing what he was saying was true. "So I guess you not going to shoot hoops with me and Mazon. There's this indoor basketball court in Virginia we wanted to check out."

"Can't fuck with it, but I'ma get up with ya'll later." When the phone dropped out of his hand and landed on his new Lebron's, he remembered he forgot to rub the fact that he had them before they came out, in his face. "I meant to tell you, I got them Lebron's."

"When you get 'em?" Ryan said. "They don't even drop 'til next month."

"You know I got the hook up." C laughed.

It wasn't even a competition when it came to C having the newest shit because he always stayed fresh. But being spoiled was etched in his makeup and he felt inspired to let a nigga know.

"Well I'm 'bout to fuck your head up right now."

"Picture you fucking up anything of mine."

Ryan laughed and said, "I'm looking at a box of Lebron's, size 13 right now, nigga."

"Get the fuck out of here."

"I'm all the way serious. I'm 'bout to put 'em on right now." Ryan bragged.

Those words hit C as hard as if someone had just talked about his mother. He was always known to get the new fashions before they dropped and the moment he saw someone wearing something he owned, he'd give his shit away.

" How the fuck you get 'em?" C said trying to conceal his hate.

"You know Mazon's father owns them Shoe City stores. So they went to some convention a few days back. I gave him a couple of hundred and he got me a pair."

"I gotta go." C said hanging up in his face.

Looking down at his feet he was enraged. If a nigga like Ryan got a hook up before he did, what was the use?

"Pull over, Wallace." C said.

"No problem."

When the Benz was on the side of the road, he took the new Lebron's off and threw them out of the window. Wallace and Kit looked at each other having seen the scene many times before. Spoiled wasn't even the word when it came to C's behavior at times.

"Take me back to my house to get my D&G's."

"I'm on it." Wallace said busting a U-turn.

It would be the last time C would ever wear a popular sneaker again. Either he wore a pair of shoes over three hundred dollars, or he wasn't wearing shit. That went for his jeans, too. So he rushed into the house in bare polo socks and changed his shoes and clothes. His conversation with Ryan inspired him to get extra fly on the world for the day. He took off his Seven Jeans and threw on his Earnest Sewn jeans feeling nobody was up on them yet. He completed his look with his custom-made brown leather jacket. Then he grabbed a few stacks of money from up under his bed and snatched his gym bag.

Fifteen minutes later he was out the door. When he finally made it to Tyland to pick up Monie, he called her house. "I'm downstairs."

"You not coming up?" She said already knowing the answer.

"You know I don't get out of my car for nobody."

She laughed and said, "I'm on my way."

When she walked toward the car C could feel all eyes on him. Tyland Towers residents hated C and the family he came from. They felt his family caused them more problems than they were worth, but there was nothing they could do about it. He was hood royalty and that's all that mattered.

When Monie got to the car C couldn't help but notice that to be a big girl, her shape was on point. Her long hair hung down her back and brushed against her leather jacket, which was slightly open exposing her ample cleavage. If a dude was in to big women, she'd be considered a dime.

"'Bout time you got here!" Monie said playfully hitting him on the arm. "You had me waiting an hour for you."

Damn she smells good. He thought.

Wallace pulled off already knowing their destination, B Smith's in Washington DC.

"I may be late but ain't I worth it?" He joked. "Now you get to look at a pretty ass nigga for the next couple of hours."

"Ugghhh, boy!" She took of his hat and threw it in his lap. "With your fake curly head ass! Tell the truth, that's a Jerri Curl ain't it?"

"You want to see the hair on my dick?"

She laughed hard and said, "You too fucking arrogant."

"Naw, just confident." He put his hat back on. "Were you able to find anybody who knows Dreyfus? I met a few rich white boys in this band and they lost contact with their other connect. I could stand to make a lot of money if I could get them a connect."

"Naw...it's hard to find him." She paused. "Just ask your mother."

"I might have to." C said.

"Nice shoes!" She commented loving the black and silver accents in his D&G sneakers. "But I know you gonna get the Lebron's."

"Fuck no! I'll leave that shit for the block niggas. I stay up on the classic shit."

"Whatever," she said, remembering all of the boxes of shoes he had at his house at the National Harbor and Emerald City. "Where's Daps? She ain't coming with us?"

"Naw...I haven't been able to reach her today." He said stealing an unconscious look at her titties.

"Ugghhh, C!" She said hitting him again. "I saw you looking at my titties."

"Please, you know I don't fuck with big girls. Don't get me wrong, you cute and all, but you gotta run the track a few times before I fuck with you."

Monie's head hung low and it was obvious that his words hurt her feelings, but C didn't care or bite his tongue. He was brought up to feel that he could say whatever he wanted and if people wanted to hang with him they had to take it.

"Well I don't wanna fuck with you either."

"Aww...sure you do."

"Uggh!" She said digging in her purse. "Here, boy." She threw a Twix in his lap knowing it was his favorite candy.

"Damn, I was just wanting one of these joints." He said ripping the candy open. "Thanks, Monie." He softly punched her chin. "You must be in my head or something."

"I'm in your heart." She said out loud.

He looked at the seriousness on her face and laughed, "You playing right?"

Monie was quiet before she said "Yes, boy! What I look like being soft on you? Anyway your best friends have been talking about you."

"What you and Daps saying about me now?"

"We was saying how you'll never get a serious girlfriend with your attitude."

"And what attitude is that?"

"You're arrogant attitude. You gotta bring that down if you want someone to see how loving you are."

C laughed, "I don't care about love, I care about pussy. Look at that bitch right there," he said pointing out the window at a girl who walked across the street. Her ass was phat and round. "I could learn to love a bitch like that."

"Well she might not want you if you don't change."

"If a bitch want me she better comply to my rules." He laughed. "I'm a king, baby. And a king always gets who and what he wants."

"Whatever, you're so spoiled you're probably right."

"I am right. Ain't no probably to it."

Monie leaned back in her seat and said, "You still trying to get Sri Lankan girls over here?"

"You think I'm playing but I'm dead serious."

"But why?"

"Look how sexy the women are," he said, pulling out the phone to show her some picture he'd saved. C had done extensive research on the women and their country. He even managed to find a site showcasing women who wanted to move to the USA. "And some of them are trained for war, too. It's very violent over there and all citizens have to be ready, even the women."

"So what, you get them over here and then what? You turn them into your soldiers or something?"

"Yep, all they need are Visas, and I'm working on that right now."

"Why?" Monie persisted.

"Because I want women on my arm no nigga around here can get. That's why."

C and Monie continued their conversation until Wallace yelled, "WHAT THE FUCK?!"

Out of nowhere a seven-year-old boy who was riding his bike rode directly into the path of their car. Wallace slammed on the brakes missing the kid by a few feet. The boy dropped his bike in front of the black Benz, folded his arms and stood directly in the front of the car. When he had their attention, a sly smile rested on his face.

"Fuck is up with this lil nigga?" Kit asked.

"I don't know but he betta move before I run his ass over." Wallace beeped his horn but the kid maintained his stance.

Kit rolled down his window and said, "Lil nigga, you betta get the fuck from in front of this car before we press that ass."

"Is that the great Lil C?" The kid said, walking toward the side of the car C was located on. "The one who think he's better than everybody else?"

"Yeah, nigga, it's me." C said through the window.

The boy stood at C's window and stared at him with hate in his eyes. "Good, 'cause I never saw a real live dead nigga before."

"Hold up! What you just say to me?"

"You's a dead nigga." The boy said, taking his finger and making a chop throat notion at his neck.

C feeling disrespected hopped out of the car and the boy ran. Cars did their best to avoid hitting the boy and C. Kit, Wallace and Monie were hot on their trail.

When the boy was far enough from them he turned around and yelled, "You don't even know how bad your life is getting ready to get do you?!" Then he laughed. "Take a good look at your friends and family because some of them won't be alive after too much longer! You fucked with the wrong family, nigga!!" He said taking off running again. "The wrong family!"

When he was out of sight, they all stopped in the middle of the street and stared in the direction the kid ran, as if he'd reappear and tell them who he was.

"Who the fuck was that?" C asked.

"I don't know. But I'ma have to tell your mom's about this." Kit said. He tapped him on the shoulder and said, "Let's go."

C didn't move. "Why you gotta tell her shit? So she can worry?"

Kit turned back around and said, "So she can know."

"You ain't got to tell my mom's nothing. She already got ya'll riding me around every fucking where I go, I don't want her worrying even more." He paused. "It was just some snot nosed brat who's jealous of me. Shit fine."

IN THE GYM

C and Derrick had just finished up on the treadmill at Gold's Gym in DC. He was replaying over and over what the boy said and wondered who he was with. What am I thinking about? It's just a fucking kid.

"You ready?" Derrick asked as his treadmill stopped. "We gotta hit the weights next."

"Yeah...I'm done." C said wiping his face with a towel. "Spot me."

When they walked to the weights C layed down on the bench while Derrick handed him a weight bar with a hundred pounds on it.

"What's on your mind, C? I know you, and you ain't been right ever since you got here. So what's up? Or do I have to ask Wallace and Kit?"

C hated how him and Mercedes always had a pipeline in on what was going on with him, because of Wallace and Kit. Eventually he would have to get rid of one of them because he knew two could keep a secret if one of them were fired.

"Nothing, Derrick." He said as sweat poured down his face.

"C, I know you. Stop lying to me. What's up?"

"You ever feel like people are out to get you, but you don't know who or why?"

"Yeah...all the time."

"Well what you do when you have that feeling?"

"You move carefully. You watch your back and you don't do things you don't have to."

"So you stop living?"

"Naw, you live life to the fullest." He lifted the weight off of C so he could rest after he'd raised it ten times. "But when you feel like people are after you, you don't do shit unless you really want to. The reward has to be worth the risk."

"I don't get it."

"For instance, when you feel like somebody is after you, you don't go to the movies for fun. You go to Mexico, Brazil, shit like that."

"I get it." C layed back on the bench and Derrick handed him the weights again. "Derrick, what you think really happened to my father? How was he killed?"

"C, didn't your mother talk to you about this already?"

"Yeah...but I just want to hear it from you."

"Black Water had him murdered, you know that."

"Yeah...I know."

"You still up at nights with him on your mind?"

"Naw! I don't be up at night thinking about shit."

"Okay, C."

"I'm serious." He said trying to convince himself of a lie. "Why you ain't been home a lot lately? Everything good with you and mom's?"

"Yeah...that's my wife." Derrick seemed nervous and almost dropped the weights on C's head. "I just need to get away every now and again. You know how it is, your mom's a firecracker sometimes."

"As long as everything's cool." C said. "She been real sad lately and I hate to see her like that."

"And you think it's because of me?"

"I don't know what it's about."

Right when Derrick said that one of C's best friends, Daps came into the gym with two large bags. She didn't see them watching her as she made her way from the front door to the girl's locker room.

"What Daps doing here?" C asked. "She got a membership?"

"That's your best friend, you tell me."

"I figured you knew, since you here every day."

"I don't know, but I do know she been working out a lot lately. A girl like that likes to keep her body in order." Derrick tapped C on the shoulder, "Now get up and add some more weight on that bar. I need you to spot me."

PITBULLS IN A SKIRT 3

"JUST 'CAUSE I'M NOT SWEATIN' YOU LIKE THE REST OF THESE BITCHES OUT HERE DON'T MEAN I DON'T WANT THE RELATIONSHIP."

-YVETTE

After playing around with my three pitbull's outside, we walked in the house. Once inside, the dogs ran around our Georgetown DC house like they owned the place until they walked into the room I made up for them. The room was decorated with large dog pillows and a floor model TV so they could watch their favorite show, I loved them so much. The moment I closed the door I thought about Chris. I know she's mad at me but I don't know what I did wrong...this time anyway. It seems like I'm making her mad all the time, even though I'm not trying to.

The heat in my house was on high, and it felt like my nose was burning inside. Chris liked it real hot in the winter and instead of arguing with her about it, I usually just went about my business like it didn't bother me.

I had just gotten us this beautiful mahogany bedroom set and the smell of its newness rang heavily in the air with her Gucci men's cologne and my wet dogs.

Walking into the bedroom, I sat on the edge of the bed and took off my shoes. My maid and cook Rosa, was preparing fresh tacos in the kitchen and I hoped to grab a few before I left. Before eating, I went into the bathroom to brush my teeth and I looked at my face in the mirror. Who the fuck am I? What is my life really about now that I don't have Thick to tell me what to do anymore? Although it had been years since I'd killed him, in the end I always felt deeply lost without him. And in a lot of ways I needed him to tell me which direction to turn sometimes.

"Where you going?" Chris asked, after I walked out of the bathroom connected to our bedroom. I didn't hear her come in.

"You hungry?" I asked, after I sat on the edge of the bed and grabbed one of my black Ugg boots from the floor. "Rosa cooking tacos tonight, the way you like 'em. With the Velveeta cheese and stuff."

"Where are you going, Yvette?"

"I'm meeting 'Cedes at her house tonight...we have a meeting. After that she wants me to go with her shopping."

"You hate shopping!"

"I know, but I still gotta go. Her and Derrick been beefing lately and she needs somebody to talk to, and you know how I feel about my friends."

Chris ran her hand through her short tapered curly hair; the edges were always shaped up nice and neat. I could tell she was about to go somewhere too because she wore her new True Religion jeans and a grey Polo cashmere sweater.

"Whatever," she paused, "Anyway, I thought the meeting was last weekend." Chris sat on the bed next to me and I turned away from her. Lately I was finding it hard to look into her eyes.

"We didn't get a chance to meet, Chris. I told you me and Carissa had a fight, or were you even listening to me?"

"You told me but you ain't say nothing 'bout you leaving tonight, Yvette."

"Well I gotta go. This is business and you know that. It's a possibility we might not be fuckin' with Tyland Towers no more so this meeting is very important." I said, standing up.

“Yvette, I thought we were hanging out tonight. What happened to that?” She walked up to me and looked into my eyes.

Damn. I had forgotten all about our date. "Oh, that's what you got dressed for?"

"Yes, Yvette. I’m dressed for you."

I walked to the mirror, placed on my four-carat Vida earrings and looked at Chris through the mirror. “Look…I can’t go out with you tonight. I got a…”

“Business to run,” she said finishing my sentence. “What about a relationship to run? You ain’t a part of that no more?”

I turned around to face her. “Chris, stop the bullshit! I’m sick of you making me choose between Emerald City and you. Because for real, if I had to make a decision it wouldn’t be nice.”

“So what you saying?”

“You know what I’m saying. If I had to choose,” I paused, swallowing hard, “I…I don’t think you’d like my answer.”

I don’t know what came over me. I guess part of me wanted her to just go on with her life. I hated that being with her forced me to question my sexuality. And it forced me to question who I really was. Every day we fought. Every day I’d threaten to leave, and every day she’d beg me to stay.

“Yvette, I’m trying…I really am, but you making me want to walk away from this relationship for good.”

“Whatever…like you’d really leave me.” I laughed. “You realized the moment you rolled up on me when we first met, that you couldn’t live without me.”

“You really believe that don’t you?” She smirked.

“I wouldn’t say it if I didn’t believe it.”

“You gonna wish you ain’t never say no shit like that to me. I promise you.”

"Well I'm saying the truth, Chris. Just 'cause I'm not sweating you like the rest of these bitches out here don't mean I don't want the relationship."

She looked at me, gave me the look that could mean so many things and walked out the bedroom. I waited for a minute. Just didn't move. I figured she would come back in the room and talk to me, but she didn't.

So I walked slowly into the living room knowing that if her coat was gone, she was really mad because she left without saying goodbye. Yep…her Gucci leather jacket was gone.

"Ms. Yvette, the tacos are done. Would you like to taste?" Rosa asked with a thick accent.

"No…just put it in the refrigerator. I'll grab a few when I come back."

Right after I said that, I heard glass crash in my bedroom. I grabbed the extra gun I kept under the couch in the living room. My dogs barked wildly at the commotion.

"MS. YVETTE…WHAT'S HAPPENING!?" Rosa said nervously holding her ears.

"Shut the fuck up, Glock, Oozie and Nine!" I said yelling at my dogs. They quickly got quiet.

When I went into my bedroom I saw my window was broken. Could Chris have carried it like that?

"Rosa, call Johnson's Handyman service, the number is on the refrigerator. Have them come fix my window as soon as possible."

"Is everything okay?" She said, still shaken up.

"ROSA! DO WHAT THE FUCK I ASKED!"

She ran into the kitchen to make the call. "And just so you know, I'm not hungry." I told her.

I saw the look on her face and knew what she wanted. Whenever she made me food, and I didn't eat it, she knew it would go to waste. Usually I'd have her throw it away and no one would get to enjoy her cooking. But Rosa had eight kids and although she wouldn't take extra money from me because she believed in working hard for her pay, she would take food.

"You know what, take the tacos home. All I'm gonna do is throw it away anyway."

"Thank you, Ms. Yvette. Thank you." She smiled, before making the call.

I don't know what happened to my window but I had to leave to meet Mercedes. I was about to grab my purse and head out the door when my cell rang. It was Mercedes and she was frantic.

"Yvette, I need you to get over here! I'm about to kill Lil C's ass!"

"Cameron. My name's Cameron!" Lil C yelled, in the background. *"I wish you stop calling me that shit!"*

"Where are you?" I asked, hating how C was talking to his mother.

"I'm at the apartment in Emerald City."

"I'm on my way."

I grabbed my keys and was on my way out the door until I ran into a familiar face outside on my steps. She looked better than she did when I last saw her and although I was sure she was clean, there was something deceitful in her eyes.

"Ma…what are you doing here?"

"I came to see you?"

Not knowing what else to say I said, "Did you just break my window?"

"No. But I saw some kids running away. Who were they?"

"I…I don't know." I said, looking as far as my eyes could take me outside. Redirecting my attention to her I said, "What do you want?"

"Yvette…baby…I came to see you. I miss you!"

"FUCK ALL THAT...THE ONLY THING I CARE ABOUT IS ROGER."

- LORETTA

The moment her daughter left the house, Loretta jumped on the phone to make a call. She was nervous because she'd never done anything like this before, but in her mind he was worth it. Walking a few feet from Rosa who had been looking at her with evil eyes, she grabbed the phone to make the call.

"I'm in her house." She whispered excited at her early victory. "I'm not sure yet, but I think I can convince her to let me stay here."

"I really can't believe it. I mean, even though you were a strung out ass bitch, you must've gotten something right for her to be so trustworthy."

Silence.

"Fuck all that...the only thing I care about is Roger. I want to make sure when I do this that you'll leave him alone. I need him to get better."

"Loretta, if everything checks out, your precious Roger is free."

"SHE HAD A BODY I WISHED SHE'D BEEN BLESSED WITH AFTER SHE LEFT MY HOUSE."

-CARISSA

"Hey, is this Carissa?"

"Yes?" I said answering my cell.

"I'm calling to see if we can fuck?"

"How did you get my number?!" When he didn't respond I hung up.

I had been receiving calls like that all day and figured I'd have to change my number sooner or later. Right now the prank calls were the least of my worries, my fast ass daughter was first and foremost.

I was having a drink in my Yacht where my girls and I spent most of our time. If I could help it, I preferred for us to stay on the Docks instead of Emerald City. Mainly because my daughter was starting to smell herself and she was chasing grown men. I was gonna have to do something about it because she's only sixteen years old, yet she act like she a grown ass woman sometimes. And then there was her problem with alcohol…I mean, just because I have a drink don't mean she has to.

"Girl, I told you that nigga dumb as shit! I don't know why you ain't believe me. I'm 'bout to go on his Facebook page right now." My oldest daughter Persia said on the phone. She was sitting on the phone in her bedroom running her fucking mouth. Her clothes were thrown across the floor and nothing was hung up in her closet. The worst part about it was, we had a maid. So what really was her problem?

"Persia, we gotta talk. Get off the phone." I said hanging in her doorway.

She put her hand on the receiver and said, "Dang, ma. I know you see me on the phone and shit. What you want?" She wasn't wearing anything but her pink bra and matching panties. Just like me, she loved to walk around the house naked.

"Persia, watch your fucking mouth! And you need to clean your room."

"Clean my room why? I mean, what the fuck we paying Evelyn for?"

She rolled her eyes and flung her long soft hair. She had a body I wished she'd been blessed with after she left my house. Her big breasts, small waist and thick pink lips had men chasing behind her and had me going crazy. If Lavelle was here…I wouldn't have to deal with this shit. And it was times like these, I wished I never gave the order to have him killed. I…I miss him so much.

As she ran her mouth, I looked at the large mirror against her wall. I'd spent five thousand dollars for that mirror, a mirror she said she couldn't live without. Now it was shattered beyond imagination due to her breaking it when she was in one of her moods. She had a problem reacting immediately on her feelings when she was mad or sad, instead of giving herself some time to cool down. Her other passion? Guns. She played with them a lot and I had to lock them up in my house to keep her out.

"Persia, get off the phone. I wanna talk to you."

"Ma…please!" She yelled. "Stop being a fucking hater."

"Bitch, I gotta talk to you so get the fuck off the phone." She didn't. "Now, Persia!"

"Sugar, I'ma call you back. My mother over here acting like a bitch," she said hanging up.

I walked into her room and she sat on the edge of her bed. The moment I sat down, she jumped up and threw on the pink velour sweatpants that were on the floor. The velvet material hugged her curves a little too closely for my taste.

"What, ma?" She said grabbing the matching jacket from under her bed. "You got me off the phone and now all you doing is staring and shit."

Even though she was mad at me she was still my baby and all I wanted to do was hug her.

"Persia…I…well, I wanna talk to you about some stuff I've been hearing."

"Like what?"

"Well, somebody told me you're not acting like a young lady should when you at the parties I host."

Persia burst into laughter and said, "I'm not acting like a lady?" She repeated. "Mama, please! How would you know what I do when you always drunk? As a matter of fact, the only time you talk to me is when you ask me to pour you *another* cup of vodka."

She got up and walked into the kitchen and I was right on her tail. My ten-year-old daughter Treasure was in the living room with her friend Bria and I could see the nervous look in her eyes. She was silently begging me not to argue with Persia in front of her company but for now I didn't care. Persia was way out of line and I had to put her in her place.

"Bria, why don't you call your mother so she can come get you, honey. I gotta talk to my daughter in private. You can come back tomorrow to hang out with Treasure."

"Mommy…we were playing music." Treasure protested.

"Treasure, go in your room!" I said pointing to her door. "And Bria, call your mother."

Treasure stomped to her room and her friend went into the dining room to place the call. I followed Persia in the kitchen mad as fuck about her attitude.

"You are getting too grown, girl. And I'm sick of it. This is my house and I can do what I want when I want and that goes for when I'm outside of here, too. But you are still my child, and although you act like a bitch sometimes, I still love you."

"You don't love me."

"Persia, I do! I just don't want you to feel like you need to give up your body just to get attention." I said walking up to her.

"Why not? You do?"

"What?"

"Ma, you fuck Slack in here and I hear you all the time begging him not to leave you. So you using your body, too. Talking about how you'll suck his dick to sleep if he'd just stay."

"Persia, are you…I mean…are you still a virgin?" I asked ignoring her comment.

"What?"

"You heard me! Are you still a virgin?"

"Yes, ma, dang!"

"Okay…that's good. Now," I swallowed, "What is this I hear about you fucking with some of the dealers at my parties?"

"Well what exactly did you hear?" She said in a sassy tone, putting her hand on her hips.

"I'm hearing a lot of shit. Like the fact that you fucking with men ten to twenty years older than you. Specifically Zulo."

"Oh well," she said rolling her eyes.

"Are you?"

"Ma, please."

"Persia, baby, I know you miss your daddy." She turned away from me and from the reflection in the window, I saw tears well up in her eyes. "Look at me." She did. "I know you miss him, but you have to watch what you're doing to yourself. He would be so disappointed if he knew how you were acting."

"Why did he have to die? Why?" I poured me a cup of liquor and drank it all while she whined. "It seems like I lost everybody at the same time. All of my uncles, too."

"It happens. The game is what the game is."

"You don't even seem like you care." She said. "Lil C says Aunt Mercedes cries all the time over Uncle Cameron."

"Please…she gave the order to kill him." I said with an attitude remembering our fight in the limo. "If anything, she crying over her husband fucking around on her. Not Cameron."

Persia's mouth hung open and it took me a moment to replay back what I said.

"Aunt Mercedes….killed Uncle Cameron?"

"Noooo!! I mean, that's what people said."

Oh my God! I thought. What have I done? I hope she'd never repeat what I said.

"Persia, don't ever repeat what I just said because it's probably not true."

"Whatever, ma." She said in a low voice. "None of that shit can bring daddy back anyway."

"You're right. But I'm still here and I love you." I smiled. "Now give me a hug." We embraced and I held on to her closely. Although I was in and out of the streets these days, nothing meant more to me than trying my best to convince my daughters I loved them.

When we separated, I grabbed a bottle vodka from the freezer and poured me a glass. As I was pouring, I noticed she was mad at me again and I didn't know why. I was just about to ask her what her problem was now, when my phone rang.

It was Mercedes and I started not to answer it. I still hadn't gotten over the fight we had. So what she saw me fucking Slack in that video. I figured somebody must've gone into his house and stole our tape. He would never do that shit to me because we fuck and tape it all the time. Anyway, the tape she showed me wasn't even the best one. When I told him about it he went off claiming he'd fuck up whoever violated and I believed him.

"Hello." I said dryly drinking my vodka while staring at Persia making a sandwich.

"Carissa, we meeting at my apartment in Emerald later."

"And?"

"And...are you coming?"

"Why should I?"

"Carissa, we had an argument and I hate myself for arguing with you, but I'm not about to kiss your ass either. So what do you want to do?"

"I'll be over."

"Good, meet me at my apartment instead of the community center. Please hurry up...Lil C giving me bullshit and before we meet I really need the advice of my friends. Okay?"

I looked at my daughter and wondered what could be worse.

"Okay." I said dryly.

"You aight, Carissa? I mean, you still not that mad at me are you?"

"No, I'm fine. But look, I'm bringing Persia with me."

"No, ma! I got somewhere to go." Persia screamed, dropping the knife she used to smear the mayo on her turkey sandwich.

"Of course she can come." She said. *"You know my niece is welcome over here."*

"Good. I'll see you later." I hung up the phone.

Five minutes later Bria's mother came to pick her up.

"Go get your fur coat and come on, Persia!" I yelled. She stomped back to her room and I said, "Treasure, go ask Bria's mother if you can stay over her house for a while."

Her face lit up with a smile. "Thank you, ma."

"Thank you nothing," I said handing her a hundred bucks. "Give that to her if she says yes, ya'll order some pizza or something."

"Okay!" she yelled running into her room to grab her coat.

When the kids were out of my earshot I called Kenyetta. "You got some blow?"

"Naw...I can't find nobody to cop from. What we gonna do? Ask somebody in Emerald?"

"Don't be stupid! All we need is the girls finding out about our habit. I'll think of something."

ON THE HIGHWAY

Bria's mother was able to keep Treasure so we left the Yacht to meet Mercedes. I was driving down New York Avenue trying to figure out what I could do to strengthen my relationship with my daughters, when we approached a light. Persia's non-stop talking on the phone was irritating me.

"Persia, give me your phone." I demanded holding my hand out.

"Why, ma?" She frowned.

"Because you're still on punishment for talking to me like you were crazy at the house."

"You mean on the boat."

"The phone!"

"Uggh, you're such a fucking hater!"

"Do you want me to embarrass you?"

She rolled her eyes. "Sugar, I'ma call you back. My fake ass mother tripping again."

She threw the phone at me and it fell in my lap. I tossed it in the back of my black BMW and waited for the light to turn green.

"Ma, you almost broke my shit."

"Persia, shut the fuck up!"

"Uggghh! I can't stand you." She said folding her arms into her chest.

"Tell me something I don't know."

In raising my kids I fucked up. Because Lavelle and me sold drugs for a living, we tried to give our kids anything they wanted in the world. We didn't want them having run over shoes, fucked up clothes and things like that. As far as we were concerned, if money was a problem, it wouldn't be a problem for our kids. But in the process of doing that, they didn't understand the importance of earning and deserving. And in the case of Persia, she definitely didn't understand the importance of respect.

We were five more minutes into the drive and I didn't even turn in her direction, the music was off and I was enjoying the peace and quiet. I was parked at a light wondering how the meeting would go tonight. That is until Persia yelled, "Oh my GAWD! Ma, is that you?"

When I looked in the direction she was pointing in I saw a picture of me naked on a light post. I drove wildly away from the parked light almost hitting another car to get closer to the light post. Once parked, I walked slowly up to the poster size picture. And there I was, naked and exposed from my face to my waist. The letters above my body read, "CALL CARISSA FOR A GOOD FUCK". My number was listed on the picture. This explains the strange calls I'd been receiving all day.

I snatched the picture off the light post and drove all around DC looking for more pictures. In the end, I removed twenty pictures. Who would do something like this to me? Who would do something like this to my boyfriend?

After collecting all of the nude pictures I got back in my car as we traveled on the way to Emerald City. Looking over at my daughter, I saw the sly smile resting on her face. After I'd just finished scolding her about her behavior, I knew she thought this was too funny.

"Don't say anything to me, Persia I ain't trying to hear your mouth."

"I won't say a word." She giggled.

MERCEDES APARTMENT
EMERALD CITY

When Persia and I got there, I could hear Yvette talking to Mercedes. But the moment Kenyetta opened the door for me they stopped talking.

"Is C here?" Persia asked Mercedes.

"No. You have his room all to yourself."

"Thank you, Aunt Mercedes. Oh yeah...I had a dream about Uncle Cameron today."

My head throbbed wondering what she was about to say.

"What was the dream about?" Mercedes asked.

"Can't really remember the whole thing but for some reason it came out that they actually found out who really killed him."

After she said that she threw her fur on the edge of the couch and stomped toward the back of the apartment.

"What the fuck was that about?" Kenyetta asked.

"I'm wondering the same thing." Mercedes said.

"That little bitch has been tripping all day. Don't listen to nothing she says." I said. Persia closed the bedroom door in C's room. "She mad at me about some bullshit."

"I'm going through it with C, too. I mean, I'm starting to think by giving them everything they wanted, that we did them a disservice." Mercedes said. "C got a fucked up sense of entitlement."

"She gonna have a fucked up something else if she keep acting like that." I said. "Anyway, where C at?"

"He just went to the store."

"Where are your girls?" I asked Mercedes trying to keep conversation going even though I was still mad. I mean, the least I could do was talk to her after Persia's antics.

"You know they at my mother's on the weekend. That bitch do anything to get paid." She laughed.

"I heard that." I said sitting down at the table without even speaking to Yvette.

"Carissa, I got a few calls about some pictures posted of you around DC. You hear about that?" Yvette asked.

I was not about to give them the satisfaction so I said, "No."

"Well people saying naked pictures are everywhere of you in DC."

"Fuck people." I said.

When Mercedes' phone rang, she ran and answered it. "Hello." She looked at us and then spoke in a low voice. "Derrick, please come home tonight." Silence. "I'm in Emerald. Maybe I can make dinner for you or something." Silence. "Oh…okay. I understand."

She hung up and walked over to us and Kenyetta got up from the table and walked to the kitchen. When she came back she had two beers in her hand and handed me one.

"So you go into Mercedes' fridge and get two beers without asking anybody else if they want something." Yvette said.

Kenyetta looked at me and we both laughed. "Look, I ain't your maid Rosa. If you want a beer go get one yourself."

"You know what, I'm not even tripping off of neither one of you bitches no more." Then she looked at Mercedes and said, "So what's up Mercedes? What you want to rap to us about?"

"It's C. He been trying to get Dreyfus' number to get a package."

"What the fuck?" Yvette said. "Did he have any luck?"

"You know Dreyfus won't be found unless he wants to be found and I ain't telling him shit."

"How he gonna move it?" Kenyetta questioned. "He wouldn't step on our toes in EC would he?"

"Naw, Kit says he hangs with some white boys in this band. I think he's moving it through them."

"C is tripping hard now." Yvette said.

"Tell me about it. He keep talking about he want to be put on in Emerald City, too. That he wanna work for us and shit like that, but you know I can't do that. I can't lose somebody else to this lifestyle, especially not my son."

"But Cameron was younger than him when he started," I said. "So why not let him help out?"

"Because he's my son and I'm worried that's why, Carissa."

"But you always said when he was ready you'd put him on. And if you ask me, I think he's ready, Cedes." Kenyetta said.

"I know and I lied." She said shaking her head. "I just can't do it. I mean, if you had kids would you put them on, Kenyetta?"

Kenyetta looked down and said, "Probably so."

"Would you, Carissa?" She asked. "I mean…can you honestly tell me you would give Persia a package and let her move it if she wanted to."

"I don't know, she would have to be more mature. I mean, you saw her. She's too young acting right now to do anything on this level. But Cameron had C counting money, measuring weight and everything. C so good at that shit that he can eyeball weight and tell you what it's worth. Plus he almost eighteen, maybe it is time."

The moment I said that, Lil C came in wearing an expensive black leather coat. I couldn't get over how handsome he was and it amazed me how much he looked like Cameron. He definitely had grown up over the years.

He gave each of us a kiss on our faces and walked to the kitchen. Then he looked in the refrigerator and said, "You ain't go grocery shopping yet?"

"No, C." Mercedes said in a defeated tone. "But my assistant will be here tomorrow. I'll have her go."

"Damn, ma, you know I like to make a sandwich when I come home."

"I'm sorry, C. I thought you were going to the store."

"I was at the gym with Derrick."

"Oh…that's where he was?" Mercedes said with a solemn voice.

"Yeah…he didn't call you?"

"Oh…yeah. He called."

"Ma, if you want me to stay here, you gotta start doing shit a mother should," he said. "I'm going to my room."

C was getting more and more bratty by the day and a part of me did not like him. I guess because he reminded me of my daughter so much.

"Oh…your cousin Persia back there." I told him. "She mad at me so she may have an attitude. You want me to tell her to come out here with us?"

"Naw…she good. I ain't gonna be back there too long anyway." He said looking at Mercedes. "Ma, we still have to finish our conversation and I need you to hear me out."

"Later, C. We can have that conversation again later."

"THE ONLY WAY YOU CAN JUMP START YOUR LIFE IS IF YOU PULL THE TRIGGER."

- LIL C

Lil C walked down the hall towards his room with a duffle full of money in one hand and candy in the other. He was eating a Twix, his favorite treat and was on the last bar. Although he didn't mind Persia being in his room, he knew how nosey she could get having walked in on her several times going through his shit.

This time before he opened his door, he put his ear against it trying to catch her in the act. Instead of hearing drawers close, he heard several clicks followed by brief silence. When he opened the door, he saw her playing with his gun by holding it to her head.

"Fuck is up with you?!" He yelled running up to her, snatching the gun out of her hands. The candy dropped out of his hand and fell to the floor. "You in here tripping that hard?"

"What's wrong?" Carissa said running into the room, Mercedes, Kenyetta and Yvette right behind her. "Everything okay?"

C held the gun behind his back and said, "Yeah...you know how she be going through my shit sometimes. Everything cool though. Ain't it, Persia?"

"Uh...yeah...I was just going through his drawers."

"Persia, get your ass outta this boy's room." Carissa said. "Don't make no sense how you don't know how to respect other people's shit."

"Naw...we cool." C combated. "Let her chill in here with me, plus I ain't seen her in a while."

Carissa rolled her eyes at Persia and said, "Look, don't act like you don't have no home training. Stay out of his shit, you hear me?"

"Bye, ma." She said, making it known she could care less about her idle threats.

Carissa threw Persia's fur coat on the chair in his room, rolled her eyes and closed the door.

"Yo, what the fuck is wrong with you?" C asked, tucking his gun back under his bed.

"I was just fucking with it. It's empty anyway."

"But why were you holding it to your head?" He waited for her answer.

Persia flopped on his bed and stared at the ceiling. "I wanted to see if I could feel how it would be if I was about to die. I be hearing all the time how people say that when they about to die, they life flash before them. I wanted my life to flash before me."

"Why?"

"'Cause I wanna feel good about life again. Right now C, I feel like nothing I do makes a difference. I miss my father."

C being able to identify with her stared at the holes in his walls. He too went through a lot of mental anguish due to the loss of his father. Little did they both know, the bitches in the kitchen had everything to do with their deaths.

"My mother don't listen to me...the dudes I fuck with only wanna fuck me...and I hate school. I'm bored, rich and alone." She sighed. "So I wanted to see if I could jump start my life some way. Can you understand that?"

"The only way you can jump start your life is if you pull the trigger." He said. "Matta fact, let me put some bullets in the gun and run that test again you were trying to do." C went under his bed, loaded his weapon and pointed it at her.

"Stop!" She yelled. "I got your point, okay? I'm not gonna fuck with your shit no more."

C shook his head and put his weapon back under the bed. Although he was mad at her for going through his shit, he understood how she felt because he was in the same boat. But there were some slight differences between them.

Lil C wasn't your typical hustler's son. He was smarter...different and harder than most kids his age. More than anything, he hated how people older than him always felt as if he wasn't smart enough to know what he wanted out of life, just because he was young. For instance, he was sick of school. Sick of the bullshit, sick of the fake bitches and sick of feeling like teachers could teach him anything he needed to know in order to be rich.

He was paid, and even as he stood over Persia, had no less than three G's in his pocket. His clothing came from the finest designers, his eyewear of choice was Blvgari and most of his jeans were imported from Italy. He had everything, but the love of a father and he missed that most of all.

Although Mercedes was harder on C's schooling, more so since Cameron's death, it was only because she was scared. She wanted to make sure he had an opportunity to go after a life she and Cameron didn't have. She made sure he took advantage of the classes Sidwell Friends, an upscale school in Washington D.C., had to offer, even when C wasn't feeling it.

And because of it, most of his friends didn't realize that he was fluent in Spanish, Chinese, and French and could play the piano like Mozart. And if art was your thing, C could paint a picture better than Picasso himself. He had the traits most people wouldn't believe the son of two drug bosses would have, yet for him it was not enough. He wouldn't feel worthy unless he had street cred.

"I know you going through some shit, but you gotta chill," C said. "You gonna fuck around and use all your lives playing dumb games."

"Boy, please. Don't act like you give a fuck about me," She said sitting up, cutting on the TV. BET's 106 & Park was on and she dropped the remote to let it play out.

"Who said I did give a fuck?" C said, always giving her a hard time.

She laughed and said, "Whatever, boy."

Although her reckless mouth bared no fruit, he couldn't get over how pretty she was. He knew they were considered cousins, because their mothers were best friends, but he couldn't lie, over time he started looking at her differently and didn't know why.

"I'm just fucking with you. But what's on your mind, cuzo? You and your moms beefing again?" He called her cuzo out loud as if that would lessen his attraction towards her.

Persia sat up in the bed and said, "C, I'm so sick of my mother's shit! I mean, I wish she would just listen to me sometimes before jumping the gun."

"The gun huh?" C said.

"Drop it already!" She laughed.

"Okay, what she do?" He said, picking his candy off the floor to throw it in the trash. Then he took off his coat and hung it in the closet.

"Somebody must've told her that I was fucking with Zulo and she in my shit." She said looking at C seriously. "I mean, she be busted, drunk and stupid and she wanna clock who I fuck? What kind of shit is that?"

"Hold up, what you mean you fucking Zulo."

"I said somebody said I must've fucked Zulo...I'm not fucking him." She laughed.

"I hope not, cause that nigga grimy and too old for you." C said. "You betta hope I never see that nigga 'cause I might put something to his ass for even coming at you like that." When she looked sad he knew she was considering dealing with him. "You were really gonna give him some pussy wasn't you?"

Zulo was an anything hustler who provided dealers with quick re-up when they were in between meeting their connects. He marked up the price of his drugs and the quality was bad but when you needed something quick he was the man.

"Maybe I was thinking about dealing with him." She shrugged.

"Persia, you gotta start acting like a lady. You royalty around here, so if you carrying it like that, you making the whole organization look bad. Niggas gotta think that getting with you is like a dream come true. And even up until the point you pick someone you wanna be with, they gotta see you as unattainable."

"Unattainable huh?"

"Yeah...beyond approach."

"Well I'm tired of being by myself and boys my age too stupid."

"There's some good niggas out there your age. I know a few of 'em."

"Hook me up." She said wide-eyed.

For some reason, C didn't want to hook her up with any of his boys. But he needed her to be unavailable to him and hooking her up might be what he needed to do.

C sat on the bed next to her and said, "Aight, I'ma hook you up with my man, Mazon. He got good paper and he good people. But don't fuck this nigga off the rip. He still a dude who might try his hand if you let him. Even though if he do some shit like that, I'll fuck his ass up and you better tell me, too."

"Is he cute?"

"How the fuck would I know?" C said standing up.

"Boy, ya'll kill me acting like you don't know if another nigga cute or not." She said smacking her mouth real ghetto like. "I ain't fucking with no eggs, C. 'Cause I break 'em."

C laughed. "Bitches like him if that's what you wanna know. But that's all I got for you."

She smiled and said, "Man, I wish our mothers weren't so close, because I'd fuck with you."

Silence.

"Yeah, whatever."

"What, C? You don't think I could be good enough for you?"

"I ain't never think about it before." He lied. "Uh...let me call Mazon, though." He said getting his phone off the dresser. And from the mirror he could see the embarrassment on her face. "You aight over there?"

"Yeah...I was just playing about what I said about me and you. I know I'm not your type plus we could never do anything like that. Right?"

"Fuck, naw! You my peoples and I know how reckless you be sometimes."

"Reckless?"

"Yeah. I heard about how you be fucking your own shit up when you mad. Instead of calming down and seeing how shit play out." Then he looked at her again. "So naw, we could never be like that because I'd kill you if you fucked with my Range."

She smiled and said, "Your loss."

He was just about to call Mazon when his cell rang. It was his homie Daps from school. He was known for saying that if he could bottle his swag, take a few drops out and mix it into a girl, it would turn into Daps. She was just that smooth.

They called her Daps because when you bought smoke from her at school, you'd put the money in her locker, and when she made sure the count was right, she'd give you 'dap' in the hallway to make the transfer. She did it so quickly and smoothly she never got caught.

A lot of white dudes were attracted to Daps in Sidwell, because she had skin light enough to be okay if you hung around her but she loved the girls.

"What's good, C!" Daps said. "Why you weren't in school the other day?"

Daps, like him, sold weed on the side to a few of the high school students. The money at school was steady but not good enough to keep him around. He needed to pump something worth the money and his time, and weed wasn't it. That's when he sold pipe dreams to some white dudes he met at a club. Now all he needed was the coke to follow through.

Through the mirror he could see Persia about to leave his room. "Where you going?" He said holding the phone to his ear. "'Cause I know you don't want to hear your mother's mouth."

"Oh...I was gonna give you your privacy since you on the phone."

"Relax." C told her. "If I wanted you out of here you would be gone."

She smiled and said, "Okay."

"Yo, nigga! You there?" Daps laughed. "Let me find out you got a bitch in your room."

"It ain't even like that." He paused. "It's my cousin." He said, not really believing the tag he put on their relationship. "But to answer your question, I'm not fucking with school no more. I'm done."

"What? You playing right?"

"Naw."

"I thought you said going to school was so easy you could do it in your sleep? So why leave now? You almost done."

When she said that, C saw Persia get up, grab the Robb Report magazine off of his dresser and skim through the pages. C only subscribed to the Robb and G Q magazines to stay up on the richest clothes, cars and real estate.

As Persia skimmed through her choice of reading material, C eyed her again. Her ass was so phat and round it almost looked fake. She had a smaller version most of her life but now it was just unreal. With the magazine in her hand, she sat back on the bed, put her hair behind her ear and as if she knew he was staring at her, smiled. What she doing to me? And why now? He thought.

He took his eyes off of her, looked down at his dresser and said, "You act like I ain't been telling you I wasn't fucking with school no more, Daps. The only difference now is that I'm serious. I'm 'bout to be king of my own empire, and school ain't for me. "

"Well if you leave, I'm going with you."

"Naw...you can't. Your peeps would fuck you up."

"What peeps? My mom's?" She paused and sounded sad. "She don't care what I do just as long as I go to church on Sunday and bible study on Thursday. Ma, not all the way right, C. She ain't paying for school anyway. The scholarship took care of that."

C laughed and for some reason, looked at Persia again. This time she looked up from the magazine, and he winked at her. Letting her feelings be known, she gave him her best Janet Jackson smile and his heart melted. Something was happening between them that he couldn't explain. They'd been around each other on many occasions, and every time they were in each other's presence, they connected in some way that was unknown to them.

When their parents sold dope, or had to leave their kids to get Emerald City in order, the same babysitter would keep them all in line. And when all the Pitbulls took an out of town trip, they'd arrange for all of their kids to be together. During these times C and Persia would go off on their own leaving their siblings alone.

"Daps, I saw you in the gym the other day. I heard you be there a lot. What's up with that?"

"Oh...uh...why you ain't say nothing?"

"You went from the front door to the locker room. You had two big ass bags with you, too."

"I'm running a marathon for breast cancer," she said. "It ain't nothing serious but I do got to be in shape."

"Well good luck, homie."

"Thanks. So where you gonna stay? 'Cause if you dropping out of school, I know your mother not gonna let you stay home."

C laughed and said, "Please, my mother don't want me to do nothing but stay home. I can be here for as long as I want."

When C's iPhone vibrated, he took it off his ear and saw a text message from this bitch named Cute Nikki he fucked with in Emerald. That's one of the features he liked about iPhones, you could get a text and stay on a call at the same time.

'Where U @? I thought U were meetin' me ova Ryan's house?'

C texted her back, 'I'm In Emerald, and I'm leaving in a sec. Whatz up?'

'Somebodee came by askin' bout U. N they say ya'll got beef.'

C texted, 'Did they say who they were?'

While he waited on her response he said, "Yo, Daps, meet me at Ryan's house in Emerald City later. And bring some friends. A lot of niggas gonna be there."

"You know the only friends I got is you and Monie."

"Oh yeah. I forgot." He laughed. "I'ma see you there."

"Love, C. All love." Daps said.

While most people said bye, she ended calls with 'Love'.

When he hung up with her he said to Persia, "What you doing later?"

"Nothing. Why?"

"You wanna hang out with me over Ryan's house? Mazon gonna be there too in case you wanna rap to him."

She jumped off of the bed and he knew Carissa wouldn't care about her hanging out with him because they knew she'd be safe.

"Yeah I wanna roll with you." Persia smiled. "But you just gotta rap to my mom's for me."

They grabbed their coats and he watched her put on her fur. "Damn, that's how you feel?"

She laughed. "Yep, so I hope Mazon got money like you say he do, 'cause I'm expensive."

C laughed and said, "Now you talking like royalty. Let these bamma ass niggas treat you like you supposed to be treated."

The response text C was waiting on to find out who came asking about him still hadn't come through his phone as he and Persia walked to the table where Carissa and them were.

"Aunt Carissa, Persia coming with me. So if you want to reach her, call my phone."

"You sure, C? I don't want her getting in your way." Carissa said.

"Naw, she family, she good."

"Okay, well...have fun." Carissa said secretly wanting Persia to sit by herself and sulk for the way she was acting.

"C, we can talk when you come back." Mercedes said.

"No doubt, ma. But let's make that conversation for tomorrow. I might be tired when I come back."

Mercedes looked sad and said, "Okay, C."

He and Persia left out the door and he called Wallace to tell him he was coming downstairs and to bring the car around. Once they were outside, they stepped into an awaiting black Mercedes Benz with smoked out windows. Wallace and Kit were in the front waiting on him as usual. Truthfully they could've walked to the building Ryan lived in but it wasn't their style.

"Everything cool?" Wallace asked as he opened the door for him and Persia.

"Yeah, man. Why you ask that shit?"

"Because we went up to the school to pick you up yesterday and you were gone." He paused getting behind the driver's seat.

"And Mercedes ain't say nothing 'bout you being out of school early." Kit added.

"My mom's ain't say shit because she ain't know." Kit picked up his cell and C knew he was about to call her. "What you doing, young?"

"I'm calling your mom's. I'm 'bout to make sure it's okay to take you anywhere."

Persia looked at C and he was heated with embarrassment and anger. "Put the phone down," C said in a low voice. "My mom's don't need to know every little move I make." He ignored him.

"Yo, Kit, put the phone down, nigga." Wallace said. "You heard him."

C could feel Persia tense up and that made him mad that she was uncomfortable. It was their first time hanging out together on some party shit and this nigga was trying to play him.

But C remained calm, because he knew Kit needed to get with the program if he wanted to get money. And he also needed to respect him, because do or die, Mercedes wasn't going to be hustling forever. Eventually she would have to pass the reigns over to someone she trusted, and who would she trust more than her own son?

Wallace looked at Kit and said, "Put the joint down, man."

C looked at Kit and said, "I know you loyal to my mom's and I 'ppreciate that shit. But I ain't Lil C no more, I'm a grown ass nigga who gonna be running all this shit soon. And there's gonna come a time when you gonna have to answer to me. Do you really want the last thing I remember to be this shit?"

Kit dropped his head. "Sorry, man."

"Fuck sorry. Just respect."

After he finished with him he sent Cute Nikki another text. He was anxious about who stepped to her about him.

"Where we going?" Wallace asked.

"Take us to Ryan's building." He was on edge waiting for her response and didn't realize it was showing all over his face."

"Don't look so mad." Persia said.

"I'm fine. You aight?"

"Yeah...you put that nigga in his place," she whispered, obviously turned on.

"Sometimes you gotta let niggas know." He told her. "I just wanna make sure you good."

The moment he said that, Cute Nikki's text came through. It read, 'C, he said his name was Tamir, and that ya'll have some unfinished business to settle. He said to tell you to watch your back.'

C had been waiting on his bamma ass to surface sooner or later. So he typed, 'Tell him he'll see me soon. And when he do he betta be ready.'

"THE REST OF YA'LL CAN GET IT HOW YOU FEEL IT."

- TAMIR

Tamir had just signed the paperwork for two brick apartment buildings he purchased in Southeast Washington, DC. Although his family knew he was buying one of them, they had no idea about the second unit or his reasoning for making the purchase. Outside of his name, the only other name on the building's was Energy's and she loved it, feeling her good credit would mean she'd carry more weight within the Klan. She was wrong. All of the women hated her, knowing that Tamir was the man to have in your bed, if you wanted to keep the good life.

"We are happy to do business with you Mr. and Mrs. Holman," Mr. Cornice said handing him the keys. "I see you have quite a large family out there waiting on you. And rest assured, you've made great purchases."

"Don't worry about all that, mothafucka. It just bet not be no problems in them buildings, because if it is...I'm coming for you. Just 'cause we buying them instead of renting don't mean they can be fucked up."

Mr. Cornice stood incredulously. "No...no, sir. There aren't any problems with the buildings at all. They're in tip top condition."

Tamir looked at him evilly due to everything he put him through to buy the properties. If it wasn't about the down payment it was about his taxes or lack thereof. Had it not been for Energy keeping her credit in tip-top condition when Black Water was alive, they would not have a place to keep their overstocked family. To say they were living large was an understatement.

Energy hugged Tamir lovingly and he kissed her passionately on the lips. He loved being where his father had been, in control, believing it made him closer to him in spirit than anyone else. So what Energy at one time was his wife, now she belonged to Tamir.

With the keys in his hand, he thought about what it took to get them to that point. They all had robbed, stolen and killed for the money necessary to get out of Virginia and into a place in DC that could keep them all together. And now, after much waiting the moment had finally arrived.

Opening the rental office's glass door, he and Energy slowly walked outside. All thirty-four siblings along with his mother Shade, and the other eight wives waited for the news. Energy keeping in tune with Tamir wore a serious expression on her face, secretly knowing the good news. They were tired of living in squalor, and places they couldn't make their own. And he learned under his father's watch that to maintain control, you have to be able to reach them all at the same time.

When he heard the sighs in their voices, and witnessed the sadness on their faces, he decided to show them the keys. The sun smacked against the silver keys, causing them to shine as brightly as diamonds. With them dangling under the winter sky, the women ran up to him landing hugs and kisses all over his face, while his brothers gave him multiple daps and pats on his back.

Energy as always was pushed to the side by the mob, never being able to fully get her respect in the family. It was because when Black Water was alive, he treated her like a cook and maid instead of a main wife. But now that he was dead, she was going to kill, beg and steal to remain by Tamir's side, and although the other women would never admit it, it was her smartest move yet.

"It's ours." Tamir said as loudly as he could. The roar of the family could be heard from blocks away...they were many. When they celebrated enough he raised his hand for them to quiet down. "Give me one minute....I gotta break some shit down to ya'll first."

When they didn't settle down quick enough Energy yelled, "Tamir said shut the fuck up! Respect him and lower your fucking voices!" When they heard her irritating utters she said, "Now go 'head baby."

The others were angry at her but Tamir liked that she was willing to do whatever was necessary to cement her position. Besides, for the longest time she had played the back seat to Shade and Shannon when she was alive. She didn't intend on doing that any longer. And because she was still relatively young, she could bare him more children and she knew that was what he wanted.

When everyone was quiet Tamir said, "We have twenty units in each building."

"Each building?" one of them said. "We have more than one?"

"Yes. We bought building numbers 2458 and 2460 right beside it."

"But why?"

"We'll talk about that later." Tamir said. "Right now I want to let ya'll know that, I got my own unit and the only person staying with me for the time being is Energy. Building 2460 will remain empty for now."

"Can we pick whichever apartment we want?" one of his twenty-year-old brothers asked.

"No. The Main Wives will make the decisions." Then he looked amongst them to spot his mother Shade and then Karen. "You two are in charge of accommodations."

"Son, I thought me and Karen were staying with you. Like we talked about." Shade said.

"You thought wrong."

The smile was wiped off of Shade's face. She thought surely he would want the wisdom and knowledge she provided when Black Water was alive. Besides she had the respect of the Klan, more than even Tamir did.

"Son, I mean...why can't we stay in the unit together?" she smiled trying to hide her anxiety of being just a regular wife. "I can cook for you, clean and everything else you need."

"But you can't fuck me, mother?" Everyone turned around and waited for her answer. Her long hair blew in her face and she shook it away to see her oldest son's eyes. Is he serious? She thought. His eyes told her he was.

"Son, what are you saying?"

"The question wasn't clear? You said you can give me everything I need...so I want to know can you fuck me, too? Because that's what I need, mama." Tamir responded.

Jesse Holman aka Black Water and the rest of the family had fucked their children's minds up so badly, that they didn't see things the way normal families did. He was fully prepared to fuck his mother if she would have agreed. Yet it would be up to her, he would not force her to do anything she didn't want to do.

All their lives, Black Water had controlled the women with money and gifts and the kids with fear and a militant attitude. To them they were normal, and people who didn't get Black Water's sick made up religion, were just trying to tear them a part. And they would cause a war like no one had ever seen if someone tried to break them up. Oh yes, it would take years of counseling to get their mental right again.

"Son!" Shade said horrified by her son's comment. "What are you saying?"

"I'm saying I need my dick sucked when I want it. I need to be fucked how I like it and I need somebody who can cook for me." He clarified not letting up one bit. "Now

I remember daddy saying before he died how good Energy was in the kitchen. But he also said how good you and Aunt Shannon were in the bedroom. My only question to you is, do you want to take her place or not?"

Energy looked at Tamir worried Shade would do whatever she had to be on top, including taking her place. "Tamir, no." Energy pleaded. "I can do all of those things for you."

"Shut the fuck up." Tamir told Energy.

"Mama, do you want to share my bed or not?"

Everyone looked at Shade and waited on her response. "Son, I can't do something like that."

"Then it's settled. Me and Energy have apartment 101. The rest of ya'll can get it how you feel it."

Hearing this, Energy rushed up to him, hugged and kissed him passionately in the mouth again. She was going overboard by filling his young mind up with more sexuality than he knew what do deal with. Her light skin, long hair and green eyes had him hooked. Older than him by ten years, she knew how to move her hips, get her mouth hot and wet and most of all, how to make him happy. She was subservient in all senses of the word and he had no doubt that if asked, she'd put her life on the line to protect his.

"Alright, everyone needs to go get settled. When you're done there's a community room in the basement. I need all of the heads of the family to meet me there. Lance and Roman, you come, too."

Lance smiled having finally gotten his chance to be heard and taken seriously. "You already know it, big brother."

COMMUNITY ROOM

Energy hung closely to Tamir's side, while Karen, Shade and the rest of the wives clung to the walls, and the available seats in the room.

"This bitch thinks she's the shit." Karen said looking at Energy who was now massaging Tamir's hands as he waited for his family members to pile into the room. "We can't let her just push us to the back. We were the REAL first wives."

"I know, but what can we do?" Shade whispered so that the other, less sneaky wives wouldn't overhear them. "I can't sleep with my own son." She paused and looked at her. "Can I?"

Karen poked her lips out and said, "This is the religion we chose. We made a promise to build our family large enough to be taken seriously and to do whatever we have to do to see that plan through. So if you ask me, I'd say yes. Fuck him better than anybody can so we can maintain our hold in this family. Because the moment I see my in, I'm taking it."

Shade thought about what she said and realized Black Water's religion was the only religion she'd ever known. When he first met his wives, none of them were smart enough to know that Black Water had taken out pages from the bible and mixed them with pages from the book of Mormon to create his sick religion. And because he was able to lavish them with gifts and money, they had everything they ever wanted. Still she was smart enough to realize sleeping with her own child was not only crazy but also wrong.

Tamir looked around his family with a serious expression on his face. He represented every perversion his father stood for when he was alive.

Whispering in Energy's ear she stood up. "Everybody settle down, our leader is ready to speak." Although she was talking to the crowd, she was looking at Shade and

Karen, angering them even more. When silence filled the room Energy sat back down and said, "They're all yours, baby."

"Bitch." Shade said under her breath.

"Thank you," he smiled. "Now...as you know we got the buildings because we had to kill, maim, and destroy many people who stood in our way. But through it all, we still haven't gotten who was responsible for our leader's death."

"But Cameron is dead." Karen said.

"It wasn't Cameron! It was his son C."

"Son, what is your thing with this boy? He wasn't even old enough to have a hand in Black Water's death."

"So you're going against me now?"

"No," she swallowed, "please continue."

He frowned and said, "Like I said, until we get the responsible parties, and their loved ones, we cannot live in peace. And I won't rest in peace." Then Tamir looked at the papers in front of him. "And since we have a place to rest our heads, it's time to move forward on our plans. First we will fuck up the lives of the people around him. And even the younger children in our Klan will have to help out. Speaking of that, good job on stopping C's car the other day with your bicycle, Roman."

Roman, the youngest person in the room smiled. In a young football player's hype voice he said, "He ain't nothing but a punk anyway! Whatever you need me to do, I'm wit', big bro! I'll lay down my life for this family!"

Tamir saw the loyalty in his eyes and smiled. "I'ma call you on that." Then he readdressed the family, "Roman has done his part and now you must do yours. I want C alive long enough to see his family tortured. And at some point, I want C brought to me. Remember, you are not to kill him at first. We have studied C and we know what he does, how he moves and the people closest to him. Now we only have to put what we know into action and move forward. And I'm ready to do that...are all of you?" They all said yes. "Okay...are there any questions on what needs to be done?" Karen, raised her hand slowly. "Yes." Tamir said calmly.

"Have you chosen which wives you'll have at your beck and call? I mean, are you getting new wives or keeping the ones your father had?"

"Bitch, please! You just mad because he chose me and only me! Let's say what this is really about." Energy yelled nervous at losing her place again.

She was so plagued with thoughts of losing position that she didn't even know that she was already the top bitch.

"Okay, LET'S SAY IT then!" Karen said. "Tamir, your father chose me, your mother and Shannon as first wives because we could meet all of his needs. And...we knew what needed to be done to prepare our children for war. Energy doesn't know these things because she wasn't competent enough to be a part of that and I think it is a bad choice for you to choose her as first wife."

Karen quickly walked up to the head of the table and knelt next to him. Her perfume was pleasing to his nose and although she was fifteen years older than him, like all of his wives, she kept herself in pristine condition.

"Tamir," she said softly taking his hand, ignoring Energy's cold stares, "let me be there for you. By right your mother should be first wife, but since she is your mother, it's only right that I'm next."

"She's right, son." Shade said wanting anybody but Energy to be on top.

Tamir looked at Karen and smiled. He knew the fighting and bickering over him would happen but thought it would be at a different time. "I've chosen Energy, and I have two more younger women I'm bringing next week to help increase our family."

"I understand." Karen said taking her place next to Shade.

For Energy the walk of shame was bitter sweet, because this was the first time that she learned other wives were coming. In her mind other women meant more competition.

"What? You didn't think it would be just you now did you?" He asked Energy.

"No...I...uh..."

"I'm keeping my father's legacy alive by having as many kids as I can so that we can grow. That's my goal. But let us not get too far off of subject, there will be plenty time to discuss who can make me happy later."

"Well are you allowing us other husbands?!" Karen yelled. "Because as it stands now, there are nine wives who were indebted to Black Water. If we can't still breed, how can we help?"

"No other men will be in our family. Only women."

"But how can we grow?" Shade asked.

"Between you there are thirty four kids. A lot of us are teenagers and those men will go out and find women they can bring into our family. You older ladies have done your part and need to fall back."

All Karen and Shade thought of was the fact that they could have no sex, and neither could see a life like that. "Son, can I ask you one last question?" Shade asked.

"What?"

"You said you bought the building next to this one...so who's staying there?"

"That's what I really wanted to talk to you about. Black Water had family down south. There are five wives in Texas and between them they have twenty kids. Five of the kids

are older than me and they're coming in a couple of days and will be living in the unit."

Everyone gasped.

"Why would you make something like that up?" Karen yelled. "Jesse would have never hidden from us the fact that he had other wives!"

"He didn't hide anything from you, he just chose not to tell you. Your purpose was to breed, not be involved in every single part of his plan. Or have you forgotten?"

"Son, what do we need them for?" Shade asked.

"If we're going to take over, we need family to help us do it. We need people who have the same blood line as dads and we have that."

The room was filled with heavy sighs. "When do they get here?" Shade asked.

"They're already here. And have been here for months. You'll meet them soon."

After the meeting was over, and everyone went about their duties, Shade stepped to Tamir. But Energy stood by his side like a loyal Pitbull with no leash.

"Energy, can I talk to my son, alone?"

"He's not your son anymore, Shade, he's a man and he belongs to the Klan. You know that."

"Energy, I respect your little position and all, but if you don't give me five minutes alone with Tamir, I'ma act like I don't respect anything about you and beat your fucking ass like I'm the heavyweight champion of the world."

Energy looked at Tamir and said, "Give us five minutes."

Energy stomped away and Shade touched Tamir lightly on the face.

"Son, are you okay?" Her voice full of concern.

"Yeah...why you say that?" He asked trying to shake her off. He hadn't shared the fact that he was HIV positive with anyone, nor was he intending to.

"Because your face looks gaunt, Tamir. Like you're losing a lot of weight." Her hand remained on his face until he griped her wrist tightly and threw it off of him. She stepped out of the line of his rage.

"Why wouldn't I be okay? Now get out of my face and do your job by getting the family in order." He said before walking out the door.

"YOU NOT LISTENING TO WHAT I'M SAYING. WE'RE ALREADY DONE, DREYFUS. WE'RE NOT FUCKIN' WITH TYLAND NO MORE..."

-MERCEDES

"So what's up, Mercedes? What is Dreyfus saying about you telling him we not running Tyland anymore?" Carissa asked me.

"He's saying a lot of shit. A lot of his words I couldn't even understand he was so mad."

Kenyetta slammed her fist into the kitchen table, startling all of them. "Man, I wished ya'll would have waited before telling him. We needed another package."

"We got enough to last us a few months. If we have to, we'll just find another connect." I said. "As a matter of fact, Kenyetta, I'ma need you to drop off one of our packages to our soldiers tonight. It's your turn."

"What? Why can't Kristina do it? She cooks all our coke anyway." Carissa said.

When Kenyetta looked at Carissa, Kenyetta said, "Don't worry. I got it."

Carissa shook her head and said. "This can be really bad for business. We need Dreyfus."

"Well it's too late now," I said. "Dreyfus is actually going to call us in ten minutes. I guess we'll see what he's talking about then."

We didn't say much more until the burner that I bought to receive Dreyfus' call rang. I didn't want to discuss business over my home line or my regular cell phone.

When the phone moved inches across the table before stopping Yvette said, "You want me to answer?"

"Naw. I got it." I slowly picked up the phone and said, "Hello." I placed the call on the cheap ass speaker and we all leaned in as it sat in the middle of the table.

"What's up, Mercedes. Are the girls there?"

"Yeah. We're all here. What's up?" Yvette said getting right down to business.

"What's up is that I can't believe how ungrateful you bitches are."

We were stunned and sat back into our chairs. Never, in any of our business interactions with Dreyfus, had he ever called us out of our names. Why would he? We were bringing him millions, way more than any of them niggas ever did under his watch.

"You must have your mother there with you or something," Kenyetta said.

"And why is that?"

"'Cause you can't be talking to us like that. Ain't no bitches in this room, Dreyfus."

"His mother? Really?" I said covering the speaker.

"Fuck him." She whispered.

"You see that's what I'm talking about, you think just because I fucked ya'll that you can talk to me any kind of way. And most of all, you think that you are in control. Well you're not, but I am."

"Well you may have fucked my friends but you didn't fuck me," Kenyetta said. "And calling us out of our names ain't gonna make us wanna stay in Tyland."

"I don't care if I fucked you or not. After all the bodies I put to rest in ya'lls names, you owe me. Or have you forgotten who brought the firepower necessary to clean up

your shit when Black Water and his crew almost killed all of you? It was me. As a matter of fact, where is Carrisa?"

We all looked at her. "I'm...I'm right here, Dreyfus."

"You and I had an agreement, so you better school your girls on our arrangement. Because ain't no backing out on me. Ever!"

When he said that we all looked at Carissa. What agreement did they have together?

"I'll talk to them about our arrangement, but it's hard for me to remember the details, it was so long ago."

"Well let me remind you." He said. *"I told you that my coming through that day you all almost lost Emerald City meant you would either owe me ten million dollars or would have to run Tyland for me permanently. You agreed to run Tyland."*

Why would she agree to something this crazy without talking to us first?

"What if we just pay you?" Carissa said.

"The price for your freedom has doubled. Do you have twenty million to buy me out?"

I don't know about them, but with my shopping habits I would be lucky if I could scrape up one million. And since Carissa and Kenyetta partied a lot, I doubt they had enough either. If any of us had the money, it would probably be Yvette.

"ARE YOU THERE?!" He yelled growing irritated by our silence.

Dreyfus didn't sound calm like he normally did. In fact he sounded up tight, angry and confused.

"We're here, Dreyfus." I said.

"Then fucking answer me!"

"Motha..."

I placed my hand on Yvette's because I saw she was about to let loose on him. "Not now." I said gripping her hand. "Let's let it play out."

"Fuck this shit!" She said getting up and walking into my room. I guess it was better to let her go than to force her to stay. If she popped off on him, we could all end up dead.

When Yvette closed the door I said, "We're here, Dreyfus."

"Good, because let me make myself clear. You bitches don't get to say when it's time to leave, I do."

"You not listening to what I'm saying," I said. "We're already done, Dreyfus. We're not fucking with Tyland no more. But it ain't like we not still gonna make you money. We still pumping in Emerald and we still use your product."

"Who you think gave you Emerald? If I wanted to get behind them niggas before ya'll killed them, every last one of you would be selling pussy off New York avenue right now."

"Dreyfus, we not fucking with it but we don't want to beef with you." I said.

"You beef with me? Picture that."

"Dreyfus, we're through. We don't want war, but if there is one, then that's on you." Kenyetta said.

Her words sounded like she was going to offer him up. I wish she hadn't, but now it is too late.

"I wonder how you will feel if I strip you of Emerald. And get someone else to run it for me." He said coldly. *"Would you still be able to talk to me as if you were my equal?"*

"I guess we gotta see." I said.

"Do you really want to go there?" He said.

Just then Yvette walked back into the room. "You know better than to fuck with us," She laughed. "We have lost everything, our men, people we love and any chance at a full life. This all the fuck we know, and if you bring somebody in here," she paused, "no fuck that! If I think you're even thinking about bringing somebody else in here, I'll have them killed. And then I'm coming for you."

He laughed and said, *"We'll see about that."*

"I JUST DON'T UNDERSTAND WHY THIS HAPPENED TO ME."

-CARISSA

It was below 20 degrees outside as me and Kenyetta rushed to my car. Thank God for my Viper automatic starter because my car was nice and warm. After the meeting, we decided to talk in my car away from the girls because we shared secrets they didn't know about.

"While you're sitting in here, start your car, girl."

Kenyetta reached into her MCM bag and hit her Viper button. Her Mercedes started up and she fell back into my soft leather seats.

"You got any coke?" She asked me.

I dug in my console and we did a few lines together. The euphoric feeling put us at a momentary ease.

"Kenyetta, you sure you gonna be able to take that package to our men tomorrow?"

"Yeah…why you ask me that?"

"Because it's not cooked. And you and me both snort coke now that's why."

Kenyetta looked at me and said, "I fucking hate you."

"Hate me? Why?" I frowned.

"Because I wasn't even thinking about getting high until you turned me onto this shit. Now I feel like most days, I can't even get along without it. Why did we even start this shit?"

"Kenyetta, I think we are both two grown ass women who made a decision. So don't try to put all this shit on me."

"But why did you even start? I mean, what made you decided to say, 'I sell coke, let me snort it, too?"

I exhaled and said, "I don't know, Kenyetta. I guess it's this lifestyle. It's so fucking hard on me. I mean, why you start?"

"Same reason."

"Well, we in the same boat."

Suddenly Kenyetta started crying and said, "I'm broke, Carissa."

"What? How?!!!"

"I been getting high and I don't hardly have no shit to show to my name. That's why when Mercedes asked us did we have enough money to buy ourselves out from up under Dreyfus, I said I didn't want to leave Tyland. I can't help ya'll if I wanted to."

"Right. I wasn't surprised though when Yvette said she has fifteen million saved. She must don't spend shit."

"I don't know what I'm going to do. I can't even afford my luxury apartment in Virginia any more. If I add up all my money right now, I might have twenty thousand dollars."

"Kenyetta, why you ain't tell me? Before it got to this?"

"I don't know, but my life is over."

"It's not, you just gonna have to stop for a while." I looked into her eyes. She didn't look too confident. "You can stop right?"

"Yeah. I ain't addicted if that's what you think."

"You sure? I mean, you did say you broke. I mean, did you mean to get broke on purpose?"

"No."

"Okay, so let me ask you again, can you or can you not stop?"

"I can."

"Okay, well stop using. And just so you know, I'm here for you. You and me are the same. We just got to get our shit in order so that Mercedes and Yvette don't find out. You know how they be judging us sometimes."

"Okay." She exhaled. "You're right. Well, let me go. My car is probably warm now, I'ma call you later."

She grabbed the bag with the package. I looked at it before she left and said, "Are you good to make the delivery?"

"I got it."

"Are you sure?"

"Stop worrying. I wouldn't fuck with our money. We're fine."

"Okay. I'ma get up with you later."

When she left I got on the phone to call Slack. Although boss shit filled my day, I still had some unanswered questions for my boyfriend. The moment he answered he sounded agitated.

"Babes, I'm so fucking sorry! Did you see the pictures somebody posted up of you around DC?"

Sometimes, but not every time, he had a slight southern accent. And since he was from DC I didn't understand why.

"You mean the naked pictures I allowed you to take of my body? Because if you're talking about those, I'll have to say yes, I saw them."

"I can't believe somebody violated like that."

"What about the videos?"

"Somebody posted the videos, too?"

"Yes, but I told you about that already. It just seemed like everything about our private sex life ain't private."

"FUCK!!! I'm soooo sorry, babes. I'ma find out who did this shit."

"Slack, are you sure you didn't do this?"

"You actually think I would do something like that to you?" When I didn't answer he screamed. *"Do you?!!!!!"*

"I…I don't know. I just…"

CLICK.

"Hello? Hello?" I looked at my receiver and the name Slack didn't appear on it anymore. He had hung up on me. Nervous about losing him I called back. "Slack?"

"What?"

"Baby, I'm sorry. I'm sooooo sorry. I just don't understand why this happened to me. I had my daughter in the car with me when we saw the posters and everything. It just fucked me up that's all."

"I know. And I hate that this is happening to you. Give me some time to get some answers. I'ma hit you back. Okay?"

"Okay." Before he hung up I said, "I love you."

He waited a few seconds before saying, *"Love you back."*

IT'S JUST THAT YOUR MOMS AND POPS SPOILED YOU, AND I THINK YOU CARE TOO MUCH ABOUT WHAT PEOPLE SAY

- DERRICK

Derrick was in the gym when he saw Daps again. Something about her secrecy as she crept into the gym raised his antennas. Like she had before, she walked into the gym with two large bags and went straight back to the locker room. She appeared to be in a hurry.

Derrick unclipped his phone off his hip and called C. "C, your peoples here again." He said walking slower on the treadmill.

"What peoples?"

"Your friend. Daps."

"Oh...she said she was working out for a marathon or something. That's why she there all the time."

"I see. But look, before you go, I saw you took all of your sneakers out of the apartment in Emerald and at the Harbor."

"Yeah...I don't wear regular sneakers no more."

Derrick laughed and said, "Why?"

"Tired of niggas having my shit on all the time."

"So you get rid of all your shoes? Including the ones I bought for you?"

"Yeah...you know how I am. What you wanted me to give 'em back to you?"

"Naw, but I been meaning to talk to you. I think you worry about what people say too much. Be careful about that trait. It's not a good look."

"Just because I don't want to wear the same shoes other niggas have in the streets I got bad traits?"

"It ain't about the sneakers. It's just that your moms and pops spoiled you when you were coming up and you gotta watch that. That's all I'm saying."

Silence.

"Derrick, I'm good. Now I'm doing something right now. I'ma get up with you later though."

"One."

"WHATEVER HAPPENED TO PLAYING HARD TO GET? SHE ACTING LIKE A FUCKING TRAMP!"

-LIL C

Ryan's house was packed when Lil C and Persia walked up in his spot. Niggas were gawking over Persia and it was making C heated. Not because they were looking at her, but because they didn't know if she was with him or not, yet they were making moves. Although both of their parents ran Emerald, Persia never mingled amongst them so they'd never seen her before. C hung around up and coming gangstas and thugs...the ones her mother warned her to stay away from. Yet there was something about them that made her want to hang around them even more. In a sense she was chasing after her first love, her daddy.

"What up, nigga?" Ryan said giving him a one-arm hug.

He was sitting in the living room with two other niggas. To C, Ryan looked like Lil Chuckee from Lil Wayne's Young Money label...down to the dreads. He was thin, with light chocolate skin and he looked much younger than seventeen.

"Where's Mazon? He here yet?" C questioned.

"Mazon!" he yelled to the back of his apartment.

"Where your folks at?" C asked.

"Out of town." Then focusing his attention on Persia he said, "What's up, Persia? You want something to drink or something? We got everything. Beer, wine, Ciroc...what

you want?" He walked toward the kitchen where the liquor was.

"Naw, she good." C said speaking up for her.

Ryan stopped in his tracks. "You sure?"

"Boy, whatever." She said to C. "I do want something to drink." She looked at Ryan. "Uh...what you got again?"

"Whatever you want."

"You got Red Bull and Vodka?" She asked.

C felt like fucking her up for being reckless in front of his friends. He told her she was royalty and that she needed to act the part yet she still didn't get it. So C pulled her to the side and said, "You doing way too much and I don't want them thinking you loose. Just fall back, aight?" She rolled her eyes. "Ryan, just give her a soda, man. She don't need all that other shit."

"Boy, you not my mother." She said all loud and ignorant like. "I drink all the time."

"Well not when you with me." C told her looking seriously into her eyes. He saw a queen in her even if she didn't and he wanted her to live up to his perceptions. "Ryan, the soda. And I don't give a fuck what she says, you bring back what the fuck I told you."

Ryan walked to the kitchen to get her drink. And C told the two niggas on the couch to get the fuck off.

"Sit down, Persia." He demanded. She folded her arms against her chest and dropped into the sofa acting like a brat. But even at her worse, C couldn't help but think about how cute she was. "I don't care about your pouting and shit."

When Mazon finally walked into the living room, C felt like ditching the whole idea of hooking them up. But the moment they laid eyes on each other, it was a wrap. They had connected and there was nothing C could do about it.

"Damn, C...this you?" Mazon said pointing at Persia as he moved quickly in her direction.

She stood up and said, "If you Mazon I came here to meet you."

Whatever happened to playing hard to get? C thought. She acting like a fucking tramp!

"This my cousin, Persia. She's Carissa daughter," C said trying to remind him about who she was and what fucking over her meant. "I wanted her to meet you."

"Good lookin' out, C." He said staring her down.

There was something in this nigga's eyes C wasn't feeling and he started reflecting on how they met. C met Mazon last year, when he was bringing some weed to Ryan to sell at his school. But Mazon wasn't anything like C and his friends. He didn't have a rack of bitches around him all the time and he seemed to be focused on something else. While females sang all around Emerald about how C and his friends were heartless, cold and players, never did anybody say anything bad about Mazon. His rep was clean and intact as far as the ladies were concerned.

In C's eyes, Mazon seemed to be more about that paper than anything else and he always told Mazon that when he got put on, that he was bringing him with him. Ryan assumed it would be him instead because they were cool, but Ryan wasn't good at reading people and making decisions like Mazon.

"Good looking out shit." C told Mazon after meeting Persia. "This right here is my peoples. Remember that shit if you think about fucking her over."

Mazon shared the sofa with Persia as they continued on without C. Done with both of them, he scanned the room for Cute Nikki because he needed to talk to her.

"Where Cute Nikki at, Ryan? She said the nigga Tamir came 'round the way lookin' for me."

"I saw her earlier. And I told her not to tell you that shit."

C staggered back a little, frowned and said, "Fuck is you talking about you told her not to tell me? You know I put the word out that I needed to know every move this nigga made. Why wouldn't you want to tell me some shit like that?"

"I figured your mind busy with enough shit already."

"Nigga...let me make it clear if I haven't already, if this nigga come looking for me," he paused, "no fuck that...if any nigga come looking for me, I wanna know."

"Man, I think this nigga's tripping off some bullshit. Who's really worried about Tamir?"

"Are you hearing me?"

"Yes." Ryan said slightly embarrassed.

C was still talking when someone came into the party. C wasn't trying to see, his ex-girlfriend Lani. They had history, history he wasn't trying to repeat. Besides, Lani broke all kinds of codes when she fucked his friend, at the time, Tamir. As far as C was concerned, she could be directly attributed to the reason he was beefing with Tamir to this day. He could never forget the time when he called Lani to check on her and his baby she was carrying. When instead of getting her on the phone, he got Tamir, for sure bad blood still brewed between them.

"What' up, Lani?" Ryan said walking up to her. "Where your twin sister, Sachi? I thought you were bringing her."

"Boy, I am Sachi! Lani heard C was here, and didn't wanna come." Sachi said looking at C with lustful eyes. Bitches ain't shit, C thought.

If he wanted to be scandalous and fuck her he could with no problems. He couldn't lie, Sachi had gotten fatter and sexier over the years. Back in the day Lani was the baddest, but now all that had changed. Lani lost a lot of weight and people were whispering that she was HIV positive.

"Fuck you invite her for?" C asked Ryan, ignoring her all together. "You know I don't fuck with them bitches."

"So what, you not gonna speak, C? Even after you had Monie Blow and her cousins jump my sister and me just because she fucked Tamir. You can't say hi?"

"Fuck you...be lucky you still walking because what I was 'bout to do was worse."

"But that shit ain't right, C! Do you know that girl is still in love with you to this day?"

"Do you know I don't give a fuck? I can't do nothing with a slut but make her suck my dick and your twin already did that."

"You act like you soooooo fucking innocent." She paused. "Let's not forget that it was 'cause of you fucking her best friend Jona that all the shit happened." She said.

C was not about to argue with the bitch about history, Lani was cut and that was the end of it. As far as he was concerned if their story was a book they had reached their last page and there was no sequel. She had gotten her ass stomped out by three heavy bitches from Tyland Towers like he promised and he was through.

C grabbed his coat and said, "Persia, let's go. We leaving early."

"What...but I'm not ready. You see me and Mazon talking."

C grabbed her fur, pushed it in her chest and said, "Get the fuck up."

His reaction told her he wasn't playing because she jumped up and said, "Mazon, I'ma call you later...okay?"

"Look, you gonna see the nigga again. Stop being hot and let's go."

As Persia was collecting herself, C could feel Sachi burning holes in the side of his head with her eyes. But he didn't know if she wanted to fuck him or if she was check-

ing his pulse for her sister, either way he wasn't interested. In his mind if you fucked one twin you fucked them all.

On his way out the door his phone rang and he saw it was Monie Blow. Persia was right behind him as he moved toward the door. He answered. "C, what's good? You got a second?"

"Naw, I'm 'bout to go to my crib."

"Well you gotta meet me first. I got a message for you from somebody I know you want to hear from."

C's father taught him to expect and to prepare for the worse. He knew Tamir was trying to get at him and wouldn't be surprised if the incident with the kid on the bicycle was related to him in some way.

"Who the message from?" He said expecting it to be Tamir since she and Tamir both were from Tyland Towers.

"I ain't gonna lie, when the message first came my way, I ain't believe it was real, C. But this shit turned out to be serious after all."

"Well who is it, Tamir?"

"Fuck no."

"Well, who? And why would somebody come to you to get me a message?"

"The person said they didn't want anybody in Emerald knowing, and since I live in Tyland, they thought it would be better if it came from me. Plus they know we hang together."

"What's the message?"

"I think it'll be best if you come see me, C. I really can't say it over the phone. Now bring your rich ass on."

"Why I ain't feeling this?"

"I don't know but, C...I wouldn't fuck with you...or anybody who would try to do you wrong. This is a message you'll want to hear, now trust me."

"Where are you?"

"I'm at my house now, but I can meet you at Peking Place in an hour."

"I'll be there." He hung up the phone.

"Persia, go wait in the car downstairs."

"I thought we were about to leave together."

Tired of her shit, C opened the door, grabbed her by her arm and pushed her out. Had he known all this shit would be jumping off tonight, he would've left Persia's thirsty ass home. Now she was gonna have to ride with him until he found out what was so important that Monie wanted to meet him right then and there.

"Mazon, come over here." He jogged in his direction. "I got a message from Monie."

"Sexy, Monie? Who look like Jill Scott?"

"You know her?"

"Naw...I know of her. She fine as shit."

C wasn't into big girls and liked his women thin and in shape. So outside of looking at her titties the one time, C never gave her a second look. "Whatever, I just need you to go make sure everything is good before I pull up at Peking's."

"You don't trust her?"

"Fuck yeah. She my peoples, but I don't know if somebody else is using her to get at me."

"I got you." He said dapping him up. "What you want me to do when I get there?"

"Just go there and don't let her see you. Fall back and just peep the scene for me. You know I got beef with Tamir and them, so I can't be sure."

Mazon flew out the door after getting C's orders, but as he was leaving out, C's homie Daps was coming in. Daps wore a long black and gold weave and she kept her body tight. Red was her favorite color so she always had something on with the color.

"You 'bout to leave already?" Daps asked. "I just got here."

"Later for this shit. We got some business at Peking's and I want you to roll with me."

"Lead the way!"

When they left Ryan's house C had Wallace drop Kit off before going to the restaurant. He didn't trust him too much after the performance he gave in the car earlier and didn't want him around. Once Kit was dropped off, he had Wallace drive him a few blocks down from Peking Palace. It didn't take long for Persia's annoyance with not knowing what was going on to set in and show in her attitude.

"Can you tell me what's up?" Persia asked. "I mean, you told me we were going to have fun, not sit in a car and wait all damn day."

C reached into his pocket and gave her a hundred bucks. "What's this for?" She said examining the money.

"Go over to that nail salon and wait for me to scoop you."

C looked at Persia seriously and she knew bucking against him was not only stupid, but a waste of time. "Hurry up, boy!" She said leaving the car in a stupid hurry.

When she was gone Daps said, "What's up with her? When ya'll start hanging out?"

"Today, and I probably will never ask her to roll anywhere else with me again." C said loving the fact that she was getting on his nerves. With her acting like that, it was less likely that he'd fuck someone he'd grown to know as family.

"I heard that." Daps laughed. "So what's up, C? Why the secrecy and why we going to Peking's?"

"It's business," C paused, looking at his phone. He was waiting anxiously for Mazon to hit him up. "Monie said she had some news for me and I gotta find out what."

"Why she just won't tell you?"

"Not sure."

Just when she said that C's phone rang. It was Mazon. "What's good? Everything cool?"

"I'm in here now. She with two other girls, they in here fussing at each other and shit. I don't see anybody else out of the ordinary."

C wasn't surprised, Monie was always checking somebody about something she didn't like, but what he did want to know was who were the girls.

"How the girls look?"

"Both them bitches 'bout the same size as Monie Blow. But the other girls look a little harder, and wider."

C laughed knowing they were her cousins. "Aight, stay in there and don't let them see you checking shit out." Then he paused and said, "Matta of fact, since you in there go get me two Twix bars and an order of General Tso's. That'll give you something to do. I'm coming in, now." C continued. "But don't come up to me when I get in there, just watch my back."

"I got you."

Just as C and Daps were leaving the car Persia was walking back toward them.

"Where you going?" Persia asked. "I'm ready to go home. That place was too packed to wait."

"Well where's my money?"

"I'ma spend it later."

"Persia, just get in the car and chill the fuck out. I'ma be right back." C said, opening the car door for her.

"Well can I use your phone? I left mine in my mother's car."

"Who you wanna call? Mazon?"

"Yeah."

"Well give him five minutes, he handling something for me right now."

"Can I use it anyway?"

C tossed it at her and walked toward Peking's hating himself for bringing her.

"You strapped?" He asked Daps.

"Fuck you gonna ask me some shit like that for?" Daps said lifting up her North Face coat, revealing her gun. "Don't play me."

C laughed as they walked into Peking's, looking around them carefully. Once inside, C saw Mazon pretending to be on the phone at a table behind Monie and her cousins. Once inside his favorite restaurant, C sat at the table with Monie and her cousins. Daps who was still unsure about what was going on, remained standing behind him looking all around the restaurant. The thing was, C didn't tell her to do any of this shit, yet she naturally fell into the role of protector.

C noticed a fake Louis Vuitton purse sat on the table and a grey duffle sat on the floor. He hoped the purse didn't belong to Monie because he would rather buy her gear for a year than to see her frolic around like a bamma bitch with fake shit.

"Hey, Daps. I called you earlier, why you ain't answer your phone?" Monie said, digging in the fake purse on the table before she handed Lil C a Twix bar.

Damn. It is hers. C thought.

"I was in the gym. But what's up with all of this secretive shit, girl?" Daps asked. "You making me nervous."

"Yeah, what's going on, Monie?" C started, opening the candy. "I got somewhere to be so make this shit quick."

"Alright...it's like this...I don't know if you know but Tyland ain't got no supplier now. And it's up for grabs."

"What you talking about? My moms supplies for Tyland for Dreyfus."

"Not no more, C. That's why I'm here. Dreyfus wanted me to get in contact with you. He's offering you a chance to step up and run shop if you ready."

"Fuck is you talking about? Even if I did believe you, it doesn't make sense that he would come to me. I ain't never ran no operation like Tyland before and I don't have the experience."

"He knows that and he wants to eventually meet with you to talk about it. I guess he heard we been trying to get in contact with him after all."

"Eventually meet with me?"

"Yeah...before he meets with you he wants to be sure you can do what he needs done. So he told me to give you three bricks. I got 'em right here." She said touching the other bag. "He said if you can move these in two days, he'd know you got what it takes and he'll meet you."

"What exactly does he want? He could get anybody to supply Tyland."

"C, I'm not really sure about all that but I can tell you what I believe. Right now since your mother and them stopped fucking with Tyland, Dreyfus will probably have somebody bring the weight by Tyland and it will be divided up and given to everybody who works for him. But sometimes people come up short and he can't take the risk anymore. Sounds to me like he needs one person he can count on to be the delivery man."

"Sounds like a glorified mailman job to me."

"I don't know too many mailmen who earn profit on their deliveries."

This was the moment C wanted but he didn't know if he wanted it like this. Going behind his mother's back and working for Tyland felt more like betrayal than an attempt at success. But he wanted it almost as badly as he wanted his father to be alive again.

"What you gonna do, C?" Monie said. "Because I know you not going to let this opportunity pass you by. You can't."

"Tell him I gotta think about it."

"He says to tell you if you said that, that he'd find somebody else, C. If you want this you have to move now."

C's heart raced with excitement but he was his father's son and would not be pushed into anything so quickly. So he stood up and said, "Well you can tell the nigga to suck my dick. I'm out of here."

Monie looked at her cousins and back at C. "I told him you'd say that. Well...not the dick sucking part but I knew you wouldn't bite."

"How you know?"

"I just know you, C. Just like I know you sent that nigga behind me who faking on the phone in here to see if this meeting was a set up." She was smarter than C thought. "But I also know you not gonna let something like this pass you by. This is big time C, so if he calls me, I'll tell him I didn't get in contact with you. That'll give you some time to think about it a little more. So basically, you got a few days."

C dropped everybody off home except Daps because he needed time to think about Dreyfus' offer. Daps was the only person he knew who could be comfortable in his silence and didn't take it personally. Because he hadn't eaten anything but candy all day, he decided to go back to Peking Palace since Mazon had forgotten to order his food.

When they walked into the restaurant this time, Haun, the owner was at the front and smiled the moment he saw them walk through the doors. There were ten people waiting in line but he welcomed him immediately.

"C, my friend, how can I help you?" Haun loved when C walked in because he'd order small but tip big, even if he was getting carry out. And because of it, he always made sure he never had to wait.

"'Scuse me, how he get to go first?" a black girl with extra large earrings asked.

"Wait!" Daps said. "You gonna get your fucking food, greedy bitch."

Daps went on her ass and C loved every bit of it. She was silenced instantly.

"You already know what I want." C told Haun.

"的命令，一般祖雞去!" Huan yelled, toward the kitchen.

C knowing Chinese knew he said, 'An order of General Tso Chicken to go!' He understood the language very well and Haun was always so amazed when they could hold a conversation. Chinese was one of the toughest languages to learn yet C knew it fluently.

"You want something, Daps?" C asked.

"You never eat all of your food so I'ma just have some of yours."

He laughed because she was right and just like Monie, she knew him too well.

"Well, how have you been, C?" Haun said.

"我很好。剛剛起步的錢." C responded in Chinese. In English he said, 'I'm good, just getting money.'

A few people around him, including the girl with the big earrings, couldn't believe how fluent he was when he spoke, they thought he was playing at first. Unlike the rest of them, Daps was use to C wowing people with his fluency in different languages. And although she didn't know Chinese, she herself was fluent in French and Spanish having gone to the same prestigious school.

"I heard that friend." Haun said in English. "Give one moment."

Remembering he had something to ask her C said, "Daps, Derrick said you be at the gym a lot. Now, I can see you losing weight, but is everything cool?"

"Yeah...I told you. I'm running a marathon." She sounded suspicious.

"You sure? You don't have cancer or nothing crazy like that do you?"

"Fuck no!"

He laughed and when the food came out C gave Haun a hundred dollar bill, some dap and walked out the door. Once they were in his car Daps decided to pick his brain.

"So what do you think about Dreyfus' offer? I know you not going to let this opportunity get away."

"I can't make a decision until I know for sure. But when I do, you'll be the first to know." C paused. "So, you want Wallace to take you home?"

"NO!" She screamed. "I mean...no, I got my car parked at Emerald. Take me there."

When they got to Emerald and Daps walked to her car, C noticed it seemed to be filled to capacity. He finally understood what was going on.

"Daps, come here." C said getting out of the car.

"What's up? You forget to tell me something?"

"Why all your shit in your car?"

"No reason."

"Daps, what's up?"

She hung her head low and said, "I ain't got no place to go, C. So I sleep in the car at night, and wash up at the gym in the morning. It's the only place I can afford right now."

"What about your peoples?"

"My mother is senile and in an elderly home. They were going to put me in a foster home but I can't fuck with it. I'm out here by myself."

C took his key off his ring and said, "This is the key to my crib here in Emerald. I'ma call my moms and tell her you going to be staying with me there for a little while."

"C, I can't do that."

"Fuck that! I can't have my friend out here like this. Take the key."

She took it and threw her arms around his neck. "I love you, C."

"Fuck all that...just don't be going through my shit."

SOME D AYS LATER

"TAMIR, YOU FEEL SO GOOD. KEEP FUCKING ME DADDY."

- CUTE NIKKI

Cute Nikki was in the back seat of Tamir's truck getting fucked from behind. Raw. No barrier disconnected his juices from hers. Although she was clueless about Tamir's real plan, she always had a crush on him and was excited that he had gone out of his way to get her attention.

*First she came home after going to the movies with her friends to discover three brand new Gucci bags in black and brown in large bags on her steps. When she opened the card on one of the gift boxes it read, **'From the nigga who been watchin' your sexy ass from afar.'** Showing off the purses to her friends, she couldn't wait to meet her secret admirer. And thinking it was C, she called him only to hear him say he didn't buy bitches purses. To make matters worse, he claimed he had a headache and could use a blowjob from her to relieve his pain. She promised to see him later and hung up on him.*

Time passed and it had been a week since she heard from her admirer. After a while she felt whoever her admirer was, learned about her connection to C and decided to leave her alone. But Cute Nikki was a money hungry bitch and hated not being lavished with gifts anymore.

One day she reluctantly walked into Phase Hair Salon to get her hair done. She brought plenty of books knowing that even though her appointment was at 2:00 in the after-

noon her hairdresser wouldn't even wash her hair before 7:00 in the evening. But this time she walked into the shop to discover she was the only one there. Tamir had paid all of the stylists off so that she could have the entire salon to herself.

When she came out of the door, looking like a million bucks, she was surprised to see Tamir was waiting in his truck to scoop her up.

"Tamir...you're my secret admirer?"

"Yeah...you got a problem with it?"

"No...it's just that the last time I saw you, you said you were trying to get at C."

"And I still am." Then he looked at her and said, "Why, you not trying to hang out with me now?"

"C's not a problem for me if he isn't for you."

Tamir smiled and after a meal and a few drinks, Cute Nikki was fucking him about an hour later. To others around the way it seemed like she was hard to get when in actuality it just took a nigga with real money to get her attention, like C.

"Damn this pussy good! You know how long I been watching your sexy ass?" Tamir said banging in and out of her wetness. Had he known fucking her would've been this good, he would've gotten with her a long time ago. Tamir's plan was simple; to have the same virus run through C's blood that ran through his own.

"Tamir, you feel so good. Keep fucking me daddy."

"Open that pussy up," Tamir said. "Yeah...just like that." When he couldn't take it anymore, he released his semen into her body, bonding them until death.

"You ain't cum yet did you?" She asked detecting the change of his motion. "I don't wanna get pregnant."

"And I don't want no more kids." He lied. "I'm just taking my time with you now. So turn around and shut the fuck up."

When she obeyed Tamir felt C really should do a better job of picking a girl. Cute Nikki marked the second one of his girls he'd fucked and he knew before long, C would feel as bad as he did on a regular basis. At least it was his hope.

"AND WHATEVER YOU DO, DON'T MENTION THIS TO C."

-DAPS

Monie watched Daps jog to the car wearing a cute red leather jacket with gold studs and her face was tight. She had picked her up from C's place in Emerald City and she couldn't wait to ask why she was there. When the door opened, a cold rush of air hit Monie in the face blowing her long hair around. It didn't take long for the heat inside her Honda Accord to warm her up again.

"Girl…its cold as shit out there!" Daps said jumping in her car. She put her seat belt on and dropped her black leather purse on the floor and rubbed her hands together for warmth. "Turn the heat up."

Monie angrily pulled off in silence. "What's wrong with you?" Daps asked after not getting a hello from her. "Don't tell me you on your period, too." She then turned the heat up herself.

"What are you doing living with C, Daps? You know how I feel about him."

"First of all you can't be my friend and think I'm doing anything with C. When you know how I am."

"You didn't answer my question."

"Oh my, Gawd! You can't be serious."

"Why are you living with him?"

Daps wondered if she should tell her the unfortunate circumstances that occurred in her life, which caused her to live with him. She didn't want the pity party but quickly realized since they were all friends, it was just a matter of time before C told her anyway.

"I'm homeless and I've been living out of my car for the past few weeks. C found out about it when he was dropping me off the other day and was letting me stay here in EC with him and his mother until I got on my feet."

Monie felt like shit now and tried to clean it up, "I'm sorry. I should've known it wasn't like that between you two. Why you ain't ask me? You could've stayed at my place."

"Bitch, ain't nobody trying to live with you and your nagging ass mother. Naw, I'll take my chances with C."

"Fuck you," Monie laughed. "But I'm sorry about thinking anything different."

"No what you need to be sorry about is the fact that you have yet to tell C how you feel about him. It's been too long, Monie. You don't know what he will say if you don't let him know."

"He's not into me. I mean...I thought I saw him looking at my breasts a while back, but when I called him on it he acted like he wasn't. Said I wasn't the right size."

"You still pretty. And it ain't like your weight all over the place."

"Yeah, but it might as well be as far as he's concerned." Parked at the light, Monie picked up a box of cornstarch from her console, and grabbed a plastic spoon. She took five scoops out of the box and stuffed them into her mouth. She was moving for a sixth until the light turned green.

"I don't see how you eat that shit." Daps said frowning. "What the fuck you get out of it?"

"It's good to me, can't explain it." She put the box down and pulled back into traffic. "I been eating starch since I was twelve."

"Anyway," Daps said changing the subject, "Tell me about this party we going to tonight."

"Oh...yeah...a friend of mine from Tyland Towers says his cousin is leaving to play basketball overseas, so his uncle who's a dealer, wanted to throw him a party at this hotel before he leaves. I think they booked like five rooms side by side and are leaving the connecting doors open so people can go back and forth."

"Any cute girls gonna be there?"

"Ughhhh, bitch." Monie shivered. "Even if there are, I don't know if any of them like bitches." Monie looked at Daps and said, "Make me understand." She paused. "You real pretty. You dress fly and you got the body size every boy wants."

"So."

"So why don't you like dudes? To me it just seems like everybody turning gay nowadays."

"Everybody ain't turning gay, Monie. It's just that people don't feel like they gotta hide any more. It's more socially acceptable to be who you are I guess." When Monie didn't bite she said, "Nobody with real sense would stay in this lifestyle unless that's how you really feel."

"But why? I mean, what is it about being with another girl."

Daps decided to take a different approach, "Okay...you know how you like boys a lot." Monie nodded. "Okay, well imagine if someone said it was wrong to like boys, and that you're supposed to be with girls."

"Ugggghh!"

"Good!" Daps pointed at her. "Keep that feeling...because the feeling you just felt, is how I feel if I had to be with a dude."

Monie looked at Daps and said, "Umph, well let us agree to disagree."

"We always do."

AT THE PARTY

Daps had a slight buzz and still wasn't feeling the scene one bit. She was on her period and was already irritated. In her opinion everyone was too ghetto and loud to be associated with her. Even if she wanted to push up on a girl, she didn't see one she was willing to give five minutes let alone a lifetime. Since she wasn't having any fun, she decided to take a few more drinks since it was all-free. And before she knew it, her bladder was on full and she had to piss.

When she knocked on the door, she heard Monie's voice say, "I'm in here."

"Monie?" Daps said frowning.

"Oh, it's you. Come on in."

Daps frowned at her offer, besides what was she going to do, sit on the toilet with her?

"I'll wait."

"Come on in, girl. I'm just rolling a spliff. I ain't using the bathroom or nothing."

Daps unable to hold her bladder walked into the bathroom, locked the door behind her and pissed. Her head leaned back as the tingly sensation of releasing her bladder overcame her. In Daps' opinion pissing when you had to go bad felt as good as an orgasm. Normally she would've been bashful about using the bathroom in front of someone else, but the alcohol had her not giving a fuck. Since she didn't have a magazine, she watched Monie roll the blunt with ease and expertise. Monie's face was void of expression as she made the perfect blunt.

By the time Monie was done rolling, Daps was off the toilet and she and Monie were having so much fun by themselves, that they smoked the joint and stayed in the bathroom. Needing a little liquor, Daps went back into the party and snuck an entire bottle of Hennessey in the bathroom...they drank it all. Although they were brought together because of their affiliation with C, this was the first time they had conversation that was not related to him and they realized they had so much in common. When people knocked on the door to use the restroom, they kindly asked them to find their way to another room where a bathroom was available. After hours of drinking, talking and smoking, they both passed out cold on the floor.

Daps was the first to awaken and was shocked at what she saw. Her face was lying on Monie's bare stomach as if it was a pillow, and she had slobbered all over her. Not only that, but her bloody tampon was out of her body and lying on the floor next to them. Seeing this she sat up straight and looked down at her legs, only to discover that her pants and panties were off and lying over the edge of the tub.

"Monie!" She said nudging her. "Oh, Gawd, please let us not have had sex." When Monie didn't awaken she sat up straight and yelled, "MONIE, GET THE FUCK UP!!!!"

Monie finally budged and when she did, she moved to the toilet and threw up. Unable to stop herself, she did it again and again until her insides felt as if they were being pulled out of her body.

When she was done Daps said, "Are you finished?"

"I think so," she said wiping her mouth with the back of her hand. "What happened?"

"You tell me. I mean, it looks like we had sex." She pointed to the tampon on the floor, sending Monie to the toilet again praying to the porcelain God.

"I may have been drunk," Monie started not being able to rid herself of the nasty taste in her mouth, "but I would never be drunk enough to sleep with another bitch."

"Then why is my tampon on the floor? And why are my pants over the edge of the tub?"

"I don't know, but put them on so we can leave." Monie stood up. "What time is it anyway?"

Daps grabbed the phone out of her leather bag and looked at the time. It said 6:15 am.

"It's morning, girl." She said. "Let me go get my shoes so we can get out of here."

"Yeah...let's roll."

When Daps was dressed, they opened the door and Daps slipped into a pool of blood on the floor. It was all over her hands, knees, and chin. And when she looked to her left she saw a man with a hole in his head whose eyes were open in her direction.

"OH MY GOOOODDDD!" She screamed.

When they looked around the room they saw bodies laying everywhere. Bullet holes rested in different areas of their flesh but the end result was the same, extreme death.

"What the fuck happened here?" Daps screamed getting up to wash the blood off of her.

"I don't know, but let's get the fuck out of here before we find out."

IN THE CAR

Daps and Monie drove in silence for awhile before Monie said, "I remembered what happened. You were..."

"Raped." Daps said finishing the sentence. "He raped me when he came in the bathroom when we were passed out. I couldn't fight him off and he took advantage of me." She swallowed. "And while he was on top of me he was touching your breasts."

"I know," Monie said hitting the steering wheel. "Nasty mothafuacka!" Then she quieted down. "If you remembered why didn't you tell me?"

"Because I want to forget it." She said looking at her seriously. "And whatever you do, don't mention this to C."

"You have my word."

"ARE YOU SURE YOU DIDN'T HIT THEM?"

-TAMIR

Tamir was having a bad day as he lie in bed in his room. The virus was moving through his system so rapidly he couldn't get out of bed. So when his brother Oscar, who was Karen's son, walked into his room, he was surprised to see Tamir in the condition he was in. Just a few hours earlier he seemed fine.

"You okay?" He asked walking up to the bed.

"Yeah...I'm coming down with something." He said wiping his mouth with a piece of tissue. "But what happened at the party? Did you get them bitches?"

Energy walked into the room carrying a cup of juice, she put it on his table and scurried out knowing they were discussing business.

Oscar waits until the door closes before he said, "We killed everybody in the party and they weren't there."

"Are you sure you didn't hit them?" Tamir questioned. "I got the word the moment they got to the hotel that they were inside. It should've taken you no more than ten minutes to reach them."

"We looked everywhere, Tamir. I got the picture you gave me and know how they look."

"What about the bathrooms? You check them?"

"Yeah...as a matta of fact, when we went into the last one, we caught this nigga coming out. We slumped him right where he stood."

They mistakenly thought that no one else was in the bathroom when they saw the man who had raped Daps walk out. After all, why would more than one person be in a bathroom at a time?

"FUCK!" Tamir yelled. Energy ran into the room thinking he needed something and he threw the cup of juice at her head. It struck her and she fell to the floor. "Close the fucking door." She quickly did.

Having no remorse he said, "Move on C next. Don't kill him though," he said leaning to his left to throw up in a bucket. "Bring him to me alive."

"You got it."

PITBULLS IN A SKIRT 3

"...IF SHE WAS GOING TO PLAY THIS GAME, I WAS GOING TO PLAY IT WITH HER."

- YVETTE

I sat in the restaurant tossing the Salisbury steak I ordered over my rice. I was trying to see if I could make a mountain with the rice or if the whole thing would fall once I put the steak on top. Basically I was losing my mind and giving my attention to something I shouldn't be, all because I didn't want to talk to my girl about our relationship.

"We talking or what?" Chris asked sitting across from me. "I mean, you ain't said shit to me outside of what you wanted to eat since we got here."

"I don't know what you want me to say. I mean, I told you I want the relationship, I just can't be how you want me to be."

"And how is that?"

"Like the other girls you use to fuck with, Chris. I'm not gay."

"Fuck!" She yelled banging her hand on the table. The rice pile I made on my plate flattened and I pushed it to the side, I didn't want it anyway. "Why do you keep saying that? If you lick my pussy, than you gay."

A few people overheard us and I was overcome with embarrassment. I looked away from her and said, "I think we should space out for a little while. Since its obvious I keep irritating you."

"But I don't want that." She said with concern. "I wanna make us work before I just decide it's not working and run, Yvette. I think that's what you want me to do though."

"Well if you don't want to space out and give this relationship time, what do you want?"

"I want you to recognize what this is between us and help me build on it. I want us to start taking trips and spending time together. That's what I want."

As she was talking to me, I looked across the way at a young couple that looked like they were clearly in love. Their relationship was traditional – a man, a woman and a child. They reached across the table and kissed one another as their child doodled on a piece of paper with a crayon. They were happy and then their realization hit me, if I stay in this relationship, I would never be able to have children.

"I need time, Chris. I gotta have time to think things through. I'm not breaking up with you. It's just that with everything going on in Emerald City, and with everything going on with my friends, I need time to breathe." I searched my mind for more excuses and said, "And then with me saying it's okay for my mother to stay with us for a while, all this we doing is just too much."

"What about with everything that is going on in your relationship? To put me on the back burner until you work things out seems like unlike everybody else, I ain't important to you."

"Stop it."

"You not telling them that you need time to step away from their situations to focus on your relationship. I'm 'sposed to be your life. We 'sposed to be working on us, Yvette."

"Just some time, Chris. I think we should revisit our relationship later this month."

"So what we doing in between that time?"

"Whatever we want."

"So if I started fucking with a bad bitch you wouldn't care?"

"I got one better than that, I want you to fuck a bad bitch."

"What?"

"That way you can see if you really want to be with me or not. Because this is me, Chris, and I'm not changing a whole lot more."

"You won't be satisfied until a nigga go up side your head like Thick. That's what you want don't you?"

"I know you mad so I'ma let that slide."

Then there was a look that came over her that I can't explain. "Aight, I'ma give you space. In fact, I'ma give you all the space you need. How much time you want?"

"Three months."

"Done."

I was relieved I'd have a three-month break even though I was sure she wouldn't be able to do it. We've done this before and the longest we've gone without her pressing me is two weeks. So three months is going to be damn near impossible, but if she was going to play this game, I was going to play it with her.

"LIKE I FEEL LIKE DEALING WITH THIS SHIT NOW."

- LIL C

Lil C who suffered from migraines badly was getting his dick sucked by Cute Nikki. She was on her knees in the tub with him, as he lay with his back against the wall. Her round yellow ass peaking out of the water wagging back and forth got him more aroused. C had learned from reading medical magazines that he could relieve migraines by having an orgasm and already the process worked better for him than any Tylenol he could've been prescribed. Cute Nikki held his balls with one hand while her mouth covered his penis.

"C, can we make love?" She asked. "I wanna feel you inside of me."

"You want it bad?"

"Yes," she said licking her finger.

"Aight...grab my condom over there."

"Fuck that...I wanna feel you. If I can taste your dick you can feel my pussy." She offered. "It ain't like we haven't' fucked raw before."

To an outsider who was aware of Tamir's plan to infect C with the virus, it would seem like she was setting him up. In actuality she was feeling guilty about her side relationship with Tamir and wanted to get C hooked with her pussy game. To hear Tamir tell it, she had the best fuck game in the business.

"Aight...get up on here." He said grabbing his dick.

Cute Nikki smiled getting excited about riding his dick when his phone rang which sat on the edge of the tub.

"Wait." He told her putting his hand out and saving his own life. He picked the phone up and said, "Hello." Cute Nikki seemed really irritated that he answered the phone.

"C, Dreyfus called me again. You want me to tell him anything yet?" Monie asked as C held the phone to his ear, his attention still on Cute Nikki.

"Don't tell him nothing yet. I don't know what I wanna do. If he really needs me, he'll wait."

"Cool...did you hear about Lani?"

"No...what happened?"

"She died of HIV complications. Her sister Sachi is fucked up. They saying Tamir infected her."

Although C hated his ex-girlfriend for fucking Tamir deep down in his heart, he still cared about her. So he took news of her death hard.

"What's wrong?" Cute Nikki asked seeing the change in his expression.

"My ex-girlfriend Lani is dead...Tamir gave her HIV."

The look on Cute Nikki's face was priceless. She hadn't even known Lani was infected let alone Tamir.

"You aight?" C said seeing how scared she looked.

"Uh...yeah..."

Focusing his attention back on the phone he said, "She ain't my fucking problem. Fuck her."

"Okay...well...I gotta tell you something else, too. But I'll tell you later."

"Tell me now. You know I hate that 'tell me something later' shit."

"Okay...me and Daps was in that hotel when all them people got killed. Me and you were talking about it when it came on the news."

"I know and you were acting funny."

"I know...I didn't want to tell you. Anyway, for some reason, I think they were coming for us."

"Why you say that?" He asked with raised brows.

"Because we were actually at the party they got killed at."

C pushed Nikki away, stood up and grabbed a towel. Then he walked into the living room portion of his suite.

"Why you ain't tell me that shit?"

"I'm telling you now and she didn't want you to know. But...but...something else happened worse, Daps was raped and she ain't been the same." Silence. "C...you still there?"

C was angry that bad news after bad news was plaguing him and he needed a break. "If she ain't want you telling me why you say something?"

"Huh?"

"Why the fuck you tell me? Like I feel like dealing with this shit now. I'ma hit you back."

Although he was off the phone, what Monie had just told him would stay in his mind for many days to come.

PITBULLS IN A SKIRT 3

"IT WAS SETTLED, IF I COULDN'T HAVE HIM, SHE COULDN'T EITHER."

- MERCEDES

I had just come from Tyson's Corner shopping because it was the only thing that relaxed me. I'll be the first to admit it, I burned the stores down and probably spent more money on clothes and purses than what was necessary. I just figured, well I guess I figured if I had the best that my husband would want me again. So the plan was to go home, call my chef and have him prepare a good meal for Derrick and me. He loved to eat healthy so I figured steamed fish, veggies and good wine would do the trick. And while the chef was preparing my meal, I'd put on my new sexy La Perla nightgown and fuck him better than I ever have in my life.

But something told me, the part that forced me to look at my relationship hard, said that when I made it to our apartment in the National Harbor, he would not be there. I was supposed to be in Emerald for the weekend on business but we needed to talk. Would he respect our relationship by coming home, or prove to me that our relationship didn't matter anymore and that it was over?

Once I made it to the elevator and to my door, I handed my assistant Vida my bags.

"Shit! Where are my keys?" I said patting the inside of my coat.

"You put them in the Tiffany's bag." She smiled. "I'll get them." Vida was a sweetheart and really effective. Not only was she organized and easy to work with she was also great on research and I don't know where I would be without her. "Here you go." She said swinging the keys.

"Whatever you do, don't ever leave me," I laughed.

"Not a chance, Mrs. Ganger!"

Once the door was open, I put my keys back into my Birkin bag, where they belonged. The moment I walked in, Derrick was sitting on the couch in our living room watching TV.

"Vida, you can leave now." He told her without even speaking.

"Oh…uh…" She looked at me nervously because he'd never given her orders.

"Go home. I'll call you with your schedule for next week."

"Thank you! Have a good day." She said running down the hallway.

I put my purse on the table next to the door and said, "Hey, baby, I didn't know you were home. Why didn't you call me? I could've come back earlier." I locked the door behind me.

He cut the TV off and said, "I see you still shopping and shit. You do that more than you do anything else."

"I know," I laughed. "But if I die, I can't take the money with me anyway. I might as well spend it." I joked. He didn't even crack a smile.

"So what you wanna talk about, Mercedes?"

I sat next to him and said, "I'ma cut straight to it because I know that's what you want." I swallowed hard. "I been hearing that you fucking with Bucky." He sighed a little and threw his head back. "Before you get mad, Derrick, let me finish. I know the shit ain't true, so you ain't even gotta bother telling me. I just want you to know what people are saying. And they're saying it everywhere, too."

"Well if you know it ain't true, why step to me with this shit? It's obvious you want something from me."

"I just…I just need to hear it from your mouth."

"So you lied when you told me you didn't believe them."

"I don't believe them, Derrick. I just need to hear you tell me that you wouldn't disrespect our marriage by cheating on me. And I need to hear that you still love me." Derrick burst into laughter and it startled me. "What the fuck is so funny?"

"Are you seriously talking to me about cheating?"

I raised my eyebrows and said, "Yes I am."

"I can't believe you, Mercedes." He stood up and walked to our bar.

Once there he poured himself a glass of Hennessy Black and I couldn't get over how sexy he was. His ripped body was still in shape and the muscles in his arms gave form to the plain white t-shirt he wore. His fuck game drove me crazy and fucked up my routine many a day when I remembered how his body looked as he moved in and out of me. I was obsessed.

"What can't you believe, Derrick? The cheating or the fact that I'm asking you about it?"

"All of this shit."

"Why?"

"Have you forgotten that you fucked Cameron in our house before he was killed? Do you even stop to think about that shit and what you put me through?" He turned around and looked at me. I could see him gripping the glass in his hand so tightly I thought it would break. "You stole a lot from me when I heard you say you'd disregarded our relationship by sleeping with him."

"So what, me fucking Cameron before he died means you can keep taking advantage of our marriage?" I stood up and walked over to him. "How many times are you going to punish me for this? How many times do I gotta scrape up my knees begging you not to leave me?"

"I didn't say I was cheating, you did. But even if I did decide to step out and get a little pussy on the side, I'd be well within my rights."

"A little on pussy on the side?" I repeated. "That's what you calling it?"

He stepped around me and went into the kitchen to get the fresh salad the chef made for him yesterday. Then he sat at the table and ate it as if the conversation was over.

I walked up to him and placed my hand on his, stopping the motion of the fork from going into his mouth. "Derrick, you scaring me." He dropped the fork and stood up from the table and I stayed closely on his heels, my heart beating in my chest the entire time. He was running from me but why? "Please…I…I gotta know if it's true or not. Are you…I mean…are you fucking her?"

As I waited for him to lie in a way that would be believable to me he said, "Yeah. I am."

I didn't even feel myself fall until instead of being at eye level, I was looking up at him. He didn't help me up though; instead he motioned to leave our apartment. The pain I felt inside was too much to let him leave me alone right now. I needed to be with him. I needed to know why he would play me like this and I needed to know where we'd go from here. So I stood up and jumped on his back causing him to fall to the floor. My mind was begging him to tell me why, but my hands and my words spoke differently. I turned violent and started hitting him everywhere.

"I GAVE UP EVERYTHING FOR YOU! WHY ARE YOU HURTING ME LIKE THIS?!" I screamed throwing wild punches all over his body. "DO YOU KNOW WHO THE FUCK I AM?!!!!"

Some kind of way I slid off of his back and he pressed me up against the wall by the door and yelled, "Mercedes, stop! I don't wanna hurt you!"

"FUCK YOU! YOU DON'T CARE ABOUT NOBODY BUT YOURSELF! DO YOU KNOW WHAT I CAN DO TO THAT BITCH? DO YOU??!!!!"

"STOP IT!" He said grabbing my wrists. The grip he had on me was uncomfortable but I didn't care, he was touching me and I wasn't ready to let him go. "I'M SERIOUS, Mercedes!"

"I'm your wife! I'm your fucking wife!" I sobbed. "I don't deserve this shit! If you wanted to cheat on me, why marry me?"

I sobbed uncontrollably. I wanted to beg him to stop the affair but my pride wouldn't allow me to do anything but play the victim.

"I know you my wife, but somewhere along the line you forgot it."

"Do you love her, Derrick?" I said wiping the tears from my face?

"Go 'head with that bullshit!"

"Do you?!" I demanded to know.

"Fuck no," he said leaving me against the wall as he stepped off. "I can never love someone the way that I love you."

"Then why cheat, baby?"

"I don't know. I mean…I guess 'cause I feel like she needs me." He said sitting on the sofa.

I sat next to him and said, "But I need you, too. You gotta know I'm nothing without you."

"You don't need me." He said looking at me seriously. "Do you know how it feels to have niggas in EC call me Mr. Mercedes? They think it's funny that I work for you. Like I can't afford to provide if you weren't with me. Like I couldn't take care of you, C and the girls."

"Fuck what they say, baby! Since when have we worried about what other mothafuckas say?"

"I'm a man, Mercedes! That shit you saying ain't good enough for me no more. I need to feel like I wear the pants in this relationship and right now I don't." He was sincere and I knew I finally tapped into why I was about to lose my husband.

"Then what are you saying? That you want me to leave EC?"

"I'm saying that you're not connected to me anymore. I'm saying that we don't bump like we should and it fucks me up. I'm saying that if something doesn't change," he said looking into my eyes, "we might not make it."

In that moment I knew what I needed to do. He needed me to be submissive and I wasn't giving him that. I could remember the times I checked him about some shit I ain't like in front of his soldiers in EC and how his face would turn flush red with embarrassment. I now understood clearly that I was losing my husband and if he left me, it would be all my fault.

"You are not going to leave me that easily, Derrick. I'm gonna fight for you. Do you hear me? I'm gonna fight for you."

"What does that mean?"

I was tired of talking so I dropped to my knees and removed his pants. The look in his eyes told me that after the serious fight we just had, he still wanted me like I wanted him.

When his pants were off, I took off my jeans and my panties and slid onto his dick. He pumped in and out of my pussy hard at first and then slowly. My juices eased all over him and dampened our brown leather sofa. He grabbed my waist and bit his bottom lip as he held onto me tightly. When he was hard enough I hopped off of him and sucked my own juices off of his dick.

"FUCK!" He said in exclamation. "Oh my, GAWD!"

After sucking him for a minute, I got back on top of him and bucked my hips smoothly. Then I ran my tongue up his neck and into his ear. He moaned as he pawed at my back. I knew my light skin would show the marks of this session and I would wear the scars proudly. This was my husband and I loved him more than I ever loved Cameron, and that was the bottom line.

"Fuck me, baby. Fuck this pussy." I said. Then I looked into his eyes, "You're my husband, not hers and she can't have you."

He looked at me seriously and said, "Fuck that bitch."

"Mmmmmmm," I murmured. Those words were like music to my ears.

"Damn, baby! You feel soooo good." He said lifting me up to lay me on the sofa on my stomach.

Then he licked four of his fingers at the same time, massaged the head of his dick and pushed it inside of me again.

"Hmmmmmm, damn, I love you sooo much, Derrick. You can have whatever you want from me. I don't care nothing about EC, I just don't want to lose you."

"You just saying that shit," he said fucking me harder.

"You can have it all. Just leave her alone, okay?"

Instead of responding he continued to fuck me viciously. I came three times to his none and suddenly I felt out of control. If he could restrain himself from cumming before me that meant he had more power than me in this relationship. Here I was, ready to give it all up for him, and I knew that made me weaker not stronger, but I was willing to take that chance.

After an hour, he finally came and we both drifted into a hard sleep on the living room floor. I could feel his warm chest against my back and the beat of his heart put me to sleep. I felt comforted as he pulled me into him. But somewhere in my sleep, I lost the feel of his touch. For a while I remained in one place, hoping he'd come back. Maybe he went to get something to drink, or went to use the bathroom. And then I heard his voice talking softly from the bathroom. Anybody else not tuned into him probably would not have heard him. But he was my everything and I could hear him clearly say, *"I'ma get up with you later, sexy. Stop crying."*

In my life I had fought wars, been gang raped and still came out swinging. But here I was at war with a bitch not fitting enough to tie my shoes, yet she was stealing my man. It was settled, if I couldn't have him, she couldn't either.

"PART OF ME, SADLY ENOUGH WAS STARTING TO HATE HER ASS."

- CARISSA

Persia begged me to get her dinner from Carolina Kitchen in Hyattsville, Maryland. I think she wanted carryout but I used the request as a reason to take her and Treasure out. We hadn't spent any quality time together and I so desperately needed to be with my girls. I was only there for five minutes when I received a few text messages about small things, but it was the message about the undelivered package to Emerald City that fucked my head up.

I got up from the table and said, "Persia, order me the smothered fried chicken and rice. You girls get whatever you want." She didn't respond because she was on her phone texting and so was Treasure. "Persia, did you hear me?"

"Yeah…damn! I said okay." She said rolling her eyes before getting back to the phone.

I shook my head and moved to a corner within the restaurant where not too many people were. I needed to have a private conversation with Mercedes. When I reached her on the phone, she sounded really sad but I didn't ask her why. I was still beefing with her and hadn't gotten over her extreme disrespect in the limo.

"Carissa…the package didn't make it to Emerald City. Please tell me why Kristina is calling me?"

"Fuck you asking me for?"

"You and Kenyetta walked out with it together that's why I'm asking you."

"We walked out together but it was in her hand." I corrected her. "You better call Kenyetta, I don't know nothing about all that."

"I couldn't reach her."

"Well you better try again."

"Carissa, is she snorting?"

"Fuck you for asking me something like that!" I yelled, scaring a little girl who had wandered a few feet over from me. "That's our fucking girl and she has never fallen that hard."

"Well you better find out what happened because I can't do it right now. I'm going back to sleep. Call Kristina when you find out something. We dry right now and we really need that package to re-up."

I called Kenyetta five times after the call but she didn't answer the phone. When I made it back to the table our food still hadn't come. I started to make a few more texts when I noticed if I got back on my phone, we all would be on the phones. This was supposed to be a time for us to bond, not make computer love.

"Give me your phones, ladies." I said holding out my hands. "I want us to spend some quality time."

"When we start doing that?" Treasure asked.

"Now!"

Treasure threw her Android over to me while Persia decided not to. "Ma, I'm not giving you my phone."

"What?"

"I'm tired of you trying to run my life. Shit…if you got a problem with me having a phone just turn it the fuck off, but don't keep asking me to give it back to you every time you get in one of your fucking little attitudes, because I'm not checking for your drama anymore. Anyway, I'm tired of your shit!"

"Who the fuck are you talking to? I'm your mother!"

"Bitch, please! I'm talking to you!"

I couldn't take her shit anymore so I reached over the table and yanked her up by her coat. But she wiggled out of it and stormed out of the restaurant. I tried to catch her, but realizing Treasure was inside by herself; I turned back around deciding to deal with her later. Part of me, sadly enough was starting to hate her ass. Yet at the end of the day, she would still be my daughter.

"I MISSED YOU..."

- PERSIA

Persia ran as far as she could until her breaths were too close together for her to run anymore. She was so mad at her mother for trying to control her life that she hadn't thought about not having her coat with her until now. She called C to pick her up but he didn't answer the phone. When she tried to reach Mazon she didn't have any luck either. With nothing left to do, she decided to call Zulo and of course his grimy ass came fifteen minutes later. When his black Yukon pulled up in front of her she hopped inside happy to be warm.

"I brought you one of my jackets," he said handing it to her. "It may be a little too big, but I want you to put it on anyway."

Zulo was way older than her but very attractive. He wore his hair in a low cut and talked real slow and mellow. A young girl like Persia didn't have a chance when it came to his chocolate brown complexion and big boy steez.

"I missed you..."

Before she could even finish talking, he stuck his finger in her mouth. And like she'd been taught to do before, she suckled it as if she could get something out of it. Getting turned on by how she ran her warm wet tongue over his first finger, he stuck more in her mouth; before she knew it she was running her tongue around his entire hand. His dick was now so hard it protruded from his pants. He released himself and grabbed the back of her head.

Without saying one word to her, she now had his dick in her mouth. "Fuck. Suck it all, baby girl. Suck that shit."

She looked up at him with her naive eyes as he maneuvered down the road. Her stomach was feeling queasy because she was hungry but she knew if she pleased Zulo right she would get whatever she wanted from him including a meal within an hour.

Persia had a problem; she was in love with power and control. And in her young mind Zulo had it. He did a good job of keeping up perceptions too by flashing his money, which he rarely spent on her along with his chunky platinum jewelry.

Zulo had Persia wrapped around his fingers and dick, and unless something happened soon, it would be no getting her back.

"...SHE DOES A TERRIBLE JOB. IN FACT, I WAS GOING TO SUGGEST TO YVETTE TO FIRE HER."

-*LORETTA*

Loretta had just left Washington Hospital Center where her boyfriend Roger was posted up in a coma. She was worried sick that he'd die. Because he was a snitch on the rise, he had gotten the living shit beat out of him after being suspected of working with the police by Judah's henchmen. And although Roger wasn't high on the hierarchy in Judah's drug operation, he did know enough to get him hemmed up if he got a mind to open his fat mouth.

So the DEA's request to Loretta, who offered to step in, was simple. They wanted her to give them information on who was supplying Roger and they would leave Roger alone. If not, they would wait for him to come around and expect him to live up to the agreement, which kept him out of jail. That's when Loretta came up with the idea to throw the cops off of Judah's trail by putting them onto her daughter instead. She knew all along that Yvette was involved with drugs, how else could she afford the expensive rehab homes she put her in? And since they didn't have a clue who was supplying Roger's miniature operation, one drug dealer was as good as the next. In other words, they had bosses and their bosses wanted to see the case closed.

In an effort to meet the DEA's demands, Loretta turned Yvette's house upside down trying to find any clues, which supported the fact that she dabbled in drugs. However, she had no idea what she was looking for. As Yvette's dogs watched her curiously, Loretta thought about the day she left the door open in the hopes that they would run away, only to have one of them close it shut with its nose. Her dogs were trained and obedient and for a while she wondered if they weren't put in charge to watch her sneaky ass.

Not finding anything related to drugs, she repaired Yvette's room as best she could and closed the door. But when she turned around she saw Chris standing before her.

"What are you doing in this room?"

Chris's height and presence scared the fuck out of her. "Who are you?"

"I'm Chris, I helped Yvette get you into rehab." She paused "Now what were you doing in there?"

"Oh...she told me about you," Loretta smiled.

"Are you gonna answer my question or do I have to call Yvette?"

"Oh..." she laughed trying to lighten the mood, "I wasn't doing nothing...just straightening up that's all."

"We got a maid for that."

"Well she does a terrible job. In fact, I was going to suggest to Yvette to fire her."

Chris suspiciously looked at her and went into the room to do what she came to do. When she collected her shit, she decided to drop a letter that she hoped Yvette would understand.

Yvette, I decided to give you the space you need from a far. I'm going to work on me and I want you to work on you. If you find you still want this relationship after a month, call me on this number 202-555-5667. I got rid of my other one. Oh yeah, I caught your mother coming out of your room. I don't know, Vette, I know that's your moms and all, but I don't trust her. Be careful. You still got my heart. Chris

With that she grabbed her things, locked the bedroom door and played with the dogs. Then she left but not before giving Loretta one last suspicious look. The moment the door closed and she heard Chris' truck pull off; Loretta picked the lock to her daughter's room and found the letter.

"DIKE!" she said with hatred in her heart.

Then she tore the letter up and haphazardly threw it in the kitchen trash right before Rosa came in to prepare Yvette's meal.

"WHOEVER PUTS YOU ON MIGHT AS WELL PICK OUT THEIR OWN BURIAL PLOT, AND I KNOW YOU KNOW THIS."

-YVETTE

When I came home from checking on Emerald, I was tired and wanted to take a nap but Mercedes said she needed me. The moment I walked through the door, my dogs jumped up on me with wild kisses and paws. I love my fucking dogs. But when I went to my room I saw all of Chris' clothes gone. My mouth dropped as I went through the closets, the drawers and the bathroom. Everything, not one stitch of clothing was left.

I ran to the phone and called her cell and discovered the number was disconnected. She went hard. Harder than I ever thought she would. I sat down to regain my breath when my mother knocked at the door. I was pissed when I remembered I agreed to let her stay with us for a few weeks…but now since Chris was gone she would be staying with just me.

"Hey, baby!" She said hugging me.

I couldn't move away because she held on to me too hard, so I hugged her back lightly. The moment we embraced for whatever reason, I felt like crying so I pushed her so hard she stumbled backwards.

"Damn, I'm sorry." She said looking at me strangely. "I was just happy to see you."

"Look, you're a fake ass mother so stop with the hugging shit. And like I told you when you arrived, you can only stay here for a month. Are we clear?"

"Yes." She said walking away.

I needed to be alone for a minute. When I looked around my room, which felt empty without Chris, I replayed our last conversation over and over. She said she would give me time to see what I wanted to do but I should've asked what that meant.

Looking through my phone, I saw her sister Seven's number and decided to call. She picked up on the first ring.

"Vette?" Seven said.

"Oh…hey, I didn't know you knew my number."

"Yeah. I got it programmed."

I was trying to feel her out, to see if behind her regular words she was saying something else. "Have you seen Chris?"

"Yeah."

"Where is she?"

"She at her friend's house."

I was enraged. The only friends she had were bitches. "Whose house?"

"Vette, you know I fucks wit' you, but Chris made it clear, she's not up for the games no more. I ain't trying to fuck you up wit' this, but she sounds like it's over."

I was embarrassed and angry, two emotions which shouldn't go together because the end result could be terrible for those involved.

"I was just calling to tell her I changed my locks and that if she wanted to get anything out of here I hope she took it already."

Seven laughed and said, "Yeah 'aight." And hung up.

I hated them dike bitches! I had my girls and that's all I needed. I gave more time to this gay shit than I needed anyway. With that I headed to Mercedes' spot.

When I made it to Mercedes' apartment I knocked on the door and Daps opened it.

"Hi, Miss Yvette. Miss Mercedes is in the kitchen, I was just leaving."

She left and I was shocked. "Daps live here now?"

"Yeah…it's a long story, too." Mercedes said.

I could tell I was in the middle of a fight between Lil C and Mercedes because her face was beet red and it was obvious that she'd been crying. I walked fully inside and locked the door behind me. Then I sat down at the table they were standing above.

"What's going on?" I asked both of them.

"Nothing," Mercedes said, wiping her tears. "I just wanna jump out of the window."

"Ma, stop being melodramatic."

"C! Watch your mouth."

"I'm so fucking sick of my life, girl. Why can't I have what I want? Why can't I have something good happen to me for a change?"

"Lil C, why aren't you and your mother getting along these days?"

"Cameron, Aunt Yvette. I go by Cameron now."

Lil C was feeling himself but I didn't care. He wasn't about to make me change what I called him most of his life until I was ready to change. I swallowed hard and said, "Okay…Lil C, what the fuck is going on?"

He sighed a little but I wouldn't have a problem putting foot to his ass if need be. And after finding out my girl had left me and carried me in a way I didn't think was possible, I would probably take it out on him easily.

"I want her to let me help her in EC. I'm tired of seeing the problems ya'll have with finding reliable lieutenants and now I'm hearing a package went missing."

"What?" I asked. "What happened?"

"I don't know. Nobody has been able to get in contact with Kenyetta."

"Whatever happened, if ya'll trusted me I could help, but she don't even wanna talk about it." He said. "Pops was fourteen when he started in the game, I'm almost eighteen."

"C, we want you to focus on school, not worry about this drug life. Do you see how many people lost their lives in this game? Your father, Thick, Lavelle, Dyson…all of your uncles are gone, baby. And what about Doctanian? He was your best friend and he's gone too." I continued. "We've lost a lot of good men for Emerald's sake and are not willing to lose you, too."

"He's not in school no more." Mercedes said. "He dropped out. It's like he just carrying the fuck out of me and won't even listen no more. I've given him everything he's ever asked for."

"What do you mean he dropped out?" I asked her. And then I turned around to look at C. "You not in school no more?"

"Naw, Aunt Yvette. I'm done."

"C, this don't make no sense!"

"Well it has to, Aunt Yvette. And since there's no way I'ma change my mind, you might as well let me help you out in EC. I'm way smarter than any of them niggas ya'll got on the block anyway."

"You gotta go back to school. You gotta get that money the right way." I continued sensing Mercedes was too emotionally drained to try anymore.

"Ya'll not in school, and look at the cars ya'll drive and the money ya'll got."

"C, not one of us knows anything else but these streets. We even tried to get a few legit businesses but shit never worked out. But you have a future."

"Look, ain't shit ya'll can tell me about life no more. I'm up on that already. Now either ya'll put me on, or I'ma get put on somewhere else."

"So you're willing to put someone else's life on the line? Because we all know whoever puts you on might as well pick out their own burial plot, and I know you know this." I said.

"Ma, I'm gonna ask you one more time," C said slowly, "are you gonna let me help you, or do I gotta help myself?"

Silence.

"C, you're breaking my heart," Mercedes cried, "I can't lose you, I'm sorry. My answer is no."

Lil C grabbed his coat and said, "I'm sorry, too." Then he walked out the door.

"YOU IN MY WAY."

- LIL C

Chewing a Twix bar, C stepped out of his silver Range Rover that he loved. It was the first gift from his mother after his father died and it was also the only vehicle he drove himself. Trying to calm his mind, he couldn't help but think about Lani's death. He wasn't sure if it was because he could've caught the disease himself if they were still together, or if he still harbored some feelings toward her. Then there was Daps, and the fact that she'd been drinking nonstop trying to hide the secret he couldn't tell her he knew...that she had been raped.

He was picking up the order he placed at Peking Place for him and Cute Nikki but the moment he grabbed the glass door, he felt something wasn't right. The restaurant was filled to capacity but when he looked around everybody looked normal including the teenage girls who were laughing and sharing a table. However, it was Huan's expression that told him something seriously was wrong. C walked cautiously up to the counter examining Huan's face.

"Hey C," he said slowly, "what can I do for you?"

"I came to get my order," C said trying to figure out what was up with him.

"Oh...it's no problem. Almost ready." Then Haun looked at the people in the restaurant. Turning around to the kitchen he yelled,

"你的生命處於危險之中。每個人都在這裡一直等著你。他們不想傷害你的意思!"

The color drained from C's face and he tried hard not to show his fear from hearing the words in Chinese, which meant his life, was in danger. Although Huan was able to play it off as if he was checking the status of his food, C was unable to act calm. He was acting unnatural and if anyone behind him bothered to look at his face, it would be a dead give a way. C turned around to look at everyone in the restaurant and chills went up his spine when he saw that everyone was staring at him. Then one of the girls blew a kiss at him and gave him a devious smile.

In Chinese Huan said, "Please act natural. Helping has placed my entire family in jeopardy." C swallowed hard, turned back around and as if a light switch flipped on, changed his body mechanics to appear like he hadn't heard Huan's warning. "Anything else, C?"

"Naw, man. That's it," he said.

"Okay, that'll be about five minutes."

He knew that must've been how much time he believed he had before whatever move they were going to make took place. But in his peripheral vision he saw someone stand up and move behind him, it was the pretty girl who blew a kiss at him. She was now behind him and he saw a gun in her hands. Then he heard a table move and he figured they were placing it in front of the door. He was cornered and he didn't have a plan. I can't believe this is how I go out. He thought, believing Tamir had everything to do with this set up. With nothing else to lose, he decided to go out swinging so he turned around to face them. But the moment he did, a cop walked up to the restaurant's door.

When he saw the table he said, "They're closed?"

"Oh no...they're open," one of them said removing the table from the door. "I'm sorry, sir." one of the girls said when he walked in.

The officer walked inside and looked at the crowd, who was chatting softly, suspiciously. Feeling nothing out of order, he walked directly behind C and got in line.

C seeing his chance to escape said, "Aight, man. I'm 'bout to go outside and get my wallet to pay you for my food. Make sure you put extra soy sauce in my shit."

But once he reached the door, one of the male Klan members blocked his exit. "You in my way." C said knowing there was nothing they could do with the cop inside.

When the cop turned around and saw the commotion the boy said, "I'm sorry, man." And he stepped out of his way.

With that C walked past the people in the restaurant who now didn't hide their disdain for him. Once outside, he moved quickly to his truck and pulled off. The moment his tires rolled down the wet street, he thought about what just happened. He had no doubt that if they shut down an entire restaurant to get at him, that Tamir and his crew were deadlier than he ever could have imagined and he needed to build his crew to be safe.

Suddenly the words Haun first said to him when he walked in the restaurant played in his mind. 'Your life is in danger. Everyone in here has been waiting on you. They mean to do you harm.'

He heard of the stories about how big the Black Water Klan moved and now he understood shit was serious. Remembering that this all started because of Lani he was glad she died and made mental notes to spit on her grave.

"YOU GONNA HAVE TO CHILL OUT C. AT LEAST UNTIL WE FIND OUT WHAT'S GOING ON."

-YVETTE

I was tired and wanted to get some sleep so badly after staying in the T-Mobile line for over an hour. I changed my cell number wanting a change because I was tired of waiting on Chris to call and since she had changed her number, I had no way of getting in contact with her. I didn't realize how many nights I would be up thinking about Chris and missing her. I guess she meant more to me than I thought.

After playing with my dogs for an hour, I walked back into my house and to the refrigerator to get a bottle of water. Pouring some in their bowls, we all drank like we hadn't had a drop of water in days.

When I looked down at them drinking in the kitchen, I noticed a small piece of paper on the floor. I picked it up and it appeared to have been torn off of a letter but when I searched the inside of the trashcan, nothing was there. Rosa must've emptied it.

Still the message was clear, '*...but I don't trust her."* Who wrote the letter and who couldn't be trusted? When my mother came in smiling with grocery bags in her hand I had my answer.

"Hey, baby. I'm cooking dinner tonight."

"Where's Rosa?"

"I fired her."

"You what? Why?"

"She wasn't doing a good job of keeping your house clean. Don't worry, I can do everything she did and more."

I wasn't going to argue with her. Instead, I took a shower and got dressed. Then I went back out to Radio shack. I decided that I was going to do a little recording of her conversations while I was gone. Before long I knew I would find out what she was really here for.

MERCEDES APARTMENT EMERALD CITY

"What? How do you know it was them?" I asked C as me, Carissa and Mercedes sat in Mercedes' kitchen in Emerald.

C paced a few feet until he stopped. "I don't know, but they shut the entire restaurant down to get at me. It was weird. I mean, we were beefing because he fucked Lani and I knew we were going to have words, but I didn't think shit would be like this. For the past few weeks shit has been happening to me."

"Like what?" Carissa asked.

"One time this kid stopped in front of our car on a bicycle, and then Daps and Monie said somebody tried to kill them at that hotel massacre that was in the news."

"C, you didn't tell me they were there! And Daps didn't say nothing either." Mercedes said.

"You gonna have to chill out, C. At least until we find out what's going on." I said.

"Can't do it, Aunt 'Vette. I got some stuff in the works and I need to be mobile."

I sighed.

"Now I'm wondering if the kids who banged on and broke my window wasn't related to them in some way." I said. "You know they blame us for what happened to Black Water."

"As well they should." Carissa said. "But now I'm wondering if the pictures that was posted up of me around town was related to them, too." Carissa said. "And the video for that matter."

"What, you fucked the Black Water Klan, too?" Mercedes said jokingly.

"Fuck is that supposed to mean?" Carissa said whipping her head in her direction.

"The only way they could've gotten that picture was if they were in the bedroom with you." Mercedes clarified. "So don't start blaming the Klan for your loose bootyness."

"Fuck you!"

I laughed and said, "I thought you said you didn't see the pictures posted."

"I eventually did," she said rolling her eyes.

"Ma…I'm 'bout to go to the gym to shoot some hoops." C said interrupting our feud. Lately it seemed as if we couldn't be in the room alone for five minutes without beefing. Our crew was falling apart. "But let me worry about this. Okay?"

"I don't have a choice do I?"

"Not really." He said giving her a kiss on the cheek before leaving out the door.

When C left Mercedes said, "I'ma put my assistant Vida on Tamir and his family. If anybody can find out where they are, she can."

"WHAT HAPPENED TODAY CANNOT AND WILL NOT HAPPEN AGAIN! WE DO NOT LOSE! EVER!"

-TAMIR

Tamir's family sat in the conference room in his building waiting on him. They knew they failed and was afraid of what would happen next. Tamir believed forgiveness encouraged more problems and decided whoever fell short would be punished. He had handed out orders specifically to take over the restaurant and when they had him in their custody, they were to bring C to him but his family had failed again.

"What exactly happened again?" Energy said breaking the silence. "I mean, you might as well get your stories together before he gets here." She sat down in Tamir's chair and rocked back and forth. "You know how angry he'll be."

"So just because you're fucking my son, it means you get to talk to us about war, too? You weren't there, bitch, so you don't get to talk to me about shit." Shade said.

"Yeah...fall back skank! Your days on top are numbered." Karen added.

Energy looked at her and laughed. "It really bugs you two that I am the head wife now doesn't it? You just can't understand how you went from the top to the bottom."

"All of ya'll need to shut the fuck up!" Lance said. "This is not what we're here about."

Lance had a dark brown complexion and he wore his hair in a low cut. A gold chain hung from his neck and he never really said much. Although Shade had given birth to him too, he lost respect for her the night they had the war in Emerald City. He felt the fact that she cried over the death of her son, his brother, meant she was weak, especially after Black Water said that even amongst them, there would be causalities and that she needed to be strong.

"Wait until Tamir gets here to speak." Lance continued. "I'm not trying to hear this other bullshit ya'll kicking right now."

They sat in their own silence for ten more minutes before Tamir walked inside. His face was expressionless as he closed the door and stood in the room with his family. He was feeling better than he had but was still very sick.

"How'd he get away?" He asked immediately taking his seat as Energy moved out of it. "How did a plan which was so well put together go so wrong?"

Shade swallowed hard and said, "We were all sitting in the restaurant like we told you. We had cleared it out and had the owner tell anyone trying to come in, that he was closed. After about thirty minutes, C finally walked up to the counter. We remained calm, just like we talked about and after a couple of minutes, I had your sister Babette walk up behind him. We were about to take him at gunpoint when a cop walked in."

Tamir had sent his mother, his sister Babette and fifteen of his other brothers and sisters to complete this mission. He chose the youngest ones out of the group who were in their early twenties, to prevent C from suspecting anything.

Threatening to kill Haun's family, they told him he must give them a call the moment C placed an order. Fearing for his family's lives, he did just that when C called. Haun had delivered but when they had him cornered, they lost him. Feeling like someone needed to pay, he walked up to his mother since she was most vocal. Seeing him approach her, she stood up and backed against the wall. Everyone around them moved out of the way to allow Tamir room to do whatever he wanted. When he stood in front of his mother, he rubbed her long silky hair and stared into her brown eyes. She was beautiful.

"I love you, mother." He said rubbing her face with the back of his hand.

"I...I love you too, son." She said shaking.

"I know you do, but you are weaker than you've ever been. Even before pops died you were fucking up. Why, mama?"

"Baby...I...I won't ever mess up again. Just..."

Before she could finish her statement, he took his hand and wrapped it around her throat. Her eyes widened and her tongue stuck awkwardly out the side of her mouth. He held his grip for a minute and sucked her tongue before kissing her passionately on the lips. He never removed his grip during the duration of the kiss. Feeling her life slip away from her, and not being ready to part with her just yet, he removed his hand and watched her fall to the floor, saving her life instantly.

When her body made a loud thud on the floor he turned around and looked at everyone. "WHAT HAPPENED TODAY CANNOT AND WILL NOT HAPPEN AGAIN! WE DO NOT LOSE! EVER! NOW BRING THAT NIGGA TO ME!!!"

"I'M HERE TODAY BUT I MAY BE GONE TOMORROW. YOU GOTTA REMEMBER THAT, BABY."

- DERRICK

The winter sun was shining inside Derrick's Benz as he made his way to Emerald City. He had long since ridden himself of any guilt he felt for cheating on his wife. He could still hear her voice in the background of his mind the night she told her friends that she fucked Cameron again in their home.

"Let me get it out in the open. A day after I got shot, Cameron licked my pussy and fucked me in my house. So now that that's out the way, can I please finish?" Mercedes told her friends.

She rattled off how she fucked Cameron in their house as if it were nothing to her friends when she didn't know he was on the phone with Yvette. Nobody bothered to ask him how he felt about Mercedes' infidelities. In fact, outside of the relationship he had with her son C, he didn't have any real friends. And anybody he kicked it with, including C, he wouldn't dare talk about their marital problems. But, he would run into the arms of the woman who made him feel like a king every time she saw his face and her name was Nakato 'Bucky' Uba.

Bucky had chocolate skin, the color of sunlight shining through honey and every curve on her body screamed sex and woman. She knew what he wanted without even saying it; she was born to seduce, to get any man to do anything she wanted. And to lock Derrick's dick down, she had done more things to him in the bedroom than Mercedes could ever imagine. Yet he wasn't sure if he loved her or not and thought their connection was more lustful than anything else. He was certain though, that there was something between them, but whether or not he was ready to leave his family was another question.

When he made it to Bucky's apartment he took his shoes off at the door and walked in. He had a key and loved how cozy she kept her home. Although Mercedes was neat and clean also, Bucky's apartment had personality and flare. From the gold curtains she'd sewn herself, to the rug her mother had given her from her hometown in Sierra Leone Africa, everything about her spoke culture. At any given time of day, he would smell spices from the incense that burned in a handmade holder, or apples she'd sliced to put in a homemade pie. Although Bucky oozed sex, and if you saw her out on the street you'd be more likely to want to fuck her than talk to her, without a doubt she was the most interesting person he'd ever known.

Derrick walked past two piles of dirty laundry on the floor by the door and hung his coat up.

"Derrick, you're home!" She said jumping up on him, planting kisses all over his face. "I missed you sooo fucking much!"

The moment she wrapped her thick legs around his waist he could feel the heat rising between her legs and his dick grew hard on impact.

"Why are you so fucking sexy?" He said holding her steady by placing his hands firmly under her ass. "You know what you do to me don't you?"

"I'm sexy because only somebody as hot," she kissed him, "and nasty", she kissed him again, "as me could take your mind off of Mercedes, and I need your mind to be on me, always."

With her words, he put her down and walked over to the couch. "Why you have to say that shit to me right now?"

"Since when have we not been real with each other, Derrick?" She said sitting on his lap. "That's one of the things you said you liked about me. I always keep it real with you, baby and leave the fake shit to your wife."

"I don't know what I'ma do about us."

"Us as in me and you?"

"Yeah...I ain't gonna lie, I'm here today but I may be gone tomorrow. You gotta remember that, baby. I don't want you getting so wrapped up in me only for me to switch up on you and leave. As much as I hate to admit, she is still my wife."

"Okay, so tell me this, what's going on with you two now? I know it must be something because you have been here a lot lately."

"You know I don't talk about our marriage...so I ain't gonna start today."

"I know, but everybody needs somebody they can talk to, Derrick. Let that be me." He turned away from her and she gently turned his head back so he could look back into her eyes. "You know you can trust me."

"I don't trust nobody," he said getting up to move toward the kitchen.

"Not even me? You got the key to my house and you still don't trust me?"

"Stop with the quips. I trust you as much as I can but not any more than that."

"Derrick, please talk to me. I want to know about everything that is going on with you."

"Maybe I should roll out. I gotta check on my spots anyway. I might be back later."

"Aight, baby." She said running up to him. "I'm done asking you a bunch of questions and you don't have to leave."

"I gotta be by myself for a while to think, Bucky. I'ma be back later."

"Stay here." She begged. "I gotta go put these loads in the washer and it'll take me a while. I can stay down there the whole time if you want." She grabbed the pack of Newport's off the counter and tucked them in her waist.

"You ain't gotta do that."

"Okay, well I'll come back while they're washing and make your favorite dinner. I just want to be your release. I'm not trying to stress you about shit."

"What's my favorite dinner?" He smiled already knowing.

Bucky swaggered to him, threw her arms around his neck and planted a sexy kiss on his lips. "Your favorite food from my country, you remember...Egusi Soup and rice. And for dessert, I'm gonna play with my pussy so it'll be so wet it will drip to my ass. And after that, I'ma let you fuck me all night long from the back. How's that sound?"

"Damn, bitch."

She smiled, walked away and said, "I knew you'd like that shit." Then she bent all the way down so her pussy lips showed in the extra short shorts she was wearing, picking up the dirty laundry by the door. It was winter but she wasn't leaving the building so in her mind shorts were fine.

Before she walked out the door he remembered something that might be detrimental to her health. Although it had been a while since Mercedes and her friends acted violently, he couldn't be sure if it was totally out of their systems.

"Bucky, I think Mercedes may be onto us. I ain't trying to scare you, but you betta watch your back."

Bucky dropped the clothes on the floor and said, "W...why you say that?"

"Just be careful. I know you knew going in what could happen if me and you kicked it. You said you could handle what it took being with me, now it's time for you to prove it." He walked slowly up to her. "I'm just letting you know."

Bucky's honey colored complexion was flushed and she was horrified. Sure she knew what fucking with Derrick meant...it was part of the appeal. But she always thought he would protect her, and make sure Mercedes wouldn't take things to a deadly level if she ever found out about them, and now she was learning that was not the case.

"Can you handle it?"

"Uh...I can handle it, baby. But...uh...let me make a call right quick. I forgot to call my cousin 'bout something earlier."

"Aight...do what you gotta do."

IN THE LAUNDRY ROOM

When Bucky made it to the laundry room, her two younger cousins Efua and Mudiwa were waiting on her like she'd asked. Unlike them Bucky had been in America all her life. When her mother left her father, instead of her wanting to go back with her mother to Africa, Bucky stayed in Emerald City. Besides, she had a very close relationship with her father before he died and wanted to stay close to his spirit. But Efua and Mudiwa were all African and their thick accents, dark beautiful skin and wide eyes made them exotic in their appeal.

"Girl, you must have trouble if you asked us to meet you here." Efua said, sitting on a washing machine.

"She's right. Why not meet at your apartment?" Mudiwa said.

Bucky placed her colored clothes in a washer and let the water run before adding the powder soap. Then she picked up the bag with her whites and did the same thing.

"It's not even like that, I just ain't seen ya'll all week and wanted to spend some time with you. What, I can't hang with my cousins?" She said shutting the washing machine lids and leaning against one of them.

"Fuck that! Tell us what's really going on." Mudiwa said.

Before they could get good into the conversation, the laundry room door flew open and in walked Mercedes, Yvette and Toi. Bucky could tell by the looks on their faces, that they meant business.

"You, bitches, get the fuck out," Yvette told Bucky's cousins before putting on her black leather gloves.

Mudiwa and Efua looked at their cousin curiously. They knew who all but one of the women was and they also knew what could happen if they didn't obey what she said. The only thing was, Bucky was their cousin, and they didn't want to leave her alone.

"Nakato, what's going on?" Mudiwa said. "Why are they so angry?"

"Make me ask you again to get the fuck out and I bet I won't," Yvette said moving the side of her coat revealing her weapon of choice, her .45.

"I'm sorry, Nakato, but we must listen. Please call us later." Efua said before both of the women hauled ass out of the laundry room.

When they were alone Yvette, Mercedes and Toi placed a washer in front of the door to prevent anyone else from coming in. Then Mercedes tied her hair into a ponytail and took her earrings off.

"Before I beat the life out of you, I wanna know what made you think you could fuck with my husband and get

away with it? What made you think that you could continue a relationship with him, and I would never find out?"

Bucky knew there was nothing she could say to avoid the ass whopping that was coming her way. But the African blood coursing through her veins meant she could never go down without a fight, so she toughened up and prepared for the worse.

"I gotta say, as fine as Derrick is, I didn't think about you at all when I got with him. Nor do I think about you now while he's upstairs in my apartment waiting on me."

Bucky removed the cigarette pack she stuck in her waist and lit one with the lighter tucked inside the pack. Then she inhaled and allowed the smoke to fill her lungs.

"What did you just say to me?" Mercedes said.

"You know why you're having problems, Mercedes?" Bucky said blowing smoke into the air.

Mercedes took two steps toward her and said, "No, why bitch?"

"Because you wanna be the man in the relationship. You are so busy trying to be in control, that you thought that alone would help you keep Derrick in line. But when he comes to my house, and he steps across that threshold, I cater to him in every way. I am cooked meals, I am sex and I am relaxation. When he's with me, it's not just my pussy that reminds him that I'm a woman and he's a man, it's how I speak to him when I call his name."

"Fuck that! Let's crush this bitch under our boots." Toi said.

Bucky laughed. "Yes, Mercedes, I'm fucking your husband, well. The thing is, I know you've always known." Then she laughed. "Now haven't you?"

"What the fuck do you have to show for sleeping with my husband? You could never be me, bitch. You will always be a trick bitch who get the scraps off of another

bitch's table. Derrick ain't leaving me for nothing, not even you!"

"Are you sure? I mean, how did you find out about me? He had to tell you. That meant I was important enough to him, for him to let you know about me. Get a good look at me, because this is the face of the woman who has the best chance at stealing your man."

"That may or may not be true," Mercedes said trying to hide her tears. "I may be staring in the face of a woman who thinks she can take my man. But the thing about faces is this...they change. So let me see how much Derrick is feeling you after I change yours."

They spent twenty minutes beating her like she couldn't imagine and when they were tired they rested and beat her some more.

When Bucky hadn't returned home after two hours, Derrick went to the laundry room to find her badly beaten. He felt horrible for putting her in that kind of danger so he carried her in his arms and out of the building. Everybody couldn't believe how lovingly he acted towards a woman other than Mercedes as he rushed her to his car. He proved all the rumors true.

Once in his car, he drove her to the hospital and prayed she'd be okay. Little did he know that Bucky was in the back plotting on how she'd get Mercedes and Yvette back. She didn't know who the other bitch was nor did she care. She would not take the ass whopping lying down.

"I DIDN'T BELIEVE MY LIE ANY MORE THAN I WOULD THINK MY FRIENDS WOULD."

-KENYETTA

When I made it to my apartment in Virginia, I was surprised to see that my stuff wasn't out on the lawn. I had allowed my life to get so far out of control, that I didn't see a way back. Unlike Mercedes, Yvette and Carissa, I needed a man. I needed one to feel like I was a human and not some machine that was used to make money. Sometimes I wondered how life would be if I died and I even grappled with the idea of killing myself.

When I made it to my house, I opened the door, threw my purse on the floor and rushed under my bed. Then I removed the coke I had stashed and inhaled a few lines. I halfway snorted the entire package I had stolen from Emerald City and had been avoiding my friends. I don't even remember how I got here, all I knew was that because of a habit Carissa started me on, my life was out of control.

Every dime I saved up was used toward the love of coke. And if I wasn't doing coke I was doing my other addiction, Cheese. Carissa and I met Slack and Cheese at the same time. It was after the last big battle in Emerald City, that almost caused us our lives, and we decided to drop it all and board her five million dollar Yacht around the states.

The day we met them we had been all up and down the east coast. We'd meet different dudes, fuck them and just when they started to catch feelings for us, we'd drop them. But when we got back to DC, we threw another party for Carissa's birthday. The moment Slack and Cheese walked in we were on pause. Immediately Cheese was attracted to me and Slack was attracted to her and since they were both friends, we double dated a lot. The only problem was, Cheese didn't want a serious relationship and there was nothing I could say to change his mind.

Now all I thought about was getting high, getting serious with Cheese and having fun. I wasn't feeling Emerald City anymore, even though it looked like I would have to move there permanently since I couldn't afford my apartment any longer. After all of the money I earned, I was having to move back to my apartment in Emerald City next week, while trying to convince my friends I was doing so because I missed the 'hood life' instead of the truth that I was broke.

Picture that. A bitch like me, who had enough money at my disposal to buy people and things off, would miss the 'hood life'. I didn't believe my lie any more than I think my friends would. The truth was every dime of the couple hundred thousand I got a month, went to getting high and living fast.

I was on my tenth line of coke when my doorbell rang. It was Cheese, and I was excited to see him. I don't know what it is about hood niggas that just do it for me.

"What up, baby girl." He said grabbing my ass and throwing his tongue down my throat. "I been thinking about that tight wet pussy all night. What's up with it?"

Cheese's slender frame and smooth bald head turned me on as he followed me into my apartment. He was so fucking fine and I could never get enough of his swag.

"I thought you ain't have time for me today." I whined always giving him a hard time.

He took his hand, wiped my nose and looked at his finger. Some coke dust was on his fingertips and he licked it off. "Got anymore for me?"

I had to be careful with Cheese, because he was liable to take all my shit if I let him. "Yeah, stay right here, I'ma get you some."

While he was in the living room, I shaved off enough coke from my stash to keep us high and horny all night. Then I stepped back into the living room, and we did line for line. The next thing I know, I was naked and had Cheese's long fat dick in my mouth.

"Damn you feel good. I bet you none of them niggas would believe I have one of the Emerald City bitches sucking my dick." He bragged. "Let me squeeze that throat," he said wrapping his hand tightly around my neck. "Tell me you love my dick."

"I love your dick," I said, in between a mouthful.

"Naw, tell me you *love* my dick again, and I wanna hear you say my name."

"I love Cheese's dick."

"Damn you sound so good. Now say…say this. Say, '*I Kenyetta, boss of EC love Cheese's dick.*'"

"I Kenyetta, boss of EC love Cheese's dick."

After I said that, he stuffed and fucked me so long you couldn't tell me nothing. As long as I had him and coke, I felt like I was in heaven, even if in our world heaven didn't last always.

MERCEDES APARTMENT

"Fuck took you so long?" Mercedes yelled the moment I opened her door. "And where have you been? You've been fucking up lately."

"I'm here but I can turn the fuck around if I gotta hear all that."

"Kenyetta, come in and lock the door." Yvette said.

Mercedes was still grilling me as I sat down at the kitchen table. "What's going on?" I asked.

"Where is the package, Kenyetta? It never made it to EC."

"I didn't want to tell ya'll, but I got robbed."

"WHAT?!!!" Everyone but Carissa shouted. Carissa looked at me suspiciously.

"I was trying to make the money back, but I can't do it. I'm low on funds."

"Damn, why you ain't tell us?" Yvette said concerned. She gently touched my hand. "I'm sooo sorry. Are you hurt?"

"No I'm fine."

Mercedes shook her head and said, "Damn! You get robbed, Black Water Klan trying to kill my son and now we have a problem with Dreyfus."

"Why?" I asked.

"He not calling me back, we may have to find another connect." Yvette said.

"But don't nobody got product like him. In all areas, hands down, Dreyfus got the best coke, weed and dope. We can't lose that connect and expect to keep our customer base." I said.

"Well we might not have a choice." Mercedes added.

"Not only that, but connects don't exactly put out ads in the paper." Carissa said.

"I know, but Dreyfus been giving me a hard time ever since we told him we weren't fucking with Tyland. The last time I went to him and told him we were out, he took his time arranging a drop off for me."

"So he's a little slow. So what!" I said.

"That ain't it." Yvette said looking at all of us seriously. "I think Dreyfus may be trying to move us out of our city."

"How?" Carissa said.

"By giving somebody else the package." Yvette said. "The other day I gave Derrick a package to distribute to his crew and they moved it with no problem. But when I checked on our other lieutenants they say they weren't able to move the weight. At first I thought they were trying to stiff us for our weight so I asked to see what they had left and it was all there. And you know we buy all of our product from Dreyfus straight up, so whatever we don't move we stuck with. He's already gotten the money off us and now he's trying to flood us out."

"So what we gonna do?" I asked feeling like doing a line.

"We gonna pull in our lieutenants, talk to them and let them know we gonna have to tighten up around here. And Kenyetta, I'ma need you to set that shit up."

"I got it."

"Tell them mothafuckas that the meeting is mandatory. They must be on time because I think Dreyfus is done with us." She said looking at all of us. "And if that's the case, we're either gonna have to get another connect or get out of the game all together."

"I can't believe somebody would be slick enough to sell shit in Emerald City behind our backs. Don't they know what we could do to them?" I asked.

"I'm just trying to figure out who would be so bold." Mercedes said.

"I bet I know who it is." Carissa said.

"Who?" Mercedes asked.

"C." She said matter of factly. "You did say he wanted to be put on, and since you didn't put him on, maybe he decided to branch off on his own."

"First of all where would he get the weight from?"

"Come on now, we all know C been selling weed around here for the longest. He coulda got that shit from anywhere."

"C may be making a little change with weed, but he would never move majorly on us," Yvette said. "I don't give a fuck what you say."

"You keep believing that bullshit if you want to, but C just like his father." Carissa challenged. "Sneaky."

"And I said my son would never do no bullshit like that. So let's be cool and think with leveled heads."

Silence.

"Have any of you ever given any thought to the fact that maybe, it's time to leave this drug bullshit alone? I mean, how far can we really get by living this lifestyle?" I said. "We made more money than any of us could ever have imagined, yet we lost everything and almost everybody we loved in the process."

"You can't be serious." Yvette said. "Just what would we do, if we don't pump in Emerald anymore?"

"I don't know…maybe open up businesses or something."

"Like what…the hair salon 'Cedes tried to open that one time?" Yvette said. "Or what about the check cashing joint that Carissa started in the hood that was robbed so many times, our employees just started giving anybody who looked like they were about to rob the place the money? Oh…I got it; maybe we can open up the restaurant again like I did where we ended up getting so many people sick, we were sued for ten million dollars. This is it for us, Kenyetta. And we ain't going nowhere."

"I ain't gonna lie. I been thinking about leaving, too." Mercedes said.

"Please don't say this is about Bucky's ass. You beat her ass for points and if Derrick still wants to get with her with a face like that, you don't need him."

"So it's confirmed?" Carissa said. I think it was the first time she asked her a direct question since the meeting and it was obvious they still weren't on speaking terms. "He is cheating on you with her?"

"Yeah." Mercedes said. I could tell she was trying to hold her feelings in.

"I'm so sorry, girl. I…I really wanted the rumors to be lies."

"Well they're not. And I ain't tell you, 'Vette, but he didn't even come home after that shit. I think this bitch got him wrapped up for real. I lost him."

"Well fuck him then! And everybody who looks like him!" Yvette said. "Chris left me too, it's hard being in power and being in love. I mean…we still got each other."

"Sometimes." Carissa said correcting her. "Lately we've been acting like we hate each other, too. The pressure is tearing us apart."

"Well let's not let it." I said.

Just when I said that, I saw them look at me with wide frightened eyes. Carissa was under the table pinching me and I didn't know why.

"Kenyetta, your nose is bleeding!" Mercedes ran into the kitchen and returned with a cool wet paper towel.

I took it from her hand to wipe up the blood. "It's nothing, the iron in my blood is kinda low. I gotta take iron pills and everything."

Mercedes looked convinced but Yvette's knowing eyes stayed on me the entire time. "You sure about that?" Yvette asked.

"Positive."

When C came home five minutes later with some news that would change the course of everything, I knew suddenly the notion that I was *possibly* using coke wasn't significant anymore.

"I'm glad ya'll all here," C said calmly. "I gotta talk to all of you."

"What is it, C?"

"I don't think you're gonna like it."

"Well give it to us straight, no chaser." Yvette said.

"BECAUSE I WRITE MY OWN STORY, AND IN MY BOOK, MY LIFE DON'T END LIKE THAT."

-LIL C

After C told his mother his intentions of getting into the drug business with or without her consent, he met with Dreyfus. He imagined Dreyfus was about six foot something and very frightening, but when he actually saw him the fear he had diminished.

After Dreyfus gave him the bricks, instead of the two days Dreyfus gave him to deliver his money, C moved them in one and was meeting him to hand over his cash. They met at the Gaylord Resort at the National Harbor which was a few blocks from his house. When he got into the suite, he was surprised when he saw all the curtains drawn. It was completely dark with the exception of one light. C walked further into the room with Daps, Monie Blow and Mazon right behind him. Although it was three of them Dreyfus had ten men guarding him.

"He over there," one of the men pointed.

"I can see that." C laughed. He shook his head and walked closer to Dreyfus who was sitting on the couch. "Here's your paper, like I told you, I moved all of 'em."

"Good job."

"Come on now, give me my props. You just gave me three bricks and I moved all of 'em in one day. That ain't good, that's great!"

Dreyfus laughed and said, "Like I said, that was good but I'm about the long run."

Dreyfus was more reserved than C thought. He believed he saw a fire that looked like over time it was slowly burning away. "Where you move your work? In EC?" Dreyfus asked.

"Naw, I wouldn't fuck with my moms spot like that. I know a couple of white boys who hang out with rock bands and shit like that. They had enough paper to lift all the work off me. And the moment I say the word, they got enough paper to lift whatever else I have, too." C smiled.

"Sounds like you got it all planned."

"You gotta understand, the game was breathed into me. Just 'cause I have a baby face don't mean I'm young in the game. Feel me?"

"You didn't have to move any of this in EC?"

"Not one brick." C wasn't sure but it appeared that Dreyfus looked disappointed that he didn't move the work in EC. "Is that a problem? That I moved the weight how I moved it?"

"Naw, but I wanted to see if you could move it in an environment like the one you'd be supplying for me. I didn't expect you to..."

"Think outside the box?"

Silence.

"That's not what I meant." Dreyfus said. "I didn't expect you to move it elsewhere."

As Dreyfus spoke, suddenly C developed a new goal. And that was, to make Tyland Towers bigger than ever before and when he had done that, he'd overthrow Dreyfus.

"Dreyfus, I didn't mean to make you think that by thinking outside of the box, I wasn't ready to supply Tyland. To be honest, I don't see why you can't get anybody to do that shit."

"What you mean?"

Daps, Monie Blow and Mazon stirred a little where they stood. They knew C could be reckless when he spoke his mind and hoped he wouldn't talk himself out of an opportunity for all of them. After all, Daps had dropped out of school, Monie had betrayed Tyland to run with the competition and Mazon had put it all on the line just to follow C.

"I mean, to me all you have to do is get the work, divide it amongst the teams and bring back the money. So anybody who can't do that, don't need to be working for you."

He laughed and that pissed C off. "What's so funny?"

"You. I just hope you're able to back up what you're saying with your performance. It ain't enough to give a speech; I need my money to be right every time."

"And it will be. But I got to tell you, there are many new ways of handling business, and someone like myself who was raised in the drug game, could bring that intellect into your operation. I am ready, because I was born to do just this. I don't know nothing else."

"You know, you remind me of your father, but I hope just like him, you don't fail." He paused. "The relationship I have with your mother won't prevent me from killing you if you fuck up."

"It's not even possible."

"How do you know?"

"Because I write my own story, and in my book, my life don't end like that."

C, Mazon, Monie Blow, Daps, Persia and Ryan were at the bowling alley shooting off some steam. C bowled a 168 and Mazon bowled a 155, everybody else was so far behind they didn't matter. C was trying not to show his irritation that Mazon was so close to his score because C hated to lose.

When Mazon bowled his final ball, he made a strike breaking C's score down. Mazon celebrated with everyone else who was sick of hearing how C was the greatest the entire game. Finally Mazon had silenced him by beating him.

As Persia, Ryan, Monie and Daps shared a pizza, C was reaching a boiling point. He sat away from everyone else and just looked at the lane he'd just lost in. Seeing he was still mad about losing, Mazon walked over to C, to give him some dap but C didn't accept. "So you gonna leave me hanging?"

"Fuck this game, nigga. I wasn't tripping off of no bowling anyway. What you need to be doing is finding ways to help me get through to them Tyland Tower niggas."

Mazon seeing C was serious said, "I wanted to rap to you about that. I been putting the word out in Tyland that you 'bout to run shop and anything going in and out of Tyland has to go through you."

"And?"

"And I'm hearing niggas not going to take you seriously. Some dudes threatening to kill you and other ones threatening to not take work from you."

C was beyond mad hearing this. "So that's what they saying?"

"Yeah. What you want us to do?"

"You ain't got to do shit." C said slyly. "If niggas take me for a joke, I'ma give 'em something to laugh at, the only thing is they might not think it's so funny."

"GAME!"

-LIL C

C was inside the indoor basketball court alone and mad that once again Ryan and Mazon were late. A lot of shit was on his mind and he was starting to doubt if he had what it took to supply Tyland for Dreyfus. Although he saw the job as easy, he hoped that after a while he'd be able to prove himself more valuable and move up in the ranks. He had no idea that the only reason Dreyfus was even entertaining him, was to get back at the women who broke their agreement. He knew it wouldn't take long before C's cocky arrogant attitude got him killed and he waited patiently to see it happen.

If C wasn't thinking about Tyland, he was thinking about the ongoing beef between him and Tamir and the fact that Cute Nikki had decided not to return his calls. 'Fuck that bitch. It's her loss.' He eventually told himself.

"Fuck! Where them niggas at? I got shit to do today." He said looking at his watch, periodically shooting hoops.

He finally made a basket when Tamir swaggered through the door alone with a grin on his face. C was immediately angry and was ready to kill him with his bare hands.

"Feel like a little game of one on one?" Tamir asked walking up to him.

C looked at the door just knowing his crew was about to flood inside. "How you know that I was here?"

"I don't think you realize how deep my family is. I got people who work here and every place else you hang. Un-

derstand C, your world is getting ready to collapse." It was settled, he would not be coming back to that gym.

"So what, you here to kill me?"

"Naw...I'ma break down your outer shell first and then come for you." Then he held his hands out. "Give me the ball." C threw it in his chest and Tamir laughed.

"What you want?" C said as he stole the ball back from him and made a basket. "Because I know you ain't come out here to play games."

"I want to know if you finally regret threatening me...you remember, the day you called and found out I fucked your girl." He shot the ball and missed and C stole it again.

"I don't regret shit I do," C said as he made a basket. "Plus I heard your dick is as weak as your game." Tamir stole the ball and finally made a basket. "You not gonna be living too much longer anyway. Don't you got that monkey on your back?"

Tamir laughed and said, "Yeah...but I fucked your recent girl, so you might have it, too."

C threw the ball across the court and stepped up to him. "What you just say to me?"

"The girl Cute Nikki...I fucked her raw." He said groping his dick. "You better get checked." Tamir laughed. "Because we may have more shit in common than you think." C balled his fist up and wanted to drop him but he held back. "Go 'head...hit me. That's a sure way to get this shit. Go ahead."

"Get the fuck outta, nigga! I'm done talking to you. If you wanna see me, see me in the streets."

When he said that Ryan and Mazon walked onto the court. Tamir and C looked at them as Tamir moved for the exit. "Take a good look at your crew." He said pointing at them. "One of them will either betray you or die within a few days." With that he walked away.

When he was gone Ryan said, "Damn...what was he doing here?"

C, feeling like had Tamir come deep he could've been dead, decided to make someone pay and dropped Ryan where he stood.

"Game!" C said shaking his hand and walking out the door.

"I HAVE PUT SOME OF MY BITCHES IN COMAS FOR GETTING ME WRONG."

-*MAZON*

Mazon and Persia had been going strong for two weeks and as far as Persia was concerned, it didn't get much better than him. Because she was spoiled, she loved the attention and money he spent on her and she loved how he was constantly trying to prove how much he was feeling her.

"What you eating, babes?" He asked as they had lunch in his favorite DC restaurant. He was skimming over the menu periodically looking into her eyes. He couldn't get over how pretty she was and was glad she chose him.

"What's good here?" She shrugged not knowing what to eat.

"Everything. But if you want breakfast, the pancakes are the best." Then he looked a little deeper into the menu and said, "The cheddar grits and eggs are good, too."

"They serve breakfast at night?"

"Even if they didn't with this kind of money," he said setting a fat wad of cash on the table, "they'd make anything for us we want. Cash changes people...and menus."

They both laughed. "What am I gonna do with you, Mazon?"

"Whatever you want to."

"Well since you know this place better than me, order my food."

Mazon ordered for her and after they ate their meals he got a beer and got Persia some sweet dessert wine. She had been meaning to ask him how C was because she hadn't seen him in days and she overheard Mercedes telling Carissa that something heavy was on his mind.

"How's C doing? I mean, is he okay?"

Mazon downed the beer on the table and started to drink the other one he had the waiter bring. "He told you?"

"Told me what?"

"That he wants me to stop fucking with you."

"What? Why?"

"I think he wanna fuck you or something." Mazon said disgusted.

"C don't like me like that," she giggled. "He got too many girls on his dick to be thinking about me."

Mazon looked over the table at her and studied her expression. She definitely appeared to be flattered by the newfound news. "Why you asking me about C anyway? Ain't ya'll cousins?"

"He my play cousin, you know our mothers are best friends so we grew up together."

"Well C's gonna be C. I mean, niggas is saying he taking shit too far with working for Dreyfus but I ain't got no problem with him just as long as he don't act brand new on me."

"And if he does act brand new? Just what the fuck are you going to do?"

"Boss or not, I'm not gonna let a nigga talk to me any kind of way."

"Boy, please! Worry about that bridge when you get to it. Because as long as he is in charge, you gotta play by the rules."

Mazon's jaw flexed and his eyes narrowed. "You wanna fuck him?"

"What? Where the fuck did that come from?"

"You not answering the question. Didn't you just finish telling me ya'll were cousins, and that ya'll grew up together?"

"Yes, Mazon. So where is all this coming from?" She paused. "I was just asking about him because I haven't seen him in a while," she said rolling her eyes, "but I don't see how you got all that from my question."

Mazon wasn't having any of it so he sat on her side of the table, and looked around. When he saw no one looking, he reached over and pinched her nipple as hard as he could through her shirt.

"Ahhhhhhhh....."

"Shut the fuck up," he said in a low voice to calm her down. He wanted her reaction to change although he didn't let up off the pain he caused. When she was quieter he said, "I don't allow my girlfriends to ask me questions about my friends, or niggas I do business with. Now don't think just 'cause C hooked us up, that I won't beat your ass for disrespecting me. Am I making myself clear?"

"Yes...yes," she sobbed.

"Now, you gonna show me the respect I deserve whenever you see my face. And if you don't," he said squeezing her nipple harder. "I will beat your ass for every day I think you even thought about doing me wrong. And let me tell you this," he said quieter in her ear, "I've put some of my bitches in comas for getting me wrong. That's why you never heard about me because none of them are around to tell the story. Am I understood?"

"Yes, I'm soooo sorry, Mazon. Please stop."

He finally let her go and kissed her softly on the lips. It didn't bother him that her tears touched his face. He loved it.

Prior to that moment she always wondered how someone so nice and so cute could be so single. Now she had gotten her answer. The nigga was crazy. He was just about to move back to his seat until seven dudes came into the restaurant.

"So we meet again." Tamir said, his brothers surrounding the table. They were so deep no one behind them could see what was going on at the table.

"What you doing here?" Mazon asked. While he was still guessing Tamir whipped out a .9 millimeter, held it to his head and pulled the trigger but it only clicked.

Mazon's breaths sped up and he immediately pissed on himself. "Now shut the fuck up and listen. I want you to do something for me." Tamir drank Mazon's beer.

Persia was overwhelmed by everything and secretly wanted her mother.

"What is it?"

"It's simple. C trusts you, and because he trusts you, he won't see us coming. So I'm going to tell you where I want you to bring him, and if you bring him to me, I'll pay you two thousand dollars. But if you don't I'ma give my brothers the money to torture you like you wouldn't believe."

"Why you ain't just take him at the gym?" Mazon asked.

"Too many witnesses...but don't worry, you're going to do my dirty work for me." Then he looked at Persia and said, "You gonna drink that wine?" She quickly shook her head no. He winked and said, "Thank you."

"WE HAVEN'T HAD AN EMERGENCY LIKE THIS IN A LONG TIME SO IT'S TIME WE GOT SERIOUS."

- YVETTE

My mother was getting on my fucking nerves and I wanted that bitch out of my house. I still hadn't even told my friends about her because it was too embarrassing telling them that the woman who gave birth to me, also was on dope and is now living in my house. Looking at my phone I read the text message again she'd just sent.

'Can you bring home some eggs? I'm hungry and want to make breakfast for dinner. Oh, and we don't have no milk either, I drank it all yesterday.'

"Fuck!" I said out loud. "I want this bitch gone."

I tried to check the recording device I hid in the room as much as I could for the past few days but still didn't come up with anything. On the days I really wanted to check it, she was in the house. It's like she knows I'm watching her. Still, I knew that if I waited, she'd reveal her sneaky ass to me sooner or later, I just had to be patient.

I was talking to myself when Derrick walked up to me. "Oh…what up, Derrick?" I said tucking my phone."

"Everybody's here," He said.

He had a slight attitude and I couldn't believe he was tripping off of the shit we did to his bitch. He was wrong for fucking with her and should be lucky we didn't cut him off all together. But with Dreyfus making threats, we needed all of our loyal men. Outside of Derrick the only other loyal men we had on our squad, who we knew for a fact would lay down their lives for us was, Dramon, Aleed, Carson, Dipbug, Kit, Wallace, Jonee, Bruce and Paul. It may have seemed like a lot but when you're in charge of five buildings with twelve floors each, it's not enough.

"Glad you were able to get everyone here and on time. I don't know where Kenyetta is." Then I paused. "Derrick, are you cool? We can still count on you right?"

I sensed his anger wanted him to get shit off his chest.

"Is this about business or my *personal* business?"

"You know what, don't even worry about it. Let's get this meeting started."

"Good…but before we get started, I wanna give you a heads up that something's off with the men."

"Something like what?"

"I'm not sure. Just take heed. There have been a lot of side conversations."

When Mercedes walked up to us Derrick walked away. Originally I was going to ask her where Carissa and Kenyetta were but I could tell she'd been crying and didn't want to bother her. Besides, I had my own shit on my mind, like the fact that Chris and me still had not spoken.

"Mercedes, are you ready?" I asked putting my hand on her back.

"Yeah why you ask me that?" She said sniffling a little. She wiped the tears, which crept up on her face and said, "I'm ready."

"Look, I know you going through shit and so am I. But I need you hard right now, can you do that for me?"

"Yvette, I might be going through something but I'm here to do my job. I don't know why you always feel like you gotta protect me. Shit don't always have to be good with me and right now I'm just having one of those days."

"All right then let's get down to business!"

As I looked out at our men I felt like I was repeating my life over and over again. How many times was I going to have to hold the same meeting? How many times was I going to say the same shit? I'm so fucking tired of this life but if I don't do this, what else am I going to do?

"All right, I need everybody to settle down." They did. "Thank you, we called this meeting for a very special purpose. We have reason to believe that within the next few days somebody will try to infiltrate Emerald City. And when they do, if they do, we have to be ready. Now we've been letting ya'll slack off a little but that shit is going to stop right now. And instead of hearing it from your lieutenants, I figured it would be best coming from us."

"Can I ask a question, boss?" One of the men asked.

"What is it?"

"Is it true that Cameron is running Tyland Towers now?" Aleed asked.

"Don't worry about all that. Stay focused. That's our problem now, we too busy worrying about other organizations when we losing control of our own. Don't ask me a question about another mothafucking crew. Worry about Emerald City."

"Sorry, boss."

I turned to Mercedes. "Mercedes, you want to say anything?"

"I'm gonna answer Aleed's question."

"You ain't got to do that shit."

"Aleed, although I appreciate Yvette's response you guys deserve the truth."

"What are you doing?" I asked.

"It's okay," she said softly, "I just want to be honest." Then she turned to him and said, "My son has decided to step off on his own, but don't for one minute think that our family isn't still intact." Then she looked at Derrick who looked away from her. "And don't for one minute think that I won't hold anybody in this room responsible for any disrespect toward him."

I decided to pick it up from there because she looked as if she was about to cry. "Over the next few days I want you to keep your eyes wide open. You need to report to your lieutenants or myself if you see anything out of order. We haven't had an emergency like this in a long time so it's time we got serious." I said looking around. "I don't want to see ya'll shooting craps, chasing bitches, or anything else that may jeopardize business. Getting fired will be the least of your worries if somebody comes through them gates that ain't supposed to be here." I said seriously. "Any questions?"

"I don't have a question but I do have a statement." Bruce said.

With that the doors opened and in came a bunch of familiar faces. Immediately they aimed guns in our direction while our men aimed at them.

"Now you have your guns turned on us, but we have ours turned on your leaders. You might want to rethink your strategy."

They looked at me and I said, "Lower your weapons."

Suddenly through the crowd came Harold. We hadn't seen his fucking face since him and his boys raped Mercedes.

"This will be quick, Yvette. Dreyfus runs Emerald City now," He said with a smile on his face. "Now as you can see you're outnumbered, so unless you and your men want to die, I'd say this meeting is adjourned."

"I LIKE THE WIT, I'M LOVING THE SHOES."

- LIL C

After receiving a negative HIV test, C felt there was much to celebrate. He rented out a ballroom in the Ritz Hotel in DC and invited a few people he knew from Emerald City and Tyland. They all came even though nobody from Tyland knew why Dreyfus would in trust young C instead of someone with longevity like Priest or Frost. In C's mind the party was to depict his 'Rise' and the fact that he was finally going off on his own.

As Super Star rapper Joe Glock performed on the mic, C waited patiently before he made his entrance. He wanted to put the party on pause when he walked through with his crew, which included Daps, Monie Blow and her cousins Lee Lee and Love. C was also able to pull some strings and send for the newest members of his crew from Sri Lanka.

When C stepped through the doors wearing a white fur coat, with his crew he called The Set, mouths dropped. All of the women came through with extra long black fur coats and one-piece dresses. Daps had a red dress under her coat and although Lee Lee and Love were uncomfortable in the gear, they still looked sexy. But it was the Sri Lankan women and Monie Blow who had people stunned.

Monie Blow was very curvaceous. The black dress she wore showed her ample cleavage, thick legs and round hips. She showed that big girls could run rings around the smaller ones any day of the week if they had a mind to. Although the women looked sexy and harmless, tucked under their fur coats were brand new Beretta CX4 Storm rifles. The weapons were light enough to carry on the go but vicious enough to lay down the entire party if need be.

"Party time, niggas!" C said holding a gold bottle of Ace champagne.

The entire party applauded with fake, 'What's ups'. Even the rap performer stopped what he was doing to show C love. C was on top of the world having gotten the response he wanted.

"Damn, C!" Mazon said walking up to him. He looked at The Set and said, "You came through like that? I'm feeling the white fur joint, too."

"I go by Cameron now, Mazon." He replied not acknowledging his compliments. "Make sure niggas know that because if I have to tell somebody again there's gonna be problems. I want everybody to refer to me as such."

Mazon heard that C had gone Hollywood, but now he'd seen it with his own eyes. "I got you. Cameron it is."

C stepped around him like he wasn't even in the room and could hear people making comments. Some were giving him his props while others were shaking their heads at how he was acting. But through it all, C didn't give a fuck. Both his mother and his father raised him as a flashy dude so he was going to do him regardless.

"Damn, C. You looking good," Sachi said, looking him up and down.

He invited her to offer his fake condolences over her sister's death but C could see in her eyes she wanted to fuck him. However, the moment she tried to step closer, Monie Blow pulled her rifle out and pointed it in her direction.

"Back the fuck up, bitch." Following suit, the rest of The Set aimed at her, too.

"Damn, C. It's like that?" Sachi said with raised arms.

"His name is Cameron, bitch. Now step the fuck off." Daps said as they moved to the VIP section specially made for him at the party.

Sachi hauled ass and people didn't know yet but they would find out soon that he instituted a new rule. No one, with the exception of a member of his crew, could step within twelve feet of him.

Once in the VIP section C sat down and The Set stood up and guarded him. He was doing the most at the party but he didn't care. Glock was on point on the mic and when he performed a song he hadn't even put out yet, bitches went crazy. If the women weren't trying to fuck C, they were trying to get at Glock. The funny thing was, with the guns The Set were toting; even a Grammy winning rapper was more accessible than C at the time.

After a few hours, C and The Set relaxed just a little to share a few bottles of champagne. He was feeling life until he saw someone with his white fur coat on.

"You aight, Cameron?" Monie asked not knowing what made him mad.

"I'm cool." He said eyes still glued on the coat. He didn't want The Set to know he was tripping off another nigga so he didn't address it verbally.

When Persia came through the door, Mazon rushed over to her and C was even more pissed because he told him to leave her alone. "Monie, go over there and tell Persia and Mazon to come see me."

"I'm on it."

When Persia stepped over to C with Mazon right behind him C was open. She was wearing a silver dress with a pair of silver Christian Louboutin high heels. She looked super sexy and C could tell by the dress that she was trying to get his attention. It worked.

"What up, Persia?" C said not taking his eyes off of her. "I like the wit, I'm loving the shoes."

Persia laughed having recognized the Jay Z verse, but little did she know, C was serious. He could tell the moment she walked through the door without even seeing the red bottoms that she was swaggering in Christians. He knew then that Mazon was making her into a girl he could have on his arm, and now C wanted her on his own because finally she looked like royalty.

"Thank you for the compliment, Cameron." Persia said slightly nervous. "I'm loving everything about you." Her comment shocked everybody and Monie was jealous.

"So you hanging out with me later?" Cameron asked making shit up as he went along. "Maybe we can go out to eat, since I haven't seen you in a while."

"She got a headache," Mazon said for her. "She need to go get some rest. I told her not to come."

"I'm talking to her, nigga." C told him. "I told you I didn't want you fucking with her anymore." Then he turned to Persia and said, "You ain't got no love for me no more where you gotta have this man answering questions for you?"

"I got love for you, Cameron." She said looking at him before nervously looking at Mazon to her right.

"Well why you acting funny?"

"Baby, go fix your makeup," Mazon told her. When she left Mazon said, "C, I mean, Cameron, I need to rap to you."

"Go 'head."

"You mind if we do it in private?"

"Yeah I mind, so what's up?"

"Okay...well somebody in Tyland says they have some information for you about Tamir. They didn't want to tell me personally but suggested that you meet them if you want to talk about it. Said it had to be done tonight and that it couldn't wait. Your life depended on it."

Monie and Daps adjusted a little not feeling his request. "Fuck they want with Cameron?"

"Yeah...why they couldn't just tell you?" Daps added.

"I know, that's what I said, but I didn't get a response."

"Where are they?" C asked in an even tone.

"They said they can meet you here tonight if you want. Do you want me to set that up?"

"Yeah. Set that up."

Mazon bopped off and Daps said, "I say you let us smoke that nigga. I don't trust 'em."

"Me either, Cameron. You see how he was moving all nervously and shit."

C didn't want to have to give an order of that magnitude but even he had to admit something wasn't right. Plus what Tamir said about one of his friends betraying him played in his mind.

"You and Daps check him out." C said to Monie. "But before you do anything, make him tell you the truth."

"I'm on it," Daps said.

They were just about to leave when Monie said, "I'm glad we doing this shit, too."

"Why?"

"'Cause he beating that girl. And I can't stand a nigga who puts his hands on chicks."

"How could you tell?" asked Daps.

"An abused woman's eyes never lie."

Mazon waited nervously in the back of the dumpster of the hotel where Tamir said he'd meet him. He was beyond nervous about betraying C and was ten minutes late because of having to go to the bathroom to shit every five minutes. He didn't want to betray his friend, but after seeing the power Tamir possessed, he decided against getting on his bad side.

Mazon grabbed his phone from his pocket. Then he typed the words,

'C, he's here. Meet me at the back of the hotel.'

He looked at the words before he sent them knowing that once he pressed send, there was no turning back. His bowels failed him again as he battled with what to do. And then his mind went back to the restaurant, and how Tamir and his crew had made a fool out of him. He knew then what he had to do. Looking at his phone one last time, he hit the send button. Fifteen minutes later, instead of seeing C, he saw the silhouettes of two sexy women walking in his direction.

The darkness hid their faces but when he saw the way the fur coats hung from their bodies, he knew who they were. He tried to run but they caught up to him and wrestled him to the ground. Although he was much stronger than them, Daps held him down with the barrel of her gun to his stomach while Monie held hers to his head.

"We ain't got long so you might as well tell us who sent you." Monie said using the heel of her shoe to step on his chest. "Who, Mazon?"

"I don't know what you talking about. It's not even like that."

"Answer the fucking question! Who told you to step to Cameron? Was it Tamir?"

Mazon cried like a bitch knowing all was lost. "I'm sorry," he wept. "I'm so fucking sorry."

Daps looked at Monie and shook her head. He was a pathetic sight to see lying on the ground in tears.

"Answer the question!" Monie said already making notes not to ask him again. The next thing he heard would be the clap of her gun.

"You don't get it. It was all a set up." He continued.

"What's the set up?"

Mazon cried some more and said, "Tamir knew C wouldn't come out himself. So, while ya'll are out here, Tamir is upstairs making a move on C. He may be dead as we speak."

Hearing those words caused the girl's hearts to drop and without wasting any more time, they filled his body with holes.

Monie and Daps rushed back to the ballroom. But on the way back, they saw people running out screaming at the top of their lungs. Some people were covered in blood while others were lying dead on the floor. It was a massacre.

"Come on, we gotta go in." Monie said kicking her high heels off. She was done with the cute shit and was now ready for whatever.

"You smart as shit for that move." Daps said kicking off her shoes, too.

When they made it to the VIP area, their jaws dropped when they saw someone laid out on the floor, the white fur coat on his body was drenched in blood.

Monie looked at Daps and said, "Please say this shit ain't true."

They slowly walked to the body but before they could reach him police rushed the area and they got the fuck out of dodge.

"I HATE YOU FOR THIS SHIT AND I WILL NEVER FORGIVE YOU! EVER!"

- MONIE

Monie and Daps walked cautiously toward Mercedes' apartment in Emerald City. Neither wanted to tell her that her only son had been killed. Seeing C lying on the floor covered in blood panged their hearts and the thoughts of losing a good friend were insurmountable. They wanted to run up to him but the cops had closed in on the hall and shut down any action leading from or to the ballroom. And because they were both carrying loaded weapons, it wasn't a good look.

"I don't wanna do this shit, Monie." Daps said stopping in the hallway. Her head Thumped greatly and she felt a migraine coming on.

Monie leaned up against a wall in the hallway and looked at the ceiling. "Daps, I know you don't, you think I want to do this shit?" She paused not long enough to get an answer. "But he was our friend and we owe it to his mother to tell her what happened."

"Well did you at least get in contact with your cousins first? I mean, we don't even know what really happened. What can we tell her?"

"Naw, I couldn't reach them, they wouldn't answer their phones."

"I can't believe we left him, Monie. We weren't supposed to leave his side, you know what I'm saying? We were supposed to be by his side no matter what, and we didn't do that."

"FUCK!" She screamed. "What do you wanna do, keep harping about that or do what we gotta do? Because no matter what we say, we ain't brining C back." Then she lowered her voice and said, "He gone, Daps. Now let's go tell his mother."

Monie stood up straight as they continued about their journey bearing bad news for Mercedes. But the moment they got closer, they heard loud yelling. At first they weren't sure if the sound was coming from C's apartment, but when they got closer to the door, they were certain that it was.

"What the fuck do you think that's about?"

"I don't know, maybe they found out already." Daps said.

When the door flew open, they were surprised to see Carissa and Mercedes fighting in the hallway. They were pulling each other's hair and hitting each other for serious points. One look at the women and no one would have ever thought that the two were best friends.

"Get the fuck out of my house with that shit!" Mercedes screamed pointing down the hall. "I'm not about to allow you to continue to hit my child!"

"You ain't got to worry about me coming to your house no more, bitch! Our friendship is long over!" Carissa yelled.

"Yeah, it was over a long time ago. When you abandoned our operation and left me and Yvette to run shit by ourselves. And it's definitely over now that you hit my son."

Carissa looked as if she wanted to cry more than anything. "Persia, we gotta go."

"No, mama. I don't wanna..."

"Persia, get the fuck out here now!"

When Persia walked into the hallway wearing the same thing she was wearing at C's party, Monie and Daps' mouths dropped and they wished they could see inside the open apartment door. Mercedes and Carissa were so enraged, that they didn't seem to notice them standing there. On the other hand Monie's heart was racing because if she was alive, maybe C was alive, too. But what about the dude with the white fur lying on the floor that fit C's description?

All doubt went out the window when C came into the doorway and said, "I'm sorry 'bout this shit, Persia." He still didn't see his friends because everything was moving so fast.

Carissa snatched Persia by her hand and they stormed down the hallway, almost knocking over Daps and Monie.

"C, get in here we have to talk." Mercedes said.

He was about to close the door when he saw Daps and Monie standing before him. Although Daps was beyond happy, Monie was angry.

Without saying anything she walked up to him and said, "Where the fuck were you?" Hot tears rolled down her face.

"What you talking about?"

"What the fuck are you doing here?"

"I stepped out of the party for a minute to take her home because she had a headache and some other shit happened that I can't talk about right now and we ended up out here. Why?"

"We thought you were dead?!" Monie cried. "We thought we lost you!"

"Dead? Fuck is she talking about?" He asked Daps still not knowing what went down.

"It's a long story." She replied.

Monie unable to get past her anger walked up to him and smacked him in the face. "I hate you for this shit and I will never forgive you! Ever!" With that she stormed down the hallway, and out of sight.

"YOUR BEST CHANCE OF GETTING HIM BACK IS TO STAND BACK AND DIRECT HIM FROM A FAR."

- DERRICK

"Mercedes, calm down. I can barely hear you."

"I caught C fucking Persia in the apartment in EC yesterday! And me and Carissa got into a fight. What is going on with my life?" She sobbed.

"I can't really talk to you right now. I'm kinda busy."

"That bitch Bucky got you so wrapped up that you can't give me five minutes of your time?!" She yelled. "I need your help, Derrick!" She paused, lowering her voice. "Please."

"Go 'head?"

"Thank you," she said, "C is out of control. And I'm hearing that he's doing too much in Tyland. What am I going to do?"

"Doing too much like what?"

"He walking around with bitches from out the country...they got guns and all other kind of bullshit like that."

"I don't know why you surprised."

"Why you say that?"

"He's a product of you and Cameron. He watched his father and how he controlled you and the girls. So he's probably creating his own pitbulls."

"Cameron didn't control anything."

"Yeah...okay. But just because he dead doesn't make what you said true."

Mercedes sighed knowing he was right and said, "But I don't want him to have this lifestyle."

"It's too late for that, Mercedes. Your best chance of helping him is to stand back and direct him from a far. Otherwise this game is going to eat him alive. He not ready for this lifestyle and I know you know that. But what else can you do?"

"I hate not having you here, Derrick. I really need you to come home."

"I think it's too early." He paused. "And as far as Persia goes," he continued getting back on topic, "C been fucking for a minute. It was just a matter of time before he got with that girl. She been infatuated with him for some time now. But watch out for her, she got more shit with her than a little bit. I can see it in her eyes."

"HE WASN'T THE SAME MAN I THOUGHT I FELL IN LOVE WITH. HE WAS SOMEBODY DIFFERENT..."

-KENYETTA

I couldn't believe it when the girls told me that we lost Emerald. And because I was going to have to live there for good now, it would be tough walking through the project knowing that I had fallen from grace. Since I had completely snorted up the stash I'd stolen, I would have to be careful whom I copped from now on more than ever.

When someone knocked at the door, I thought it was Cheese so I opened it wide. It was and I smiled when I saw his face. Damn he fine.

"Hey, baby." He said kissing me gently on the lips, gripping me in a full body hug. "I came by to see if you needed any help moving."

"Naw. I'm fine." I said being reminded of what I had to do, move back to the projects.

I walked into the living room and sat on one of the boxes. "I don't even think I have enough room to put everything in EC. My place there is so fucking small."

He walked up to me, knelt down and said, "You gonna be okay. Don't trip off of none of that shit."

"I know, but it's so hard." I hugged him gently around the neck and he looked up at me. His eyes were so seductive that I knew what he wanted from me, but I wanted to hear him say it. "Why you looking at me like that?"

"Because..."

"Because what?" I smiled.

"Because you one dumb bitch."

"Huh?" I laughed.

Before I could do anything else, he had his hands around my neck. And while maintaining his grip on my throat, he stood up and continued to squeeze it tighter. His grip lifted me off my feet as I clawed at his hands with my nails.

"W...why?" I whimpered as tears ran down my face. "I loved you."

He smirked and instead of telling me what I had done so wrong, he maintained a tighter grip on my throat. He wasn't the same man I thought I fell in love with. He was somebody different and had I not spent the last few months snorting coke maybe, I would've seen him for the man he was.

The moment I reasoned that my life was over, a face I recognized stepped inside my apartment. Dropping me to the floor, he got back over me and gripped my throat tighter. The woman stood over me and smiled. It was Shade, and I recognized her right away from when Black Water told me he wanted me to be a part of his Klan. Her black hair still as long as it was the night I last saw her. The same night her son, Nathan was killed in EC's community center.

"I've been waiting so long for this. And finally, after all these years," she continued while Cheese continued to choke me, "My wish comes true. Don't worry, I'ma send those friends of yours right behind you."

I tried to speak and I guess curiosity got the best of her because she said, "Let her go for a second."

Then she stooped down and said, "What you say, bitch?"

Taking a second to arrange my words carefully I laughed and said, "The only person…I'm gonna be seeing next…IS YOU."

Angry I didn't beg for my life she stood up and said, "Kill this bitch now!"

"MY DAUGHTER IS NOT INTO YOU! LEAVE HER THE FUCK ALONE!"

-LORETTA

Loretta stood in the doorway staring into the bedroom her daughter set up for her in her house, which use to belong to the dogs. The new comfortable queen size bed, the drawers, phone, pens and designer penholder on the desk all bothered her. She knew the personal phone line Yvette conveniently set up for her was there to record her phone conversations, but she would not be caught slipping.

Still, too much time had passed and she hadn't given the police any valuable information so she would have to continue to snoop around. They were pressuring her and she was starting to think that the moment her boyfriend woke up from his coma, he would be thrown in jail.

When Yvette's phone line rang she moved out of the doorway and walked to the living room to answer it.

"You have a collect call from, Chris. Press five to accept the call or to decline the call hang up or press 9 now." Trying to figure out why she was in jail she accepted.

"Hello." She said with her hands on her hips. Yvette's dogs eyed her suspiciously.

"Vette...is that you?" Chris asked.

"No it's her mother." She said sitting on the sofa.

"Where's Yvette?"

"What did you do to get locked up?" Loretta laughed. "Trying to impersonate a man?"

"Since you being nosy, I gotta rack of speeding tickets I forgot to pay and they suspended my license. Now where the fuck is 'Vette?"

"I don't know, but I do know she got your little letter and guess what...I'm still here. She also told me to tell you that if you called to leave her alone. She's done with you and has taken a stroll back on the normal side."

"What?"

"Find another pussy to lick, bitch!"

"I know you there to hurt Yvette!"

"You really are pressed! That's my daughter why would I want to hurt her?" Loretta laughed. "Face it, she's not into you! She told me herself. Now leave her the fuck alone!"

Click.

After she hung up the phone she took off her shoes and laid back into the cushions. Feeling remorse for her deceit was not something she was capable of. She needed things to move quickly in her direction and she needed it to happen soon.

When one of Yvette's dogs stared her down, she took her anger out on it. "Fuck is you looking at?"

"Grrrrrrrrrrrrrrrrrrrrrrrrrr." The dog growled showing all of his teeth.

"Stupid, ugly dog." She laughed sticking her tongue out at the animal.

The dog inched closer. Believing the animal wouldn't bite like Yvette promised, she decided to taunt the dog by throwing her shoe at it. Ten seconds later the animal jumped on her on all fours and bit a chunk out of her arm.

"Hellllllpppp!!"

"I WANT TO THANK OUR FAMILY FROM THE SOUTH WHO CAME THROUGH WHEN WE NEEDED THEM THE MOST."

-TAMIR

The Black Water Klan had their ears fixed on Tamir's words as they prepared to celebrate a victory won; they had finally killed one of the infamous Pitbulls. Although the victory was sweet, most wondered who the girl sitting in the chair to the right of him was. They knew at some point he'd explain her existence but for now they'd just have to wait.

Tamir and his family sat in their meeting place discussing what needed to happen next. Champagne bottles littered the table in front of them and they all had champagne flutes in their hands. Finally he executed a plan that worked.

"Settle down everybody," Tamir said with raised hands. They did. "First I want to thank our family from the south who came through when we needed them the most."

"Not a problem," Cheese said. "We're just happy to be here."

"We're happy to have you." Tamir continued. "I trust you like the apartments we have for you and your family?"

"Fuck yeah. Ya'll laced the hell out of them mothafuckas, too. We good." He nodded. "Definitely."

Tamir smiled and said, "Where is your brother?"

"He's still undercover waiting on your word. We didn't think it would be smart to have him around us now, since we put that bitch down."

"Yeah, you're right." Tamir said suddenly feeling ill again.

"You okay?" Energy asked.

"Yeah...just gotta sit down for a minute."

He was trying to keep it together because nobody in his family knew that he was HIV positive and he wanted to keep it that way. Not only did he not want people feeling sorry for him, he also didn't want people thinking that he'd be replaced so easily. It had taken him forever to get to a position of respect and he was not going to have it taken away from him. After all, he had succeeded in doing what many wanted, killing a boss of Emerald.

"Before everybody goes to their apartments, I want to introduce you to the newest member of our family." Then he put his hand on Gia's shoulder. "This is Gia, and she's my second wife."

"See, we're losing our place," Karen whispered in Shade's ear. "We gotta step up."

Shade was overcome with anger as she took in everything that was happening. Here she was, being pushed even further to the side, by her own son at that. She had decided then that she would do whatever was necessary, even if it meant sleeping with her own child.

"I want you all to make her comfortable, because she's pregnant with my child."

Some of the family members were happy while others weren't. Energy stared her down from the sidelines with daggers in her eyes.

"Bitch," she said under her breath. "You better watch yourself."

While everyone continued on with his or her idle chatter, Tamir stood up and pulled Cheese to the side. Out of earshot of everyone else he said, "I want you to orchestrate the move on Carissa next. From there we'll work our way to C."

Cheese smiled and said, "I'll let my brother know."

"THE FORCE OF HER KNOCK AGAINST MY DOOR LET ME KNOW SOMETHING WAS UP."

- MERCEDES

I needed a day. Just one day to try to make myself understand why my best friend would put her hands on my child. Fuck was she thinking about? I didn't like walking in on Persia and C fucking any more than she did, but it is what it is. I mean, how could they not have a connection, they were together all the time.

As I sat on the sofa, I decided that I was going to ask Derrick to move out. He didn't bother coming back home after we jumped Bucky, so I figured he was where he wanted to be. I still can't understand for the life of me, how a basement bargain bitch was able to take my husband so easily. My friends said it was probably sex related, but I knew it went deeper.

And then there was this shit with losing Emerald City. What was I going to do now that I wasn't boss anymore? I didn't have any legitimate skill sets. I tried the business shit and it didn't work. I was fucked.

I was about to make myself a sandwich after not eating since yesterday when a heavy pounding found its way on my door.

"Who is it?" I yelled running up to it.

I was still in Emerald City only because I found it easier to be here then at the National Harbor.

"It's me!" Yvette screamed.

The force of her knock against my door let me know something was up. When I opened the door, I saw her standing there while Carissa was in a ball on the dirty hallway floor crying hysterically.

"Yvette...what's going on?" I asked looking at her, then at Carissa. "Why Car crying like that?"

"You...you gotta sit down," Yvette said trying to force her tears back.

"Naw, I'm not sitting down." My hand still on the doorknob. "Tell me what's up."

And then, as if by some crazy moment of clarity, I suddenly understood what was happening. So I shook my head over and over and back peddled into my apartment. When thoughts of what they were about to tell me crept back into my mind, I backed up further. As if walking away from them would make things easier to digest.

Yvette came in slowly and Carissa crawled halfway into the doorway but she couldn't move any further. Her body forced the door to remain open before she collapsed where she was and cried out in anguish.

"Yvette, where's.... where's Kenyetta?"

"Sit down, Mercedes. Please."

"Fuck that! Where is Kenyetta?"

"She's gone," Yvette said dropping to her knees. "She's fucking gone!"

"I MEAN, WHO ELSE CAN PUT A NIGGA DOWN AS COLDLY AS YOU DO?"

-LIL C

Lil C had arranged to meet with Persia about what happened between them. He didn't know if it was a good or bad thing yet, but he did know that the course of their relationship would forever be changed. But first he had to meet with Monie because he still hadn't spoken to her since she smacked him the other day and he wanted to clear the air.

"Wallace, take me past Monie's house." C said as a Louis Vuitton bag sat to his left.

"You going alone?" he said worriedly.

"Yeah. I'll be fine."

Wallace drove past Tyland's gates and they both saw the stares placed upon them as they entered. C hated how they mocked him and felt he had something for them but first he had to get his crew together which was obviously falling apart.

C got out of the car and walked to Monie's apartment with the bag in his hand. When he made it there, he was about to knock on the door but felt himself hesitating. Why was he nervous all of a sudden to deal with her? When he realized he was being ridiculous, he knocked and Monie's loud mouth mother Tanta opened the door wide.

"COME ON IN, LIL C! I AIN'T KNOW YOU WERE OUT THERE!" She hugged him up and he could feel her

grip him tighter than she should have. "I SEE YOU STILL LOOKING GOOD."

He was about to tell her not to call him Lil C but knew it was worthless. "Thanks, is Monie here?"

"Yeah, she in the back." She said pointing with her extra long manicured nail.

"Is that bag for me?"

"No...it's for Monie."

"Lucky girl."

C walked toward the back of the apartment until he made it to her room. He knocked first and then Monie said, "Come in."

When he walked into her room he couldn't believe how sexy she looked. She was wearing a pair of thin grey sweat pants that hugged her thick legs and phat ass, and a white t-shirt. He could also tell she wasn't wearing any underwear.

"Cameron!" she yelled jumping up. "I didn't know you were in here."

It was the first time he'd been in her room. Normally they'd meet up at one of his apartments, whether it was in Emerald or at the National Harbor, but now that he was in her room he felt himself everywhere. His pictures were on the dresser, on her wall and everywhere else. The moment she saw where his eyes roamed, all over his pictures, she was filled with embarrassment.

"Cameron.... what are you doing here?" She asked bringing him back.

"I got something for you." He said handing her the Louis Vuitton bag.

Her eyes grew big as she opened the box and pulled out her first genuine designer bag.

"Cameron...I can't believe..."

"Fuck that...I never want to see you carry a fake purse again." He said remembering her inauthentic Louis Vuitton the day they met at Peking's.

"I thought you didn't buy females purses."

"You ain't just a female. And I fuck with you."

She smiled and said, "Thank you...this means a lot to me."

C walked all the way in and said, "I wanted to talk to you about what happened. Why did you act like that?"

"I don't know."

"Don't tell me you don't know. I could've fucked you up behind that shit. My own mother ain't ever put her hands on me. Ever."

"Cameron, I was worried about you. When we came back into the party and saw all that blood on that dude's white fur, I thought you were dead."

"So you react in violence, by putting your hands on me?"

"I'm sorry, but you one of my best friends, if something were to happen to you," she said flopping on the bed, "I don't think I'd be able to take it."

C sat on the bed next to her. "Well I'm fine." He said softly hitting her in the face with his fist. "But I need you hard. I don't need you breaking down like that when shit hit the fan."

"What do you mean when you say you need me hard? I mean, I know what you mean, but I want to hear you explain it to me."

"Monie, you my nigga. I fucks with you. Tough."

"I'm your nigga?" She repeated disappointedly.

"Yeah. I mean, who would've thought a bitch I had beat down my ex-girlfriend could become one of the closest people in my life. And you know I must be feeling you because I never get out of the car to walk anywhere."

"I know, I'm still shocked you in my room."

"You should be...because this tells you I fuck with you."

She smiled. "Cameron...I gotta, I gotta tell you something that I been meaning to tell you for a long time. But I'm scared..."

"Tell me."

"Okay," she swallowed hard. "I been meaning to tell you..."

"Before you do that, I forgot to ask you how that all ended? With Mazon?"

Monie had never come so close to baring her heart. And now that she had, she could tell it wouldn't be received well so decided against telling him how she felt about him. She knew they could never be like she wanted, and that she would have to keep her mind on business if she wanted to stay in his life.

"We killed him. Daps ain't tell you?"

"Naw...I got Daps her own place so she been back and forth. We haven't really discussed the details."

"Before we killed him he said Tamir sent him. Turns out you were right and we deaded his ass right where he stood. Had you stayed in that party, your life would've been over."

"Tamir said one of my friends would betray me. I just can't believe that nigga was gonna set me up like that. And that I almost let him stay with Persia. I would've died if something happened to her.

"I almost died when I thought something happened to you." She paused trying not to look into his handsome face. "But tell me what happened with you. How did you end up in EC that night?"

She knew part of the story because her cousins told her he dismissed them fifteen minutes after her and Daps left to see what Mazon wanted. But beyond the dismissal, they didn't have any more information for her on why C left the party.

A sly smile came over C and he said, "After ya'll left, I told your cousins and them to go home. Persia said she wanted to talk to me but she wanted to do it in private, plus she was saying her head was hurting." He smiled. "I could tell by the look in her eyes what was really up though. So, I figured we'd go back to my spot in Emerald since my mother said she was going to be at our crib at the Harbor. One thing led to another one and the next thing I know we was fucking."

Monie's heart dropped to the pit of her stomach. She had waited too late and now she'd never know if they could be.

"Did you...I mean...was it good?"

"Fuck yeah!"

That hurt Monie a lot. "What do you like about her?"

She figured if she knew what attracted him to her that if he ever tired of Persia, him and her could be.

"She got a banging ass body for one." He said. "You know I like my women fit." It seemed like everything he said out of his mouth didn't make her feel any better. "And I'm not sure what else it is yet. Outside of fucking her, I don't know much else about her."

"But ya'll grew up together. Ya'll practically cousins."

"We not fucking cousins." He scolded. "And don't let me hear you say that shit again."

"Okay."

"Even though we grew up together, we didn't know each other like that. I mean, we talked every now and again, but it was mostly about bullshit. I'm trying to see what she's like outside of how we usually kick it."

"I get it." She said in a soft voice.

"Look, I gotta roll. I forgot I'm supposed to be picking her up." He stood up and said. "But don't lunch out on me

again. I need you." She smiled. "I mean, who else can put a nigga down as coldly as you do?"

When C had Wallace pull up in front of Carissa's building he thought somebody was chasing Persia when she ran toward his car.

"What the fuck?!" They both said gripping their weapons.

She rushed in and threw her arms around his neck.

"What's up, Persia?" He said. "Why you crying?"

"Kenyetta is dead! Somebody killed Aunt Kenyetta!"

MERCEDES WAS CUT OUT OF MY LIFE FOR GOOD!

-CARISSA

I buried my best friend. My sister, and if God could take me right now in this moment, I'd gladly die with her.

"We ran out of juice. Do you have anymore?" Mercedes asked me as we stood in the kitchen of my Yacht.

"No." I said coldly.

"How long are you going to be mad at me, Carissa? Doesn't burying one of our sister's change anything for you? I didn't even get a chance to tell her I loved her and now she's gone. Do you really want something like that to happen between us?"

Before I could respond to her Yvette walked in. "They out of juice."

"FUCK THEM MOTHFUCKAS!" I yelled. "HALF OF THEM DON'T EVEN CARE THAT WE PUT OUR BEST FRIEND IN THE GROUND TODAY! ALL THEY CAN THINK ABOUT IS FUCKING JUICE!"

Yvette leaned on the counter and put her head down while Mercedes leaned on the refrigerator. Just then Toi came into the kitchen and said, "They out of juice."

I was so mad all I could do was laugh. For that moment we all did.

"Did I just say something funny?" Toi asked.

"Naw. You good." I told her.

"Look, I know you guys don't know me like that, and I probably don't deserve to say anything about Kenyetta because I barely knew her. But…I just wanted to say that I know before she died that she knew how much you all loved her. And ya'll gotta keep her spirit together by staying on point."

"What you mean?" I asked.

"I know ya'll been falling apart. You don't dress the way you use to and the glimmer in your eyes is not there anymore. It's been gone for a minute."

"She's right." Yvette said.

"Well look, I'ma leave ya'll to it. I just wanted to say my piece."

When she left I went up to Mercedes and hugged her tightly. We cried for a minute before Yvette jumped in and hugged us too. We were missing a part of our flow and there was nothing we could do to get that back. She was gone. She had passed and she would be missed.

After we had a good cry, we separated and held each other's hands. I didn't want to fight with my sisters anymore. They meant too much to me for this shit.

"So what are we going to do now?" I asked releasing their hands.

I needed answers because after all these years it didn't make sense that Kenyetta would no longer be in my life.

"Well, we start by acknowledging that she's not here anymore. That's the first thing." Yvette said. "It took us a long time to get over Stacia's death because we kept expecting her to knock on our door, accept our calls or come sit on the steps of Unit C with us. Before we can do anything, we have to admit that she is gone."

"I know we gotta do that, but I'm not ready to do that now." I said.

"Me either." Mercedes added.

Just when she said that, I saw Lil C holding Persia. She was crying in his arms and he held tightly onto her.

"Mercedes, how are we going to put an end to that?" I said nodding in the direction they stood. From the kitchen we could see their embrace.

"I don't think we can." She said. "It ain't for us to say nothing. I guess we gotta let them be.

It made me mad that she was taking such a lazy attitude toward what was brewing between our kids. I didn't want Persia dating a drug dealer, and I definitely didn't want her dating Mercedes' son. Don't get me wrong, I love Lil C, but I also knew he was spoiled and would never be able to take care of her like she deserved.

"Mercedes, we can't allow this. I don't want him with her."

Yvette said, "Can we do this later? Today is supposed to be for Kenyetta."

"You need to talk to her!" Mercedes said. "She beating a dead horse about C fucking Persia. Drop it already."

"I know why you taking the attitude you taking."

"Why is that, Carissa?"

"Because you're so use to giving him whatever he wants, that you won't stop at anything, even if it means giving him my daughter."

"Bitch, please! You act like your daughter too good for my son."

"Well she is!"

"Persia ain't nothing but a fucking whore!"

I gasped. I couldn't believe she said that, but I really couldn't believe Persia and C were standing in the doorway. Hearing what Mercedes had just said about her, Persia stormed away and C was right behind her.

"I want you off my boat! And outside of doing what we have to do to clean Kenyetta's apartment, I never want to see you again."

Mercedes leaned on the counter and said, "Come here."

I did and she spit in my face, "BITCH, FUCK YOU!"

Mercedes was cut out of my life for good!

"SHIT IS CHANGING WITH ME. I'M AT A POINT IN MY LIFE WHERE I CAN'T GO BACK TO DOING WHAT I WAS DOING."

- LIL C

C held a meeting with his primary crew, which consisted of Daps, Monie Blow, Lee Lee, Love, Nimali, Hinni and Dayani. C loved the Sri Lankan sisters because they were use to war and were trained in combat in their country. Seeing a body drop due to a command would be nothing for them and they would do it with ease.

C knew he made a wise decision by hiring all of the women. After the multiple attempts on his life, and after Kenyetta's death, he knew nobody was off limits. Although it wasn't said, he knew his mother thought Dreyfus had something to do with the death, but he would place money on it being Tamir. The only reason he didn't say anything to her about it, was because he didn't want her to worry more than she already had about him.

He spent the past week being there for his mother. Derrick was around for a couple of days, but after they started arguing, he left her again. C didn't want his mother to have to go at things alone in her condition, so in between making deliveries to Tyland, he stayed with her at her apartment at the Harbor.

When she cried, it was her son's shoulder that caught her tears. They had grown closer than ever and she was thankful to have him in her life. Now it was time to get down to business and C welcomed the change. Although he loved his mother, it was depressing being with her day in and day out, but he would do what he had to do.

In an empty apartment in Emerald City, C dispatched the women of his crew known as The Set. It was cramped in the small apartment but it was the only place C could find where he'd have an ounce of privacy.

"Monie, as far as you know, who would you say is in control of Tyland right now?"

"You are."

"You know what I mean. They're about to run out of product any day now and I got the package from Dreyfus. But before I do anything, I need to know who's who."

"Dreyfus ain't tell you who to make the delivery to?"

"Yes...but I want to know who's really in charge. I don't wanna just be delivering packs. I'm positioning myself to RUN Tyland."

"Did you tell Dreyfus your plan?"

"No, but since there was always an issue with packs coming up missing and money coming up short, he'll appreciate me for it later."

Monie took a sip of her beer and said, "I get it, well, you got five major players over there now. I mean, any nigga with a package to move think he in charge. But you can count the people with influence on one hand." She paused. "The first one is Frost. He's cool, but he afraid of being broke. He the type of nigga who saves up everything he makes, including his coins because he say he gonna get his own business one day."

"Why they call him Frost?" Daps asked.

"'Cause he got a little grey hair on top of his head even though he young."

Everyone but C laughed.

"Continue," he said getting back on point. He wasn't feeling the jokes.

"Okay...well from what I can tell I think he's loyal, Cameron. He seems to be about his money and I don't think you will have a problem from him or his men."

"Alright. Who else?"

"Then there is Detroit. And yes he's from Detroit," Monie laughed. "He seems to be laid back but I don't know a lot about him. From what I can tell, he's about his money and he loves his mother."

"Yeah, like seriously." Lee Lee added. "On Sundays you can see him dressed in a suit taking his mother to church. Since I've known him he hasn't missed a Sunday. I'm telling you now don't look for him in Tyland on church day 'cause you won't find him."

"He even missed a few days because she was sick before," Love, said. "As long as his mother's cool and he's getting enough money, you won't have a problem from Detroit."

"Aight, well who else?" He asked.

"You got Nick and Docks and they're troublemakers." Monie said. "You gonna have a problem with them but it shouldn't be anything you can't handle."

"Okay...anybody else?"

"Yeah, Priest."

"Why they call him Priest?"

"I don't know. I never found out. I can ask him if you want." Monie said.

"Naw. What you know about him?"

"Just that he been bucking against Tyland Towers and your mother and them since Black Water got killed. Priest ain't gonna let up easy, Cameron. He hate young niggas and feel they're best suited for block work, not boss work."

"Yeah, you may have to lay him down." Lee Lee said.

"You want me to do it?" Daps asked.

"Naw. Hold fast." C started. "Monie, set up a meeting with them for me. Tell all five of them I want to meet with them in Tyland tomorrow. Let 'em know it's about the future of the business." He paused. "Daps, you go with her."

"No problem, Cameron. You know I'm all over that shit."

C and Persia had been seeing each other for the past week. Since their families didn't want them to be together, they chose to be together in secret. After meeting with The Set, he called her and told her he was sending Wallace to pick her up and bring her to the Ritz. He was feeling her and he couldn't deny that it wouldn't be a lot that could keep them apart.

When C walked into the hotel room, he caught the solemn look on her face. Having seen it before, he feared the worse.

"What's wrong?" He said taking off his fur coat. "You don't feel too good?"

"Cameron, what happen to Mazon?"

"Mazon?" C said frustrated. "Why are you even asking me about him?"

"Because people are saying you killed him. Is it true?"

"You answer the question. How could I kill him when I was with you the night of the party?"

"Who said he was killed the night of the party?"

C had made a mistake he wouldn't soon repeat. He figured her to be cuter than she was smart and didn't think he'd have to formulate his lies. But more than anything, he didn't think she'd trip him up on his own words.

C walked up to her and put his hands on her shoulders, "Babe, let's worry about us. If the nigga's dead this is the first I'm hearing about it. But I don't want you getting all rowed up over no bullshit."

"I thought ya'll were friends."

"We were, but now we ain't." He paused and said, "I'ma go get in the shower. I got a few moves to make but then I'ma be back later. You staying with me or do you want me to have Wallace drop you off home?"

"I'm staying here. My mother too pathetic for me to go home."

"Cool."

C got in the shower and when he was done, he opened a few shopping bags he had Wallace bring in earlier that day. He rarely wore the same clothes twice. Once he was dressed, he walked into the kitchen part of the suite, he saw Persia rapping on the phone. When she saw him come in, she abruptly hung up.

"Who was that?"

"Nobody." Persia lied setting her phone down.

"So we lying to each other already?"

He was mad at her but couldn't deny that she was so fucking sexy. The white shorts she wore clung to her round ass and the thin t-shirt exposed the browns of her nipples. Her long hair was brushed calmly down her back and she had on just enough makeup.

"No, I'm not lying to you."

"Okay who was it?"

Before she could even finish her lie, he snatched the phone out of her hand and saw Zulo's name.

"I thought I told you to stay away from that nigga."

"You did!"

"So why you not listening to me?"

"Cameron, it's not that big of a deal."

"You wanna fuck with this nigga or you wanna fuck with me?"

"You! Why you say that to me?"

"Because you better act like it."

"Okay, Cameron. I got it." She paused walking into the living room area to sit on the sofa. "So what time are you coming back? I don't want to stay here all day by myself."

"I gotta check on my mother first and then I'll be back."

"Cameron, don't be over there all night. Last time you put me up in a hotel you said you'd come back but you never came."

"My mother needed me that night and I had to stay with her."

"Well I need you tonight. You gonna stay with me?"

C smiled and said, "Yeah, but if I ever find out you lying to me about anything, I'm cutting you off, Persia. I can't have liars around me now. You got it?"

"Yeah." She said standing up.

"Now keep it wet for me. I'ma be back when I can.

C was almost to his car when he ran into Derrick. He had Bucky with him and he felt like dropping him for the disrespect. He knew him and his mother were beefing and decided to stay out of it but even this was too much for him to bite his tongue.

Spotting C Derrick said, "Bucky, go wait in my car for me. I gotta rap to C."

Derrick walked up to him and he said, "Lil C, can I holla at you for a minute?"

"Yeah," C said watching Bucky walk to Derrick's car. "We can step in my ride."

Wallace was sitting in the car patiently waiting. "Wallace, step out for a minute. I gotta talk to Derrick."

"Okay, before I forget, Kit wanted to know if you needed him for tomorrow."

"Did I call him?" C said.

"Naw...but I was just asking for..."

"Tell the nigga he fired. I'm done with him, he questions my authority too much."

Wallace got out without another word leaving them alone.

"Be careful of how you treat your people, Lil C." Derrick said.

"Cameron." C said cutting him off.

"Cool. I can respect that. I wouldn't want niggas calling me Lil anything either."

"Good, now what the fuck do you want with me?"

"What I want with you? I thought we always had a bond."

"I did too, but the way you doing my mother is filthy. And then you wifing some clucker?"

"Cameron...me and your mother have been having problems for a while. The only difference now is that we aren't faking it anymore."

"Yeah whatever."

Derrick smiled already knowing how C was. "I heard a rumor that you taking over Tyland Towers."

"For once the rumors are right."

"I don't think you ready."

Cameron looked away not realizing that his words would sting him so hard. Had he thought about it long enough, he would've realized after his father died, that Derrick was all he had. He was the one who gave him the last pieces of what it took to be a man. So Derrick's opinion whether he liked it or not mattered.

"Dreyfus must've thought I was ready, or he would not have put me on."

"Dreyfus is mad with your mom's, Cameron. You gotta think. Why would he put someone as young as you on? It doesn't make any sense."

"I ain't got to think about shit." C shot back. "He put me on and the why's don't matter to me."

"Well they should." He paused. "Look, I'm not trying to make you mad. But had Mercedes still been fucking with Dreyfus on that Tyland Towers shit, you would not be working for him right now. He thinks you're going to fail or worse, get killed. When that happens, he figures she'd come crawling back to him."

"Maybe or maybe not. But had moms took me seriously I would not be dealing with him."

"You right and I always believed when you were ready to do what you wanted, you would do just that. I just ain't know you had your mind all the way made until now."

"Now you do."

"Cameron, I know you are ready for the business aspect of this game. I remember your father spending time with you and showing you what was what. I just want you to know that passing the product and collecting the profit ain't it. There's more to it."

"Like what?"

"This is a people game. You have to learn how to get people to do what you want them to do, but not because they fear you, but because they respect you."

"Fuck respect." C said. "I'm taking it back to the Roman times." Derrick was confused at his statement. "I was studying that shit real heavy when I was in school and I got it all figured out. I'm like Julius Caesar. Just like me, his people expected that when he finished school he'd get a modest job and build his career. But we both realized one thing and that's money is the key to everything." C laughed to himself. "And just like me, his father Lucius died when he was a teenager."

"You just don't get it."

"Naw...naw," C said slowly. "You don't get it. Shit is changing with me. I'm at a point in my life where I can't go back to doing what I was doing. And if people got a problem with that, they need to get the fuck out of my way."

Derrick gave C some dap and said, "Alright, young nigga. Good luck on your thing, and if you need me, know that I'm here."

"Indeed."

"...SHE'S CAUSING A PROBLEM BETWEEN ME AND SOMEONE I LOVE."

- MERCEDES

When we walked into Kenyetta's apartment, we couldn't believe how nasty everything was. We knew she was not the same, but this apartment did not speak to the fly, eccentric and fun loving friend we'd all known.

"Lock the door, Mercedes," Yvette told me. "We don't want whoever came in here and killed her, to come in here and fuck with us next."

I locked the door and we all stood in her living room. Fresh blood stains where they found her rested on the floor. Although they said the cause of death was due to asphyxiation, they also said her fingertips had been cut off. We guessed to get rid of the DNA from her scratching whoever was killing her.

"Anybody tell her boyfriend, Cheese?" Yvette said.

"Yeah...my boyfriend told him." Carissa said.

"Well...let's get to work," I said hating the sound of her voice.

"I'll work in the bedroom," Carissa said looking at Yvette. We still hadn't spoken since the funeral and I would just as soon leave it that way.

"Aight."

"So what do you want to do with her clothes?" Carissa asked. "Throw them away?"

"Throw them away?" I asked acknowledging her for the first time since we drove over there together. "You want to get rid of our best friend that easily?"

"You're not the only one who lost somebody, Mercedes. We lost our best friend, too. I hate when you try to make stuff out to be about you." Carissa flopped on the couch instead of going into the bedroom.

"I know you lost a friend too, I guess I'm taken it a little harder than you that's all."

"Let's just chill out for little while and think things through. It's not important that we take her stuff out of her apartment today." Yvette said.

"So what is important? Because I'm confused right now." Carissa said.

"Well, if you ask me I think we should look into who the fuck killed her. Why don't ya'll wanna talk about that shit?"

"Because it could be anybody." I said.

"We need to look into this shit to find out what the fuck went on. Let's put our heads together, who would kill her?" Yvette said.

"Do you think that Dreyfus did this?" Carissa said.

"FUCK NO!" I yelled. "He wouldn't do no shit like that!"

"Why wouldn't he?" Yvette said. "He cut us off of everything. And I don't know about ya'll but I can't even show my face in EC no more."

"So what can we do about it?" I asked. "I mean, he's Dreyfus. If he did do it, we can't put a move on him like that."

"Or can we?" Carissa said. "He got dick and balls just like the rest of them niggas we killed. So what makes Dreyfus any different?"

Silence.

"I can't believe we just buried Kenyetta. I can't believe that a member of our family has been killed again." I said.

"Well believe it. We buried her and she's gone. And I might sound like I don't give a fuck but that's not the case." Carissa and I broke out in tears and Yvette looked at us displeasingly. "I can't believe my girls are this fucking weak now. When we get here? When did we get to a point where we aren't strong enough to do what was necessary to survive? Kenyetta may be gone and I might be mean, but right now our lives are in danger. Niggas just totally disrespected us and we might be next."

"Do you understand that Kenyetta, our best friend, was murdered recently? We're not talking about some average nigga in the hood, Yvette. We're talking about a friend we've loved most of our lives. I know you hard bodied and we need you to be that way sometimes, but are you that cold that you can move on without at least grieving?" I said.

Her jaw tightened and she said, "So what would you have me do? Cry?" Yvette said looking at us. "Let's say I cry right now, and then you cry some more, and then you cry, then what?" She looked at both of us. "How far will we get by acting like sissies? Somebody has to be the one to push forward and I'm that someone." She paused. "Now I love Kenyetta just like y'all, but if I fell apart like you two how much better would that make me or this situation?"

"So it sounds to me like you already have a plan." Carissa said.

"Do you? If so what is it?" I asked.

"I'm not feeling C working for Dreyfus, and we need to try our hardest to do what we can to stop him."

"You know C gonna do what he want to, Yvette." I said.

"Yeah, including fucking my daughter."

I was so tired of hearing her mouth that I made a decision. I was going to do whatever I had to do to end their possible relationship. I didn't want to give this bitch the satisfaction of thinking my son needed to be with anything she popped out of that pussy."

"You know what, Carissa, give me a few days, and trust me, that relationship will be done."

She seemed uncomfortable about my promise. "What does that mean?"

"Nothing, I'ma prove to C that she ain't worth his time."

"Ya'll finished?" Yvette asked.

"Yeah, go 'head." I said.

"I think we should step to Dreyfus again. See if we can do anything to call a truce at this point. Once we're there, we can feel him out and see if he was involved in her murder."

"Yeah…and maybe even get Emerald back." Carissa said.

"I don't want it back." I said.

"Well if there's a chance for me to get it back I want it, but that's not my concern right now. My only concern is keeping my friends safe." Yvette said.

"Okay. I'll set up a meeting with Dreyfus." Mercedes said.

"Don't do it yet." Yvette said. "Before we do anything, we need to get our households together. Let's focus on our personal lives and lay low for a few days. I don't think any of us should stay in EC right now either. Carissa you stay on your Yacht, I'll stay in Georgetown and you at the Harbor, Mercedes. When we meet back up, I need my crew to be hardcore again. Can't nobody fuck with us when we got the right mind. So get it together. You got a week."

After the meeting with Yvette I realized I had to do something to break up C and Persia and I knew just what to do. I was waiting on the outside of a deli and was freezing my ass off. I would've waited in my car, but I wanted to be somewhere public when I met him. It's not that I was scared of him, but I didn't really know him like that either.

Five minutes later, Zulo came walking up to me in a black Burberry coat and blue jeans. He was attractive but it made me mad that he was fucking Persia. Zulo had to be at least thirty-two years old.

"What's up, Mercedes? Why you wanna meet out here?"

"Look, this won't take long."

"You need me to do something?"

"Yeah, I need you to step to Persia. But I need you to step to her hard." A guilty look rested on his face. "Look, I know you fucking with the girl or have fucked with her. I'm not out here judging you or anything like that. But she is causing a problem between me and someone I love. So I need you to consume her time. Fully."

"Okay." He said shaking due to the cold. "What's in it for me?"

I dug in my pocket and handed him one thousand dollars. "That should be enough for wining and dining. And since I know you fucking her for free, that's more than a fair price."

He smiled and said, "After I finish with her, she won't have eyes for anybody else. Believe that."

"I'M GONNA BE READY FOR YOU WHEN YOU GET HERE. IT'S GONNA BE JUST ME AND YOU."

- CARISSA

I was in my Yacht, and on my fifth cup of Hennessy waiting on Slack to come over. I didn't have any more coke, and hoped when he came over he'd bring some with him. Yvette had given us a week to get shit together, and I decided I'd quit before then.

After putting my gun in my drawer, I thought about how it had been a while since I'd seen him. He said he couldn't come to the funeral because he was out of town, and I understood. After the fight me and Mercedes had, I was glad he didn't come anyway. Damn I couldn't wait to see my boyfriend. Slack said he wanted to spend some time alone with me, and I wanted to spend some time alone with him, too. I needed to feel his touch.

My youngest daughter Treasure was at her best friend's house spending the night and Persia was in the living room with her friend Sugar. Her mother said she was coming to get them both so that me and Slack could spend some time alone and I couldn't wait till she got there. But already it was eight o'clock and she hadn't shown. Slack would be here in an hour.

When my phone vibrated, I walked into the living room and scooped it up. It was Slack. His text message read, *'I'm on my way. We still on for some alone time right?'*

Fuck! Where was Sugar's mother?

Not really wanting to lie I responded, *'I'm gonna be ready for you when you get here. It's gonna be just me and you.'*

When I walked into my living room I saw Persia and Sugar. I was still kind of mad with her because she didn't come home 'til three in the morning. When I asked her where she was, she said she got caught over Sugar's house and couldn't get a ride back to the Docks. But I didn't believe her. I would've pressed the issue a little more if I thought she was with C, but he was over Yvette's house in Georgetown helping her put up her lights for Christmas. With everything going on, it didn't seem like Christmas would be in two weeks.

"I can't believe ya'll are still here," I said. "I figured you'd be gone by now."

"Well we're not gone." Persia snapped.

"Fuck is wrong with you?"

"Nothing, ma." She said rolling her eyes.

"Don't tell me nothing! What is wrong with you?"

"She just mad because C popped up on her and Zulo hanging out at a restaurant yesterday."

"Uugghhh, bitch, why you say something?"

"Language!" I screamed which meant I wanted her to watch her mouth.

"This bitch is so fucking big mouthed!"

"Fuck that, what does she mean you were out with Zulo and C caught you?" I said not believing their little relationship was coming to an end already.

"Yeah, and how C know I was going to be there, ma?" She said with a lot of sass in her voice. "It's mighty convenient that he knew exactly where I was going to be."

"Well it wasn't me..." I said going off into my own thoughts. "Because I never know where you are."

And then it dawned on me; Mercedes posed idle threats about ending their relationship the other day, maybe this was her way of doing it.

"If anything it was your Aunt Mercedes."

"Aunt Mercedes?"

"Yeah, she didn't want ya'll to be together so maybe she fixed the situation to happen."

"But why doesn't she want me to be with him?" She said choking back tears.

"I don't know."

"And why did she call me a whore?"

Out of everything, I knew she was hurt by that comment most of all. And although I was mad at Mercedes, I didn't want them to be mad at each other forever. After all, we were still family.

"She didn't mean it, she was just mad. Don't charge that to her heart."

"Whatever," she said wiping the tears off of her face, still angry.

"Are you going to help us get the last of your aunt's things out of her apartment tomorrow?"

"I said I would," she said. "So I don't even know why you would ask me that. I loved her, too."

"You sure that's the only reason? Or the fact that you want her Birken bags?"

"Ma, I do want the bags but that's not why I'm helping out."

"Whatever, just make sure Sugar's mother brings you back in enough time to leave."

"She will," Sugar added. "And I'm sorry about your loss, Miss Carissa."

Sugar was a sneaky girl who was fake enough to be likable when she was in my presence. But fake or not, I smelled her ass the moment I saw her conniving eyes.

"Thanks, Sugar."

"Okay, ma, we'll let you know when Mrs. Michaels gets here. So can you get outta our face now please? We're busy."

"Busy checking Facebook. You need to stay off the internet, Persia."

"You mean stay off of it like you?"

"What is that supposed to mean? I ain't got no Facebook page."

"You might not have a Facebook page but you still on the internet."

My curiosity was peaked and I had to know what she was talking about.

"What you mean? I said I don't have a Facebook page and if I have one on there, it's fake."

"I'm just playing, ma, dang! You don't have a Facebook but you do have a video up on Hood Celeb Bang Out."

"A video up?" I said feeling my face heat up.

"Yep, of you and Slack. He posted it. So you see, ma, you got a lot of growing up to do, too."

I stopped what I was doing and said, "Show me! Show me right now!"

I didn't know how to use computers that well. We never had to use them on the block. So I needed my daughter, who I didn't want to look at me having sex, to pull it up. It took one minute for her to go to the page and show me the video and my heart throbbed with anger. It was a different video than the one Mercedes first showed me.

"What! How can these people allow this shit?"

"I don't know. They got all kinds of hood royalty on this page."

"And you knew this shit was up there for how long?"

"A couple of days. Why?"

"You don't think nothing is wrong with your mother's pussy being out for all to see?"

"It ain't your pussy it's your mouth."

I smacked her and said, "Persia, get the fuck in the room now!" Her friend jumped out of the way to avoid my wrath and she probably should have.

"Why you hit me?" She sobbed.

"Because I'm sick of your mouth! And tomorrow I want you to report this video for me on that site! Do whatever you have to, just make it go away!" I yelled stomping away toward my room. "And if I find out it's still on there, I'm holding you personally responsible!"

When I got to my room my world and my head was spinning. I needed to slow down and I didn't know the first place to start. I guess since I believe Slack was the culprit, I would start with him. He would have to answer for the shit he did to me and I wasn't taking anymore of his *'I don't know who's trying to break us up'* bullshit either!

Fifteen minutes later Slack came over and he was already high. My liquor high had worn off and my feelings were over the chart. After I let him on the Yacht he stepped in and smiled. Something seemed eerie about him and it made me slightly uncomfortable. And when he moved, I saw the handle of his gun peeking from under his shirt.

"Hey baby," I kissed him trying not to let on to what I just saw. "Sit down. I'm gonna make you a drink."

"Hurry up back, we gotta talk." He said watching me turn the corner.

"Okay. I'll be right back."

When I was out of his eyesight I leaned up against the wall and tried to catch my breath. He was here to kill me I just know it, but why? While he was waiting for me in the living room portion of my Yacht, I went to look for my gun in my room but it wasn't there. Knowing Persia had an obsession with guns, I crept softly toward her room trying not to alert Slack as to where I now was on the boat. From her halfway opened bedroom door, I could see Persia and Sugar sitting on the bed and I could also hear Sugar begging her to stop.

"Please stop. I hate when you do that." Sugar pleaded.

I slowly pushed the door open and saw Persia holding the gun to her head, playing. She had done this plenty times before and I figured I should get her help. And I was mad at myself for being too buzzed to remember to lock my gun drawer when I put it back earlier.

"Persia, what the fuck are you doing?" I yelled.

"It's not loaded, mama!" She said putting the gun behind her back.

Just when she said that Slack walked into the room and aimed a gun in our direction.

"I thought you said we were alone?" He questioned.

"What are you doing?" I sobbed.

"Fuck all of that, you coming with me. And I'm not leaving here without you." He paused. "The only question is, do you want me to kill just you, or all of you bitches?"

"NO! I'm coming by myself." I said holding my hands out in front of me. I turned to my daughter. "Persia, I want you to stay here. I'ma be okay."

"Mama, no! Please don't leave."

"COME ON, BITCH! I'M TIRED OF FUCKING AROUND WITH YOU!"

I quickly gathered myself and followed Slack to the door, but right before we were about to leave, a bullet pierced his shoulder and he fell to the floor dropping his gun. I turned around and Persia dropped my gun and stared at him.

"I'm sorry!" She screamed covering her mouth.

"DON'T BE, BABY!" I said rushing toward him to grab his gun. When I made it to him I shot him again in the other arm."

"Persia, call your Aunt Yvette, and tell her we got business over here I need her help now!"

"I SEE YOU TOTING A LITTLE SOMETHING THERE BABY BOY. I'M GLAD I AIN'T HAVE TO BLOW THAT MOTHAFUCKA OFF."

-DAPS

Priest stood in the doorway looking at his ten soldiers get his money in Tyland Towers. His money came quickly and easily because he was able to secure ten of the hardest block soldiers in the area. They were loyal, ruthless and as money hungry as he was. As far as he was concerned nothing needed to change. Now that he didn't have to worry about the bitches that ran shit after Black Water, he could get his money with no problem. He wasn't concerned about the rumor that C was taking their place because as long as the youngin' stood back and out of his way, there would be no problems.

"That's him?" Daps asked Monie.

"Yeah."

"He look like he may give us a problem." Daps laughed.

Monie grabbed her gun and said, "Let's find out."

In a sexy swagger, they walked up to him as he stood on the corner talking to his men. The moment he saw their faces he grew irritated.

"What?" He said before they even got within ten feet of him.

"Cameron wanna meet with you tomorrow."

"Well, tell his little ass I'm busy."

Monie looked at Daps and said, "Nigga...ain't nobody asking if you busy or not. I'm telling you Cameron wants to meet with you. Your next question should be where."

"Where?"

"The meeting is in building 1010 and you best be there or else!" Daps added.

"Or else what? What the fuck ya'll think you gonna do to..."

Before he could finish his statement he felt pressure against his balls, where his dick rested to the left.

"If you don't wanna be there fuck it. But if that's the case, we ain't got no use for you now do we?" Daps said. Monie smiled having liked Daps follow up flow.

"Aight." Priest said slowly raising his hands. "Now can you please move that shit?"

"Naw." Monie said. "Not until you understand how shit is going down in Tyland from now on. Keep that shit right there, Daps."

"I'm right on 'em."

"I don't like your attitude so I'ma warm you up now before you meet Cameron. He is running shit in Tyland and if you or any of your niggas got a problem with that I can solve it for you right here. Are we clear?"

"Yeah."

"Now, remember the meeting. You better be there."

Daps removed her gun and smiled. "I see you toting a little something there baby boy. I'm glad I ain't have to blow that mothafucka off. It would've been such a waste for the ladies."

With that they walked away.

"I AIN'T GOTTA GIVE THEM SHIT. I HAVE SPOKEN; NOW GET YOUR MEN IN ORDER."

- LIL C

C was in the building waiting for the men who would either help him in his plans for Tyland Towers, or get buried for trying to get in his way. C knew he had to be serious about the direction he was taking because he knew if he didn't no one would take him seriously.

In the room they held their meeting no other furniture outside of a single table and chairs were present. It was large enough to fit everybody invited and members of The Set stood in various parts of the room to provide security for C.

Nimali, Hinni and Dayani stood behind C and they were strapped and ready to go. Daps, was on the door and Monie Blow, Lee Lee and Love were at the far end of the room next to the windows.

Five minutes later, the Tyland Tower members came straggling in one by one. Lee Lee put cups in front of them and poured some Hennessy Black in each cup. C heard they favored the drink and wanted them to be relaxed. Everybody got a cup in front of them with the exception of Nick and Docks. He heard things about them since his meeting with Monie Blow and decided his hospitality to them would not begin.

"You forgot my cup." Nick said.

"Yeah...mine, too." Docks added.

"Nigga, shut the fuck up." Lee Lee said stepping up to them before standing against the wall.

"Look, fuck a cup!" Priest yelled, angry Nick and Docks were acting thirsty...literally. Then he directed his attention to C. "Now what is this about, young blood? 'Cause as long as I'm in here, I ain't making money out there. And the purpose of business is to get paid."

"Yeah, so what, you think you run Tyland now because you in charge of the package? Still don't mean we gonna bow down to you." Nick said.

"This nigga actually expects a dude from Emerald could get respect from us," Docks laughed looking at Priest who remained straight faced.

Priest sat back into his chair and shook his head. Nick and Docks were doing the most to embarrass him and Tyland and he wished they would shut the fuck up.

"Man, fuck this shit!" Nick said. Then he tapped Docks on the shoulder and said, "This some bullshit. Let's bounce."

"We out." Docks added.

Both of them made moves for the door until Priest said, "Sit down." When they didn't obey him he turned to them and said, "I said sit the fuck down. The least we could do is hear the little nigga out." They both sat down.

"I don't expect you to like me." C said in a low but authoritative tone. "Matta fact, I don't want you to like me, but you will respect me and the way I do business. We gonna be tightening up on the sells around Tyland. No more getting paid directly outta your cut. From here on out, the money is going to be collected at the end of each day, and we gonna pay out based on the sells of the organization as a whole."

"The way we do it now, we work off of a package and take out our cut before the money is collected." Nick said.

"Yeah, and because of that shit right there, packages come up missing and money comes up short. That shit ain't happening under my watch."

"Nigga, I'm not 'bout to give you the paper before I get mine." Nick said. "It don't make no sense."

"So you telling me you not gonna get with how I'm running shit?" C asked.

He laughed and said, "Look...back in EC..."

Before he could finish his sentence Lee Lee put one in the back of his head and followed up with another bullet for his partner Docks. Both of their lifeless bodies slumped at the table as reminders that C wasn't playing games.

"WHAT THE FUCK IS YOU DOIN', CUZ?!" Priest yelled standing up next to Detroit and Frost.

"Sit down." They didn't move.

"I'm tired of begging you niggas. You gonna start hearing less from me and feeling more. I'm starting to realize that the only thing ya'll can get with is the clap of my gun. So if you don't sit down, you 'bout to hear a round of applause."

Everyone sat down when the women raised their weapons in the air.

"Young Blood..."

"Cameron. The name's Cameron." He said cutting Priest off.

And then it dawned on him, they didn't respect the name his father was born with or the name he'd also given him. Because of it, C decided to take things to another level.

"Okay...okay, Cameron..."

"No fuck that! From here on out refer to me as Young King. And Tyland Towers as Camelot." He said naming it after his father. "I'm tired of niggas thinking because I'm young I'm soft. If anybody addresses me as anything other than Young King or Your Highness, matta fact, if any of

your soldiers even look me in my face, I'm burning them down."

C could feel The Set looking at him crazy but he was done fucking around.

"Young Blood..."

All you heard was the cock of weapons in the air.

"KILL THIS NIGGA!" C ordered.

Monie held the gun to Priest's head and Frost jumped up and said, "King...please. Don't do this shit. We feel where you coming from but killing one of your best is not a good move."

C's jaw clenched as The Set waited on his final word.

Reluctantly he looked at his crew and said, "Drop 'em."

They all lowered their weapons but Monie asked, "Are you sure?"

C nodded. Then he turned his attention to Priest, "I'ma give you that one, but it will be your last." Priest swallowed hard having gotten away with his life.

"King, I think you going to have a lot of people bucking this new order." Priest said. "Maybe you should go a different route and give niggas a chance to get with the program before you change it."

"I ain't gotta give them shit. I have spoken; now get your men in order. We meet back here at the start of every week." C paused. "But I should tell you, shit is changing around here whether they like it or not."

The moment he said that his phone vibrated. It was a message from Persia and he started to ignore it. But when he read her words he stood up straight and said to The Set, "Come on ya'll. We got business to tend to."

"What about them?" Daps said.

"The meeting is adjourned. Go make my fucking money."

"WE HAD BIGGER FISH TO FRY, AND HE WAS LYING IN HIS OWN BLOOD ON CARISSA'S FLOOR."

-MERCEDES

"Where this nigga at?!" Yvette yelled as we walked through the Yacht holding our guns.

"In here!"

We rushed in the direction of Carissa's voice and when we made it to the room she was in, we couldn't believe the sight. On the floor lied Slack screaming his heart out begging us to let him go.

"Let's get him out of Persia's room." Yvette said.

We took him to Carissa's spare room and laid him on a big piece of plastic paper so we wouldn't ruin her floors before we threw his ass overboard. Yvette having a memory like an elephant, couldn't wait to flip him over to see if the tattoo she saw on the video was on his back. And sure nuff, NC was tatted on his skin.

"Fuck does NC stand for?" I asked.

"North Carolina." He said, sweat pouring down his face.

"You from North Carolina?" Carissa asked. "I thought that was for Nations Capital. Like you told me."

"I lied." He said, his face expressing the pain he was in.

"Told you I was gonna kill this nigga," Yvette said reminding me of our conversation in the limo.

"Who sent you? And don't start lying to…" Before I could finish questioning Slack, C rushed into the Yacht with Daps and Monie and five other girls I didn't know.

"C, what are you doing here?" I asked walking up to him. "I don't want you here right now."

"Persia called me and told me what happened."

We all looked at her. "I'm sorry. I was scared and wanted him here with me."

"Stop lying! The only reason you told him was so you could see him." Carissa said. Persia shrugged neither admitting innocence nor guilt. "You should've taken your ass with Sugar!"

"C, we got it taken care of." I said.

"Why he try to kill Aunt Carissa?" He asked looking into my eyes.

"We don't know yet."

"Who the fuck are you really?!" Yvette said kicking him in the stomach.

"Slack."

"Nigga, I said who are you really? I know you with someone but what I don't know is who." Yvette continued.

"I'm just a friend."

"Monie and Daps, get on this nigga." C ordered.

All of sudden all of the women aimed their guns at his head. We all looked at C impressed with the women and their use of firepower.

"As you can see you about to have more trouble than you need. So what you wanna do? Yvette said."

Realizing he wasn't about to tell us what we needed I figured it would be best to get our kids out of there.

"C, get out of here. I don't want you around…"

"Ma, I'm not about to leave you in here with this nigga." C told me.

"C, please! Go now and take Persia with you." I ordered.

"I don't fuck with this bitch no more!"

"Lil C! Don't you call my daughter out of her name!" Carissa yelled.

"I'm sorry, Aunt Carissa, but me and Persia are done."

"C, I managed to take care of myself for years. Now I'm asking you to leave. We got this under control." I said.

C looked at me with a frustrated stare and said, "Aight, but I'm leaving my girls here."

"Cameron, you can't be by yourself." Daps yelled.

C turned around and said, "Monie come with me."

With that he walked out of the door. Persia appeared irritated with his departure and stormed behind him. I didn't have time to deal with either one of them right now. We had bigger fish to fry, and he was lying in his own blood on Carissa's floor.

"...I'MA LET YOU GO. BUT I NEVER WANT TO SEE YOU AGAIN, PERSIA. EVER."

-LIL C

C was almost to his car when Persia came barreling out of her mother's yacht. C and Monie continued to walk to his truck and were trying to avoid an altercation with her but feared it was inevitable.

"Cameron, we need to talk!" Persia screamed running behind them.

"Get in the car, Monie. I'm coming."

Monie walked two steps closer and said, "You know I'm not leaving you."

C didn't feel like arguing with her because he knew it was fruitless. She cared about him more than any human should care about another and after the near death attempts on his life, she would never leave his side again, not if she could help it.

"What do you want, Persia? I'm done with you. I don't fuck with people who not loyal."

"I am loyal, Cameron. I could've betrayed you but I didn't."

"Fuck is you saying? Were you or were you not with the nigga Zulo?!"

"I'm not talking about him."

"Well, I am."

"Cameron, I'm so sorry about Zulo. I didn't know you were going to be there and I don't like him more than you. I want to be with you, baby. Can you forgive me...please?"

"Fuck you, not knowing I was going to be there. You should not have been with the nigga to begin with. Now it's over, get the fuck out of my face!"

C turned around to walk to the car and Monie was relieved. She didn't want him being around her longer than he had to. Unconsciously C opened the door for Monie and she got inside the front passenger seat. The gesture came so smoothly that she didn't want to draw attention to it because for the first time ever, he treated her like a lady instead of one of his niggas.

"Cameron," Persia said grabbing his arm. "Don't walk away from me, plllleeeassse."

"Get the fuck off of him!" Monie said from the truck.

"Easy, I got this, Monie." C said calming her down with a wave of his hand. "Because it's nothing this bitch can say to make me want her back."

"But your mother set me up. She arranged for Zulo to take me out just so we wouldn't be together. Then she told you to be there so you would catch me."

"My mother wouldn't do no shit like that." C said getting into the driver's seat.

"She did, Cameron. Think about it. How did you know I was going to be there?"

He took his key out of his pocket and put it into the ignition. Monie was in the passenger seat and couldn't believe the feeling. The way C was treating her, for the first time ever, she felt that maybe there could be something between them after all.

"Bye, Persia."

He was driving off the Docks until she yelled. "YOUR MOTHER KILLED YOUR FATHER!"

C threw the truck in park causing Monie a medium case of whiplash.

"Don't listen to her, Cameron. Let's just go."

Getting out of the Range, he walked up to her and wrapped his hands around her throat. "Bitch, what did you just say?"

"It's true," she said clawing at his hands. "She didn't want you to know because she knew how much he meant to you." Her voice was low but her words were powerful. "Ask her, if you don't believe me."

C looked into her eyes and saw truth. Lies could be all over the place and often hard to spot but the truth was always visible upon first sight.

He released her and said, "Because of all of the shit that's going on now, I'ma let you go. But I never want to see you again, Persia. Ever."

C walked to his truck replaying what she'd said over and over in his mind. If what she said was true, this would change the course of the relationship with his mother forever.

"BABY, WHY WOULD YOU ASK ME SOMETHING LIKE THIS?"

-MERCEDES

We tortured the nigga Slack before we ended his life only to find out that he was with Tamir and they had been trying to kill my son for the longest. And to think, all of this shit started over a girl. Then we learned him and Cheese were the cause of my best friend being taken from us at the orders of Tamir. I don't know where Tamir was, but he fucked with the wrong family. I had Vida working diligently to find out where he laid his head and before I rested, I had plans to see that his life and the lives of his family members was over. First I had to warn C, so I called him over to talk about it. But when he answered the phone he sounded different, like something was on his mind.

When C finally got there Derrick was just leaving with the last of his things. We made a decision to cut the fake relationship off and I was ready for it. He was barely here anyway and since he was sleeping with another bitch, I felt it was best for us to part ways.

"Later, C." Derrick said leaving.

C didn't respond, just paced back and forth with blood shot red eyes. He didn't even speak to me and I could tell he'd been drinking. The smell of alcohol floated out of his pores.

"Have you been drinking?"

"Yes. I got a lot of shit on my mind and if I didn't drink first, somebody could've gotten hurt." He said looking at me seriously.

"How did you get here?"

"Wallace. Now I have to talk to you."

"C…baby…what's wrong?" I walked up to him and touched him on the shoulder. He shook me off and stared at me intently. "C, what's going on?"

My words seemed to hit him hard because he stopped in his tracks and smirked. Rubbing his head he said, "I'm about to ask you something and I wanna know the truth."

I walked up to him looking softly in his eyes and said, "Sure…anything, baby."

"Ma, I'm not fucking around this time." He pointed at me. "I need to know the truth and if you lie to me," he said boxing the air missing my face by inches, "if you lie to me, I'll never speak to you again. Ever."

"I've never lied to you about anything, C and I'm not about to start now."

He swayed a little and said, "Is it true…that you…I mean…"

"Just say it, son." I said walking up to him putting my hands on his shoulders again.

"Did you kill my father?"

I sat down where I stood not realizing the couch was several feet away from me. He stood over top of me and I crawled to the couch backwards pulling myself up on it. He rushed toward me.

"I don't know what you're talking about."

"Answer the question, ma." He said standing so close to me now I could feel his hot breath.

"Baby, why would you ask me something like this? I mean who told you that?"

"Persia! Now are you gonna tell me the truth or what?"

"I wanna tell the truth. I just want to know why you think I'd be responsible for some shit like that."

"You really not trying to answer me."

"C, I told you Black Water was responsible for his death. As a matter of fact, Cheese was with the Black Water Klan and was responsible for having Kenyetta killed and almost Carissa."

"You still haven't answered me."

"C….please!" I begged.

"You can't even repeat the lie you told me for so many years."

"Baby, please…I'm soooo sorry." I sobbed. "I was trying to protect myself. He was going to kill me."

He stood straight back up and said, "You gonna be hearing from me soon."

"C, don't leave!" I said running behind him. He walked out of the door and slammed it shut.

First Derrick and now my only son had abandoned me. I couldn't understand how Carissa could tell her daughter something so cold about me and I had all intentions on finding out why.

"...WHAT I SAW HURT, ANGERED AND SHOCKED ME. LORETTA WOULD DEFINITELY HAVE TO PAY."

- YVETTE

"Ughhh, what are they even doing around here?" a dumb bitch said to Mercedes and me as we were walking to my gold Range Rover in Emerald. She had three girls with her who I use to punish when I first moved around here. And now that she thought I had fallen from grace she wanted to pop shit! "You don't run shit around here no more. Be gone bitches!"

They all laughed as they taunted us.

"Who the fuck you talking to?" I said walking in their direction with my hand on my heat before Mercedes grabbed my hand pulling me in the opposite direction.

"Let's just get in the car," Mercedes said. "We don't need the bullshit." I was going to step to her anyway when she said, "Please, with all of this shit going on with C, you know I don't need this right now."

Once we made it to my car I was just about to pull off when the chic with the mouth threw the fuck you sign up and walked off. Mad as shit, I revved up my engine.

"Yvette, please don't. She's not worth it."

"Well let me see about that!" I said as I ran up on the grass and hit her from behind.

The moment her body fell face first into the grass, I felt I'd taken shit too far. But with so much on my mind before that moment I really didn't care. When she got up from the ground, looked at us and ran away screaming, I thanked God for the small favor. Mercedes and me laughed for about five minutes as she got the fuck out of dodge.

"Bitch…you tripping hard now." Mercedes said relieved we didn't kill someone in broad daylight.

A FEW DAYS LATER

It had been almost a month since I last spoke to Chris and I missed her every day. And because she was gone, for some reason I began to appreciate my mother's company. Especially after having to put my dogs down for turning on her. Can't believe I had managed to lose my best friend, my dogs and my lover in little over a month.

Still, there was something I needed clarity on before we could work on a mother-daughter relationship. I needed to know what her real purpose was for moving in with me. Loretta was normally ALWAYS there but since she hadn't returned from the doctor yet for her follow-up visit for the bite, I decided to check the recording device I planted in her room. Although they offered me a phone recorder when I went shopping, it was the penholder, which held a spy camera small enough to go undetected, that I bought. Removing the holder from her room I went into mine and looked at all the footage. What I saw hurt, angered and shocked me. Loretta would definitely have to pay. There goes the mother-daughter bullshit.

TWO HOURS LATER

"Baby, can I make you some lunch?" She asked when I came inside from taking a long walk.

"Sure." I took my shoes off and sat at the table.

Yeah…I got plans for you bitch. I thought.

"Here, drink some coffee. I grounded the beans and made it from scratch." She said bringing the pink cup to the dining room table I sat at.

"Thanks, ma." I smiled, eyes on her the entire time.

"No problem, baby."

Bitch. "Ma, why did you come back?"

"Do you want me to leave?"

"No…I didn't say that. I just want to know why you would show up now."

"I came back because I didn't have anywhere else to go." *Lies!* "I know it doesn't feel good hearing me say that but I want to be honest. And because I'm clean, I knew hanging out with my old friends would just pull me back down. So after begging the lady you paid monthly for my rehabilitation to give me your address, I figured I'd come here. And I'm happy I did."

I bet.

"Do you have a man, ma?"

"No!" She laughed, her tone heavy with guilt. "I'm too old for all of that."

I shook my head. "Ma, do you ever feel bad for abandoning me…for killing my baby sister Andrea by leaving her in the Laundromat during the dead of winter, and for dropping my sister Cecil off on the side of the road all alone? Do you regret any of it? Ever?"

"What?" She replied scratching her head. "Of course I do."

"Do you ever wonder if Cecil is still alive?"

"She's not. She's dead. They found her body a long time ago."

I hadn't known that and irritated with the newfound news I got up and tried to reach my friends again. This bitch was working my nerves and I would deal with her soon enough. While Loretta prepared lunch, I called Carissa and Mercedes again. We needed to talk about what we were going to do to earn money now but the moment I placed the call, there was a knock at my door.

"I'll get it," my mother said.

When she opened the door, Carissa and Mercedes were standing there. "Hello." Mercedes said strangely. "Is Yvette here?"

"Yes…come on in."

After all this time I still hadn't told them about my mother and now here I was, having to let them know the bitch was alive like this.

"Let's talk in your car, Mercedes." I grabbed my coat.

"You not going to eat?" Loretta asked me.

"Naw…I'm good." I said shutting the door.

"Who was that?" Mercedes asked when we sat in her car, me in the front, Carissa in the back.

"That was my mother."

"Your mother?" They both said at the same time. "I thought you said she died." Mercedes said.

"She was dead to me. She was strung out on drugs for the longest, and all of a sudden, out of nowhere, she showed up on my doorstep clean."

"Well…are you happy she's here?" Carissa asked.

"The bitch is trying to frame me as the drug connect for her dying boyfriend. Apparently she's too afraid of Judah, her real connect, so she would set me up instead."

"Evil!" Mercedes yelled.

"I got a plan for her though. I'm not even worried." I paused. "Were you able to get in contact with Dreyfus?"

"He won't answer my calls. I mean, after all this time and all the money he made with us, he doesn't give us the courtesy of a return call." Mercedes replied.

"Okay, was your assistant able to find out anything about his cleaning staff? And how often they come to his property?"

"Yes. We were even able to get the janitor uniforms. So if Dreyfus doesn't want to talk to us, we'll break into his house and talk to him." Mercedes said.

DREYFUS COMPOUND

We rented a white Ford Company van from Next Day Car Rentals to drive onto Dreyfus' property. We knew this was going too far, but we had to talk to him. We also realized that this major move could cause us our lives, but it was a chance we were willing to take.

"YEAH, BITCH! I GOT YOU NOW!"

-BUCKY

"Bitch, drive slower! You're gonna let them see us following them." Efua told her cousin Bucky.

Bucky was nervous on account of the bitch ass shit she was doing. The wheel shook nervously under her ghetto manicured nails and sweat poured down her face.

Wiping the liquid off her brow with the back of her hand she said, "They don't know it's me and they definitely don't know what I'm about to do." Bucky paused as she maneuvered in the white Honda she was driving, some yards behind them. "I wonder where they going though."

"Who cares? I'm just happy you finally gonna be able to get them." Mudiwa replied.

"I think we could've handled this a different way." Efua said.

"No we couldn't! I had to do it like this, to keep people out of my business."

"Humph. It couldn't be me." Mudiwa paused. "Where your phone at? Because the moment they stop we got to put in the call."

"I got it right here." Bucky said raising her outdated cell phone. "Yeah, bitch! I got you now!" Bucky said.

TAMIR

Tamir looked at the women in his California King sized bed and grinned. To the far left was Energy, her yellow skin illuminating off of the glow of the lamp next to where she layed. Next to her was Gia, the beauty in her face still personified by her youth, and then there was Karen whose age had not touched the curves of her body or the smoothness of her face. And finally there was his mother; a woman who had given him the very life he breathed. Crawling into the bed, the women pulled him into their naked bodies as if they were welcoming him into another world of sick lustful passion. The softness of their breasts and the feel of their warm legs soothed him as they waited to discover who would be fucked first.

He had been doing better physically having finally taken the doctor's advice and medicine. So his natural cinnamon colored skin was returning and he was pleased it hid any evidence of the disease coursing through his blood. The disguise was helpful for those who still believed that they could tell if someone was healthy upon first sight.

Energy, Gia and Karen all fought to be taken first, but it was Shade who won the fight. Reaching over to his mother, she softly kissed his lips and pulled him on top of her. Their sick, vile sexual connection was heightened by the fact that they should not be together. Still Tamir was pleased in all senses of the word by her stimulating touch. For a brief moment, he thought about C and Mercedes, and he wondered how many times they'd been sexual with one another. He never once thought that what he was doing was wrong, he was raised this way.

PITBULLS IN A SKIRT 3

The battle was not over and although they managed to kill Slack, Tamir knew it was part of the game. But soon he would be taking Mercedes' life, while leaving C alive long enough to grieve her death. And then he'd kill him too.

"GET RID OF HER. I'M NOT TRYING TO HEAR HER SHIT."

-LIL C

C was sitting on the couch in the suite he rented and was eating a Twix bar. Monie had finally convinced him to eat something else outside of candy even though he didn't want to.

"I ordered your sandwich, Cameron. You gonna eat it when it gets here right?"

"I told you yes. Stop asking me."

It had been days since C had spoken to his mother and she was heavily on his mind. Instead of going back to his house, he was hidden in a hotel room with Monie who waited on him hand and foot. And the days she couldn't stay with him, she'd call Daps over to make sure he was okay. C took the news of his mother's betrayal harder than he thought and he hated her more for it. Although the news broke him down, he knew eventually he'd have to face Mercedes again.

When Monie picked up some trash in the room, C looked at her and said, "You know I appreciate what you doing for me. You ain't have to do this."

"Where else am I going to go, Cameron? I can't be anywhere you not."

C and Monie looked at each other and it was obvious something was brewing between them.

"Come over here. Sit next to me." C said.

Monie's heart thumped in her chest as she moved toward him. The moment she sat down, a few raps on the door startled Monie and ruined any chance she had at finally letting her feelings show.

"Uh...let me get that." She said getting up.

"Yeah...hurry up. We got some things to talk about."

Even though she ordered room service, in her opinion the knock was too heavy. So she grabbed her gun and moved cautiously to the peephole. The moment she saw Persia's face, she shook her head.

"It's that bitch again. What you want me to do, Cameron?"

"I should've never brought her ass here before." He spat. "Get rid of her." C walked to the bedroom in the suite. "I'm not trying to hear her shit right now."

When Monie opened the door Persia pushed her way inside. "Where the fuck is Cameron?" Monie felt like breaking her fragile neck for interrupting them.

"What do you want?" Monie said closing the door. "He told you he didn't want to see you no more and that if you wanted money, you had better put that baby shit on Zulo." Monie folded her arms and rested on the back of her heels. "You know...the other nigga you fucked."

"But it is his baby!" She screamed in her face.

"Persia, you betta get the fuck out my face."

"I'm sorry, I just gotta talk to him. I can prove it's his baby if he just talks to me."

"Look, Cameron said he's not trying to see you. So you gonna have to leave." Monie held the door open.

Persia frowned and looked down at the table. When she saw the Twix wrapper she grew enraged. "Tell him he's gonna wish he hadn't fucked with me!"

"Yeah whatever...kick rocks bitch."

"YOU'RE GONNA WISH YOU DIDN'T FUCK WITH ME!"

- PERSIA

"Was he inside?"

"No." Persia said softly. "I think he had his driver pick him up or something."

"But his car is here."

"I know." She paused. "But can I do something to the car before we leave?"

"Yeah."

Persia had them drive her to the gas station to buy a gallon of water. When she got outside of the convenience store portion of the station, she poured the water out on the ground and filled the jug with gas. When they drove her back to the hotel she jumped excitedly out of the car to step in front of C's silver Range.

"Make it quick." The driver said.

Not having a lot of time and feeling rushed by her new friends, she doused his truck with gas and lit it with a match. "You're gonna wish you didn't fuck with me!"

A smile spread across her face when she watched it go up in flames. C had fucked with the wrong person and she hated herself for having sex with him.

When the fire got out of control, she ran back to the car, but not before becoming aroused after seeing the damage she'd caused.

"You just gave me an idea." The driver said. "Let's go back to the gas station and then on to our next stop."

"C IS MY BEST FRIEND AND I CAN'T BETRAY HIM."

- DAPS

Daps was walking to her apartment building when people she didn't see ambushed her from behind. When they turned her over, she was immediately doused with liquid and once she saw Tamir's face her heart dropped.

"Why are you doing this?" She asked as members of the Klan held her down. She could barely see.

Tamir stood over her. "We haven't done anything yet."

"Whatever you want me to do I will do. Just please don't hurt me." She said convincingly.

"I'm glad to hear that...now all you gotta do is tell me where C is." Tamir paused. "But if you don't, you're not going to have a choice."

"I don't know where he is." She sobbed uncontrollably. "I haven't seen him all day." She lied.

"I really wish you didn't say that." Tamir said, angrily.

With a wave of his hand he ordered that she be burned alive. Karen flipped a matched, smiled and dropped it on her body. Her body was instantly covered in fire. Daps screamed her heart out as the fire peeled her flesh back as if it were never there to begin with. Before long, she couldn't feel the pain anymore as she felt her life slip away.

“I BET YOU HE GOT SOMETHING DOWN THERE.”

- MERCEDES

It was easier than we thought to get on Dreyfus’ property. With the makeup wiped off of our faces, our hair pulled back and a show of the janitorial uniforms we’d stolen to the guards at the station, we had no problems. After all, thanks to my assistant Vida, we knew exactly what time the cleaning staff was due to clean his mansion.

Once on the property, having been there before, we moved to the front door and knocked. When no one answered we decided to twist the knob. Sure enough the door was open.

“Rich dumb mothafuckas.” Yvette said.

Once inside the house, we went right to the room Dreyfus frequented. We could smell wood from his fireplace burning. And when he saw us, the blood looked like it had drained from his face.

“What are you doing here?” He said.

“Where are your bodyguards Dreyfus?” Yvette said.

“Why, do I need them?” Yvette laughed and he said, “I let them off early…it’s a mistake I won’t make again.”

“We came to talk business with you.” Yvette said coming out of the janitorial uniform, feeling more comfortable in her jeans and t-shirt underneath.

“So you come onto my property without asking?” He stood up grabbed Yvette’s uniform and threw it in the fireplace to watch it burn.

“You wouldn’t answer our calls.” Carissa said.

"We don't have any more business together. Isn't that what you told me?" He looked at all of us. "This better be important."

"Dreyfus, we want to know why you cut us off? And more importantly why you stole what we helped build in Emerald City." I said.

"I told you the moment you gave back Tyland what intentions I had on doing. You just didn't believe me."

"What has happened to you? You use to be a man with honor and integrity. Has all that changed?" I asked. "And then you get my son tied up in all this bullshit! Why?"

"Don't worry, he'll be dead by the end of the week. He's doing a better job than I thought he would and I don't want him under any delusion that I'll be keeping him on a permanent basis."

"Did you say dead by the end of the week?" Carissa asked walking up to him. I'm glad she was able to move because my feet were planted. I was frozen still with the possibility of losing my son to death.

"The moment I give the order, it'll all be said and done."

"So the order hasn't been given yet?" Yvette said grabbing the poker from the fireplace.

"No, but it will be."

Right when he said that, Yvette drove the poker through his chest. Blood gushed everywhere as he continued to fight for his life. That's when Carissa hit him on the head with the wrought iron shovel from the fireplace. Seeing the work my friends had put in for me, I took the lamp on the desk and hit it over his head. And just like that he was gone. The three of us had committed and accidental murder and there was no turning back now.

"What have we done?" Carissa said dropping the shovel.

"We just killed Dreyfus," Yvette said releasing the hold on the poker which was still stuck in his chest. "That's what we did."

"I'm sorry, ya'll. I didn't know things were going to turn out like this."

"We couldn't have him kill C," Carissa said. "We couldn't." I walked up to her and hugged her tightly. "I'm sooo sorry about what I told Persia." She continued. "I was drunk when I told her. I'm so sorry."

"It's too late for sorry's. He's mad but I know he'll get over it. After all, he's my son."

"Fuck that…we need to figure out what we're going to do with this." Yvette said brining us back to reality.

"We have to get rid of the body." I said. "Now Vida said his cooking staff will be here in a couple of hours. So whatever we do we have to do now."

"Alright, but since he's already dead let's find out if any money's in the house."

We ran all through the house and came up empty-handed. But when we reached the basement, where five pitbulls roamed, we knew something valuable was down there. And since Carissa and me were scared, we ran back to the top.

"I bet you he got something down there," I yelled to Yvette who was still at the bottom. "But unless we kill his dogs, how we gonna get to it?"

ROOF! ROOF! ROOF!"

"I'm going inside." Yvette said.

"Fuck no!" I begged. "You gonna get hurt."

"I love dogs. You just gotta know how to talk to 'em."

Against our wishes she went into the room within the basement. At first the dogs barked wildly, but after a minute, they were silent.

"You think she okay?" Carissa asked me.

"I don't know…I hope so."

"Should we go down there?"

"And do what?" I paused. "Get our asses chewed off?"

When we saw Yvette coming back up with three bags we smiled and hugged each other, it was our first embrace since the day of Kenyetta's funeral. I guess Yvette's love for animals finally paid off. Once upstairs, she placed the bags on the floor and opened it. Two were filled with several kilos of pure coke and the other was filled with money.

"Ya'll...I think we just made a come up." Yvette said one of the dogs following right behind her.

"Yvette, get that dog!" I yelled as I jumped on Dreyfus' dead body and Carissa jumped on the couch to get away from the animal.

"Go back!" She yelled to the animal pointing at the stairs. When he walked back down the steps she locked the door. "Ya'll some punks."

"How much shit you think that is?" Carissa asked as our feet met the floor.

"Enough to put us back on top in another hood." Yvette said.

"I agree." I said.

The moment I said that, I could hear police sirens moving quickly in our direction. And before we knew it their bright lights could be seen from the white chiffon curtains. The funny part about it was, there were only two cars

"Oh shit! We fucked!" Yvette said.

"They can't know we killed him!" Carissa said. "Maybe they're here to arrest him on some drug shit."

"Well ain't nobody gonna be arresting his dead ass today." Yvette said.

"Maybe they know we broke in. What we gonna do?" Carissa replied.

"We can say we're with the cleaning crew." I reminded them.

"But I don't have a uniform." Yvette said. "He burned it."

"Oh, my God!" Carissa said. "Here, Yvette, take mine." She was moving to take hers off.

"No! I'll give her mine."

"No," she said calmly. "I'm going to have to go out there and see what's going on. You guys put his body in the bed upstairs."

"But what are you going to do?" Carissa asked.

"Move him! We have to hurry." She directed.

Once we drug Dreyfus' dead weight up the stairs we came back down. We straightened up as best as we could and wiped our fingerprints off of everything. If we could make it out of this okay, we knew we'd have to take his body with us, there was no other way.

Five minutes later, the cops knocked on the door. "I'm going out." Yvette said.

"No…please don't." I begged.

"I have to. It's either me alone or all of us."

"But they're going to lock you up." I advised.

"Well if I don't go out there they're going to lock us all up." Yvette explained.

Knowing we couldn't stop her we hugged her closely. "I love you, Yvette."

"I love you, too." She said. "But if they lock me up, I'ma need ya'll to toughen up. I don't want to come back to no weak ass bitches. If I can go hard, both of you can, too."

"You know we will." I said hugging her again.

"I love you so much." Carissa said.

"Let me go talk to them, if they take just me, then you know what you have to do with the body. Call the Vanishers and get rid of it."

"We got you." I said.

When Yvette stepped outside, the cops immediately ambushed her. Carissa didn't like what they were doing and rushed outside too. I was coming right behind them until I saw Bucky and her cousins. I knew exactly what was going on now. The bitch must've been following us and pressed charges for the ass whooping we put down on her, so I hung back. There was no doubt that this was a petty crime she was trying to check us for.

"What are you doing here?" Carissa questioned the cops.

"Can we come in?"

"Do you have a warrant?" Carissa asked.

"We have reason to believe that Mercedes Ganger is in there, too. And we're here to arrest her."

"Well this is private property, so unless you present a warrant, you have to leave now."

The cop angrily said, "Let's go."

Bucky smiled having seen Yvette carried away in handcuffs. Although she wore a smug look on her face now, she wouldn't be wearing it for long.

"DAMN, BITCH, I DIDN'T KNOW YOU WERE TRIPPING OFF OF ME THAT HARD."

-YVETTE

When I was taken to jail and told what it was I was being charged for, I had to laugh. The bitch Bucky actually filed charges. And then she was too embarrassed to do it in Emerald for fear of being labeled a snitch, instead she had us followed and called the cops. I wasn't concerned, in fact I was relieved, I knew we could beat this petty shit in a matter of days.

I had spoken to Mercedes and she already told me, using the money we'd stolen from Dreyfus, she was getting us the best lawyer around. He was so good that he managed to get Mercedes off on her own personal recognizance until the trial and promised that I would be out tomorrow. Since neither of us had ever been in any trouble. I think that's comedy considering all the people we killed.

I was just settling in mentally until I saw someone who made me fall back into my cell. I knew everything about her. Whether it be the way she liked her coffee, or the way she liked her favorite meal. We had spent the last few years of our lives together and I missed her so much.

I walked up to her and said, "Chris, what are you doing here?"

At first I could tell she was happy and shocked to see me and then as if she remembered how I treated her she said, "Do I know you?"

"You playing right?" I asked thinking she was joking.

"I don't know you. So step the fuck off." She told me walking away from me.

"So you that fucking mad you wanna try and play me in jail? Damn, bitch, I didn't know you were tripping off of me that hard."

She stopped in her tracks and said, "Bitch, I wouldn't fuck wit' you again if I was paid to. Now get your rotten ass out of my face."

"C, YOU GOTTA GET OUT OF HERE."

- MERCEDES

I was visiting my younger daughters over my cousin Vickie's house. Although we didn't get along too well, she was great when it came to my kids. I had been in her house for five minutes when Carissa showed up unannounced.

"We have to talk and we have to talk now!" She said on the other side of the door.

"Carissa, please don't tell me this is not about Persia again. I mean, I got your message but you don't have to call me like you a manic. Yvette and me had a long day after beating that assault charge bullshit on Bucky. I just want to be with my girls."

"Mercedes, this can't wait, now can we go outside please?" She said looking at Vickie standing behind me. "Hi, Vicki."

"Carissa…" She said walking off.

I walked outside, down the steps and listened impatiently to what she had to say. "What's going on?"

"Persia's missing. I haven't seen her in weeks." She said crying.

"Soooooo?"

"So the last time I talked to her she said she was running away and that if C won't answer her calls, she didn't want to live anymore. She's taking the breakup really hard."

"What do you want me to do? First you tell me to end their relationship and I do it! Now you want me to bring them back together?" I paused. "Because of their relationship C doesn't want to talk to me no more."

"This isn't about us! And just so you know, I didn't think she would tell him. Like I said, I was drunk when I told her, but she must've remembered."

"It doesn't matter. He hates me now and I think it's best for them to stay apart."

"Well, I don't. She's fucking pregnant, Mercedes!" Carissa added.

"She's what?"

"You heard me."

"You know what, fuck this shit!" I said walking back toward the house before a bullet whizzed by Carissa's head.

"What was that?" I said until another bullet flew by us. It wasn't long before I realized they were shooting at me.

"Duck, Carissa!" I said taking my own advice.

"Fuck was that?!"

When another bullet crashed into Vickie's van, shattering the window, we hid behind another car too afraid to move.

"Who do you think it is?" Carissa asked as we heard footsteps rush in our direction.

"I don't know but they obviously want us dead."

"I'm scared, Mercedes."

"Me too, but I'm gonna try and peak to see who it is."

"No…" She said pulling me back down.

"Just give me a second." When I finally scooted up, my heart dropped when I saw my son moving in our direction with a gun.

"It's C." I said sliding back down behind the car. Feeling the life snatched from me, realizing he wanted me dead, my head banged heavy. "I can't believe its C."

I was just about to look him into the eyes before he killed me when I saw him and Wallace rush past us. When

I turned into the direction they were moving, I saw Tamir with a gun aimed in our direction. It had been him firing at me all along. It wasn't long before C and Wallace ran up to him and shot him in the head. When his body dropped Carissa and I rose from behind the parked car.

C apparently still angry, pumped two more bullets in his head. Dogs barked wildly in the background as I took the gun from his hand and said, "C, you gotta get out of here."

"Fuck that!" He told me giving me an evil stare. "I don't want you saying shit to me."

"C…your mother is right, we have to go." Wallace said. "Come on, man."

"Just so you know, you dead to me." He pointed in my face. "And if you didn't give birth to me, I'da let this nigga slump you and your friend, too."

With that C walked out of my life.

"ENERGY? WHAT ARE YOU DOING HERE?"

-SHADE HOLMAN

Shade Holman decided to treat herself to a nice long massage, especially after having to bury yet another child. And although Tamir's death rocked the Black Water Klan to its core, it wouldn't stop what needed to be done and that was to build on Black Water's principals, but unlike under Tamir's rule, the focus for them now would be getting money. And Shade had stepped up to her rightful position in charge.

Lying on her stomach on a massage table, she waited patiently for her therapist to enter her room. And because she had been so tired, the therapeutic music forced her into a light sleep.

When the door opened Shade kept her eyes closed and said, "I want a long back massage and when you're done, you can spend the rest of that time on my feet."

"No problem," the woman said in a light voice.

The moment she placed her hands on her back, Shade exhaled. The touch of another human being soothed her and she wanted it to last. But when the woman moved too closely to her neck, she got nervous.

Her eyes flew open and she said, "What are you doing?"

"Massaging you." The woman said in a high voice. Only this time, Shade recognized her tone immediately.

"Energy? What are you doing here?"

"Settling old debts," she said gripping her throat harder.

From the position Shade was in, she was at a disadvantage and could not fight her off. Besides, Energy was crazy and there was nothing more she wanted in life than power. She knew that with Tamir's death, it would be just a matter of time before they got rid of her. So for five minutes straight, with everything she had, she choked Shade until her soul left this world, and her eyes remained closed permanently.

"YOU SHOULD'VE NEVER FUCKED WITH ME TO BEGIN WITH."

-ENERGY

Energy power walked to her car to avoid suspicion. The rush of killing her archenemy shoved her to the brink of insanity. Once at her white Ford Expedition she quickly pulled off and thought about her victory. With Shade out of the picture now all she had to worry about was Karen, Gia and the latest addition Persia, who was new in the Klan and if anything, would warm to her influence so she didn't see them as threats.

"I told you I was going to get your ass, bitch!" She ranted off to herself. "You should've never fucked with me to begin with."

She was delusional as she cursed the woman for ever having entered her life. Once on the highway, she decided to put on her favorite CD to relax. But when she noticed traffic approaching ahead, she lightly tapped on her brakes to prevent hitting the car in front of her.

Tap.

The brakes failed to halt the car.

Tap. Tap. Tap.

The brakes had failed again and she knew something was desperately wrong. When she tapped again and noticed the pedal had gone straight down with no change in speed, she realized that someone had severed her brake cords.

"Oh my Goooood! Not like this..."

SLAM!

She had driven smack dab into the back of a tow truck, which carried an empty flatbed; her head was taken completely off her body.

"IF I COULD GO BACK, I WOULDN'T DO IT AGAIN IF IT MEANT LOSING C."

-MERCEDES

After everything that was going on, we decided to go to a lounge to get something to drink. We were different now, more bitter, more angry and ready to do whatever necessary to stay on top. In a VIP section at the Luxor lounge, we shared a bottle of ACE and was looking for the waiter to order another bottle. The buzz was a welcoming sensation to what we'd been feeling for so long, extreme depression and irritation.

"Can you believe Kenyetta's dead?" Carissa asked. Yvette rolled her eyes hating topics, which pulled out emotion. "I mean, after all this time, it still don't make no sense to me."

"I can't believe it either…but at least we got one of the members of the Klan, that bitch Energy." Yvette said. "She can't even have an open casket funeral." She paused waving her hand for the waiter to come over again. "But what I want to know is, what happened to Shade?"

"She must've gotten on somebody else's bad side and finally got what was coming to her." I said.

I was just about to dig into the next bottle of champagne with them when Derrick called. He had been calling me nonstop lately but I hadn't taken his calls. I decided today I was going to finally answer.

"What?" I said coldly.

"I can't believe you answered. I been worried about you after hearing about you being down the jail. Look, I ain't know Bucky was going to carry shit like that. What happens in the streets stays in the streets and she forgot that."

"Derrick please," I laughed. Hearing his name caused my friends to look at me. Nobody knew better than them what I went through when he left me. "I don't give a fuck what you and that bitch named Bucky do together. Her days are limited. The only reason I don't step to her now is because we just won our case in court and I don't want this bitch snitching, again. But trust me, her day is coming." I said spotting a nigga on the floor who looked like he had enough cash and swag to handle me for a few nights.

"Can I see you?"

"I'm not trying to see you right now, Derrick."

"Ever?"

"I don't know about ever, but I know not right now."

"Hang the phone up on that nigga," Yvette said.

"Yeah…fuck him." Carissa added.

"Tell your girls I said hello."

Since I never fully got what his reason was I decided to humor him. I put my finger up to them to stop their adlibs and said, "Derrick, why did you really leave me? I don't wanna hear lies or anything else you think I may want to hear. I want the truth."

He took a few seconds before he replied and then said, "Aight…I'ma keep it one hundred. It seemed like every nigga ya'll fucked with has come up missing or dead. I didn't want a fight to eventually cause my death, that's the real reason."

I believed him. "Well thanks for being honest, but don't ever call my phone again, I don't fuck with punks."

When I hung up on him, I looked at my friends. "Got closure?" Yvette asked.

"Yeah."

"Maybe we ain't cut out for relationships." Yvette said. "Maybe we should just stick to what we know, the pursuit of power."

"Deep but true," Carissa said.

"Any word on Persia?" I asked skipping the subject.

"She eventually called me and said she lied about being pregnant. I don't believe her though." She paused circling the rim of her drink with her finger.

"Why would she lie?"

"I don't know. But because she's a minor I reported her as a runaway, I really don't think they gonna help me get her back though."

"I'm sorry about all of this." I said.

"Yeah…me, too."

"It's hard as shit raising kids and having a full time job…or in our case, full time drug operation. If I could go back, I wouldn't do it again if it meant losing C."

"Me either." I paused. "But I have some good news for ya'll. I got the address on where the rest of the Black Water Klan lives. I say we pay them a little visit."

"I'm with that." Yvette replied. Then she looked around and said, "Anybody looking for Dreyfus' yet?"

"No…once we took his body out of the house, the Vanishers did their thing and got rid of it. But my thing is this, the cops, Bucky and her cousins knew we were there. It's just a matter of time before we have to answer to when he doesn't show up. I started the rumor that he needed a break and went on an extended vacation, but what happens when he never shows up?"

"Right. So what are we going to do for money now?" Carissa asked.

"I want Emerald back," Yvette said. "And I know ya'll do, too."

"I don't." I said. "Like we said earlier, the less responsibility the better."

When Carissa grabbed my cup and started sipping from it I said, "Bitch, that was my glass."

"No it wasn't! I put mine right there."

"Bitch, I'm wearing clear lip gloss. And you're wearing whore time red lipstick! See!" I said picking her glass up and showing her. "You put your lips on my shit."

"Fuck you!" Carissa said pushing the glass over to me.

"I don't want that shit now!"

"Then why you say something?"

"You know I'm so sick of you two arguing all the time. When is this shit going to end?"

We both looked at each other and decided not to answer. I was staring to believe that me and her would always have a love hate type of relationship.

"Sorry, 'Vette. She just burns me up sometimes." I said. "But I'm serious. I'm not trying to run Emerald nomore."

"But with Dreyfus gone, both Emerald and Tyland still need product." Carissa said. "We short."

"If it would be possible to be their supplier without the responsibility, I'd be with it." I said.

"Again we don't have Dreyfus. So we can't supply shit." Carissa said.

"I got a plan for that. But I don't want to give up on Emerald. Just so ya'll know." Yvette said.

"SHUT THE FUCK UP, BITCH! I'M NOT PLAYING YOUR GAMES ANYMORE."

- YVETTE

At first my mother looked pitiful as we stood around her hunched over body on the floor. Looking at her, I tried my hardest not to feel bad about the bite mark on her arm, instead I remembered how she was the cause of my relationship ending, firing my maid and me putting my dogs down. I had just run down to her everything I learned after watching the camera tapes and she burst into tears.

"I thought you rigged the phone," she said.

"Well you thought wrong."

"So what are you going to do to me?" She asked looking up as we stood over top of her.

"I'm going to help you get your boyfriend off the hook,"

"Really?"

"Yes…and in exchange for my help you're going to give me Judah's number."

"But…I can't…"

"You don't have a choice. I have you on tape talking to your friend about how you were afraid that if you didn't set me up, Judah was going to kill you and the cops were going to lock up your boyfriend. It's all here." I said showing her the tape.

"I'm scared…" she sobbed. "Please don't do this to me, they'll kill me." Her tears got heavier and louder.

"Shut the fuck up, bitch! I'm not playing your games anymore."

Proving the entire act was fake she stopped crying and said, “Okay…what I gotta do?”

"OH NO...I TRUST YOU."

-LORETTA

After receiving Zulo's number for a package, Loretta placed the call to meet him. Before meeting her, he grilled her about whom she knew and whom she was with. She said she'd gotten his number from Mercedes who vouched for his quality of product and that she needed the package for a friend. Since he felt he and Mercedes were on good terms, he trusted the woman. Later that day in front of a 7-Eleven, Loretta got out of her car and slid into Zulo's.

"Where's the money?" He asked eager to make a little change to go to Vegas the next day.

"It's right here," she said handing him an envelope stacked with one hundred dollar bills.

Zulo accepted the money and took his time counting it. When he was done, he handed her the overcooked crack she requested.

"Thank you," she said, nervousness all over her face. "I'll be in contact."

"You not going to look at it? To make sure it is right?"

With her hand still on the door's handle she said, "Oh no...I trust you."

"You trust me?" he said growing heavy with suspicion. "In this business you don't trust shit people say."

"Well I trust you. Besides, Yvette vouched for you."

"I thought you said, Mercedes made this arrangement?"

Before she could answer he took out his gun and shot her in the middle of her head. If he hurried, he'd have time to meet up with these dudes he knew to clean up his mess and get rid of the body. But the moment he backed up, five cops blocked him.

"FUCK!" He yelled shooting her again. "I knew it was a fucking set up!"

"...AFTER SEEING THAT FINE ASS NIGGA, I GOTTA GET MORE BATTERIES FOR MY VIBRATOR."

-YVETTE

When we finally met with Judah he wasn't sure if he could trust us and we were unsure if we could trust him, but luckily our reputations preceded us and he agreed to meet. Judah towered over me like a basketball player and his complexion was a golden yellow. He was the finest man I had seen in a long time.

"What happened to Dreyfus?" He asked as we spoke on a roof of one of his houses. He was into real estate in Baltimore heavy. "After the millions you made him, I'd think he wouldn't wanna lose the business."

Then he looked at me differently, in a way Thick use to look at me when we first got together.

"Shit happens, he went his way, and we going ours." I said.

"Why did you do that for me? You know, throw the Feds off my trail?"

"Everybody wants something," Carissa said. "And we want your product."

"Yeah...we still have a demand to meet." I said.

He smiled at me again and I turned away, his attention was turning me on and I hated the feeling brewing between my legs. I was afraid of men like him and never wanted to love again.

"Okay…you've more than proven you can be trusted. And I'm sad to hear about what happened to your mother." He said to me.

"Fuck that bitch. She got everything she had coming."

He smiled slyly and said, "Gangsta…I like you a lot." He gave me that look again and said, "Okay…I'm gonna give you my best price. If you like my product, we can arrange to meet up again for future purchases. Deal?"

"You got a deal." I said.

"I hope so, Yvette. Because I definitely would love to continue our relationship."

"You mean business relationship." I corrected him.

"Yeah…whatever." He winked walking away.

IN MY TRUCK

As we walked to my truck I thought about the meeting with Judah. For some reason, I knew he was going to be something else but I didn't know how. Did he want to do business with us or just me? I guess all would be revealed soon.

Once at my truck Carissa moved for the front seat and so did Mercedes.

"I was here first," Mercedes said holding on to the door's handle.

"You rode in the front on the way over here." Carissa said pushing her a little.

"That's because I always ride in the front. When I drive, she rides in the front of my car." She said pushing her back. It wasn't long before a pushing match occurred.

"JUST GET IN THE FUCKING TRUCK!" I yelled at them. Mercedes sat in the front and Carissa reluctantly sat in the back. "This shit is getting so old between you two."

Silence filled the vehicle for a few minutes.

"It looks like we back on." Mercedes said.

"Yeah…it does," I said still stewing about how they were acting. "And I called C, he's willing to take our product to supply Tyland and Derrick is the point person for Emerald."

"What about Harold?" Carissa asked.

"Without Dreyfus, he don't have shit. We own the product so we own Emerald." I laughed.

"For now anyway." Carissa said.

When I looked at Mercedes she looked sad. "What's up, Cedes?"

"C talks to you, but he won't say shit to me. His own mother."

"Just let some time pass between you two. Things will be okay."

"I hope so. I miss him so much, ya'll." Mercedes said.

"He knows." Carissa paused. "So Yvette, Judah seems to be smitten with you."

"Yeah…that nigga act like he didn't even see us."

"It don't even matter. I ain't paying none of these niggas no mind out here no more. I'm all about my paper."

"So you're still on some gay shit even without a woman in the picture?" Carissa said.

I started to swell on her but I was use to her shit.

"It's not that, it's just that I don't feel like all the mental games right now."

"We understand girl," Mercedes said. "But if you got a chance to feel something, you gotta take it."

I wasn't going to tell them I still missed Chris because I knew they wouldn't understand. "But before I go home I gotta make one last stop at the store."

"Why is that?" Carissa asked me.

"After seeing that fine ass nigga, I gotta get more batteries for my vibrator."

We all laughed.

"Tell me about it bitch!" Mercedes laughed.

EPILOGUE

Yvette, Mercedes, Carissa and Toi looked at the buildings they learned were owned by the Black Water Klan. They were scoping the scene so that they could come back later and finish off the rest of the sick family.

"Where the fuck is everybody?" Toi said looking at the buildings. "We been out here for twenty minutes and not one soul has walked out."

"I don't know, but this is definitely the address." Mercedes said.

"Maybe they're inside fucking each other," Carissa laughed.

"Oh shit! Is that Persia?" Yvette pointed looking at her walking out of one of the buildings with a woman. Her stomach large.

"Yeah...but what the fuck is she doing here?" Yvette said. "I didn't even know that she knew them."

"Oh my God," Carissa said covering her mouth. "That's my baby and she's still pregnant!"

"Right...but with whose baby?" Mercedes said to no one in particular.

"Don't fucking start with me! You know whose baby she's carrying." Carissa said. "Your grandchild at that."

"If it's true, C not gonna want her anywhere near these fuckers." Yvette said.

"Fuck this, I'm going out there." Carissa ran up to Persia in the street and was almost hit by a car.

"Watch where the fuck you're going!" the driver yelled before pulling off.

"Fuck you!" Yvette said smashing the horn in her friend's defense.

"Baby, what are you doing here?"

"Ma? How did you find me?" She said putting her hand over her eyes to shield the sun.

"Don't worry about that, you're still my daughter and you're coming with me!"

"I can't, this is my family now."

"Fuck that...I want to take care of you and your baby, honey. I'm sorry about everything we've gone through, please come home."

"I'm not going anywhere! Leave me alone!"

When other Klan members heard the commotion, they came out .of the buildings and flooded the street. The girls knew shit had gotten way too serious now.

"Let's go break this shit up." Yvette said, Mercedes and Toi were right behind her.

"Fuck are ya'll doing here?" One of the men said. "She doesn't belong to you anymore."

"What kind of sick shit is this?!" Mercedes asked. "You can't just take a child and think shit is sweet. She is a fucking minor!"

"We can take better care of her than her own mother can," said another woman.

"I don't know what the fuck is going on, but I am not leaving here without my daughter!" Carissa cried out, the crowd was so thick now no one could drive on the street.

"Where's Cheese?" Someone yelled.

"He's not here!"

"Somebody go get Karen!" Another said. "Tell her we got outsiders out here!"

"Yeah, get Karen, bitch! Like we give a fuck!" Yvette said.

"Karen must be their fake ass leader." Mercedes said. "Ya'll packing right?"

Toi and Yvette put their hands in their purses, "You already know it." Yvette said.

"What's going on?" Karen's voice rang through the crowd.

"We got trouble over there!" Another person said as the crowd parted from the entrance of the building where she exited, to the place Yvette stood.

But when the woman stepped to Yvette neither one could believe their eyes.

"Cecil?" Yvette said recognizing the sister her mother had left on the side of the road many years ago.

"Oh my, God! Yvette...is that you?"

PITBULLS

IN A

SKIRT 4

KILLER KLAN

CARTEL PUBLICATIONS
BRINGING OUR STORIES TO LIFE
WWW.THECARTELPUBLICATIONS.COM

The Cartel Collection
Established in January 2008
We're growing stronger by the month!!!
www.thecartelpublications.com

Cartel Publications Order Form
Inmates ONLY get novels for $10.00 per book!

Titles		***Fee***
Shyt List	________	$15.00
Shyt List 2	________	$15.00
Pitbulls In A Skirt	________	$15.00
Pitbulls In A Skirt 2	________	$15.00
Pitbulls In A Skirt 3	________	$15.00
Victoria's Secret	________	$15.00
Poison	________	$15.00
Poison 2	________	$15.00
Hell Razor Honeys	________	$15.00
Hell Razor Honeys 2	________	$15.00
A Hustler's Son 2	________	$15.00
Black And Ugly As Ever	________	$15.00
Year of The Crack Mom	________	$15.00
The Face That Launched a Thousand Bullets	________	$15.00
The Unusual Suspects	________	$15.00
Miss Wayne & The Queens of DC	________	$15.00
Year of The Crack Mom	________	$15.00
Familia Divided	________	$15.00
Shyt List III	________	$15.00
Raunchy	________	$15.00
Reversed	________	$15.00

Please add $4.00 per book for shipping and handling.
The Cartel Publications * P.O. Box 486 * Owings Mills * MD * 21117

Name: ____________________

Address: ____________________

City/State: ____________________

Contact # & Email: ____________________

Please allow 5-7 business days for delivery. The Cartel is not responsible for prison orders rejected.